BOONE COUNTY LIBRARY
2040 9100 805 409 7

D0292083

Manifest Destiny

Rick Robinson

Headline Books, Inc.
Terra Alta, WV 26764

Manifest Destiny

By Rick Robinson

Publisher Page
P.O. Box 52, Terra Alta, WV 26764
www.publisherpage.com

Tel/Fax: 800-570-5951
Email: mybook@headlinebooks.com
www.headlinebooks.com

Publisher Page is an imprint of Headline Books, Inc.
Front Dust Jacket Design by Kevin T. Kelly www.kevintkelly.com

ISBN 0-929915-96-8
ISBN 13 978-0-929915-96-8

Library of Congress Cataloging-in-Publication Data

Robinson, Rick, 1958-
Manifest destiny / by Rick Robinson.
p. cm.
ISBN 978-0-929915-96-8
1. Elections--Romania--Fiction. 2. United States. Congress.--Officials and employees--Fiction. 3. Kidnapping--Fiction. 4. Communists--Fiction. 5. Romania--Fiction. 6. Political fiction. I. Title.
PS3618.O33367M36 2010
813'.6--dc22

2009054130

PRINTED IN THE UNITED STATES OF AMERICA

To my Mother and late Father

(and all the rest of my family and friends who continue to make me believe in myself)

I would remind you that extremism in the defense of liberty is no vice! And let me remind you also that moderation in the pursuit of justice is no virtue!

Barry Goldwater, 1964

I saw an interesting thing today. A man was being arrested by the Military Police; probably an urban guerrilla. Rather than be taken alive, he exploded a grenade hidden in his jacket, taking the command vehicle with him.

It occurred to me: the police are paid to fight, and the Rebels are not.

Michael Corleone, *Godfather II*

Prologue

August 24, 1814
The War of 1812
Washington, D.C.

Admiral George Cockburn stood on the steps of the United States Capitol and surveyed the scene around him. Washington was burning. The night sky was ablaze with fire as Federal buildings, including the nearby Naval Yard, burned. Black smoke blocked out the evening stars and burned Cockburn's lungs and eyes as British troops under his command were taking control of America's capital city.

The victory taking place before him was bittersweet for Cockburn, as he had not been entirely happy with the decision to attack Washington in the first place. He had grown up in the military, putting out to sea at the young age of 14. Military tactics ran through his veins and consumed his every waking minute. His troops had limited resources in what was coming to be known as the War of 1812, and he knew that an attack on Washington was not the best tactical move for the war effort. Holding the city would consume precious resources and troops. Cockburn felt that the taking of Baltimore, which was a thriving seaport, was far more important to a final British victory.

From a military standpoint, it made no sense to capture Washington. Cockburn was well aware, however, that revenge for the Battle of York demanded otherwise.

The defeat of the British at York had been weighing on the minds of Cockburn's superiors for nearly a year. In the late summer of 1813, the shipping lanes of Lake Ontario had rested firmly in the hands of the British. They had controlled the shoreline along Canada, as well as a small port on American soil. American leaders had devised a plan to gain control of the lake. A flotilla, which included 12 schooners of men, had moved on Upper Canada's capital city of York (today's Toronto).

Expecting an attack on Lower Canada, British troops were taken totally by surprise when the Americans landed about 6 miles west of York. Initially, there was no British resistance whatsoever and American forces came ashore without incident. Things quickly changed as Americans made their way to the city. They were met by British-backed Indians defending the outskirts of York. In the ensuing skirmish, the Indians suffered heavy losses.

The remainder of the next two days was a disaster for the British. The British sent reinforcements to assist the Indians. The reinforcements literally got lost. Whenever and wherever the opposing forces actually engaged in combat, the attacking Americans inflicted substantial casualties on the British.

The battlefield setbacks were further compounded by a series of bad command decisions on the British side. Despite heavy losses, the British military leaders refused to agree to articles of surrender. This created a delay that gave the American military regulars *carte blanche* to do as they pleased in York. American troops pillaged the city. Some of them set fire to the Parliament building. A soldier hoisted the white powdered wig of the Speaker of the Parliament, declaring it to be his scalp. Homes of Indian sympathizers were looted. And the Royal Standard, a regal mace symbolizing the Crown's authority over Upper Canada, was stolen from the Parliament. It was taken back to one of the American ships as a trophy of victory (and actually remained on display at the Naval Academy in Annapolis, Maryland, until it was returned by President Roosevelt in 1934).

When its defenders finally agreed to surrender, York was in flames and the British were humiliated.

Baltimore might have been a better military target for Admiral Cockburn, but his orders were clear. "On account of the greater political effect likely to result," the orders were given that Washington was to be burned. America's capital city and its nation's citizens were to suffer the same humiliation that the British had felt at York.

As Cockburn made his way into the city, he was surprised to find it largely deserted. An evacuation preceded the British invasion. The only resistance the British encountered was a 15-minute engagement involving sniper fire from a lone house about two miles from the Capitol.

The British troop's first stop in the city was the Navy Yard, the Washington home of naval operations. The Navy Yard contained everything from command leadership to ships and supplies. There Cockburn's job had been easy. It was already on fire. American forces had set the yard ablaze themselves so that the stores of munitions and supplies would not fall into the hands of the enemy. After the fire was set, the American forces had fled—the Navy Yard ablaze in their wake.

After letting his men rest for several hours, Admiral Cockburn then led a procession of troops up the smoky streets to the empty Capitol building. As he stood on the steps of the grand structure, he reminded himself that it had only been a year since the Americans had pillaged York. To the men he led, however, the humiliation at York was seared into their memories as if it had happened only the day before.

I've done what they asked of me, Admiral Cockburn thought to himself. *I've captured the Capitol. Now payback for York is at hand.*

The Capitol building which the troops entered in 1814 had a much smaller footprint than the one which tourists visit today. The dome had not been added yet, and the building ended on the east and west sides at the hallways which today lead to the House and Senate chambers. It may have been smaller in size, but, for its day, it appeared just as regal.

The troops followed Cockburn into the building and, like children exploring a new house, they began scurrying to and fro throughout the halls and rooms. A young British officer, impressed by the grandeur of the structure, approached Admiral Cockburn and pleaded that the building be saved. For a brief moment, Cockburn considered the young man's request. Then he called his troops to assemble on the floor of the United States House of Representatives, the lower chamber of America's youthful legislature.

Cockburn went to the chair of the Speaker of the House and sat down, the Mace of the House of Representatives to his right. The seamen who had followed Cockburn into the room were rowdy, but they quieted themselves as Cockburn stood and inspected them from the seat of power. As an old seaman, he knew the nature of the men who surrounded him at this moment in time. He cleared his voice and spoke, calling a question.

"Shall this harbor of Yankee democracy be burned?" Cockburn shouted.

The British on the floor of the House replied in unison: "Aye!"

Orders were given to torch the building.

Chapter 1

A Sergeant at Arms shall be appointed, to hold his office during the pleasure of the House, whose duty it shall be to attend the House during its sitting, to execute commands of the House from time to time, and all such process, issued by authority thereof, as shall be directed to him by the Speaker. A proper symbol of office shall be provided for the Sergeant at Arms, as such form and device as the Speaker shall direct, which shall be borne by the Sergeant when in the execution of his office.

Order of the House of Representatives, First Congress, First Session dated April 14, 1789

"Office of the Sergeant at Arms," Robert Patterson said in a matter-of-fact tone as he picked up the receiver. "Patterson here."

"Hey, Bob," said Julie Bernstein, the Parliamentarian. "I didn't expect to hear your voice. I figured you'd leave early tonight."

"I thought about it," said Patterson, "but only briefly. I let Donna go home early so she could get ready for her vacation. She needs a break."

"So do you, Bob," Bernstein replied.

"Aw, it's not that bad," he sighed. "Besides, you know I like the Capitol on nights like this. There are not many people around. Solitude can be a good thing."

"I guess," replied Bernstein. "Anyway, you'll get to head home soon. They just started on the last Special Order. Congressman Thompson from Kentucky is doing fifteen minutes on the Presidential elections over in Romania.

Apparently, his Chief of Staff is headed over with one of the institutes during the recess to monitor the voting."

"That's a helluva way to spend the recess," replied Patterson.

"Yeah," said Bernstein. "It sure isn't a weekend on the Maryland shore. Anyway, Thompson just started, but I don't think that he's going to use all of his time. You've probably got 10 minutes. Come on down to close us out."

"Sounds good to me," said Patterson. "I'll be right down." Patterson hung up the telephone and looked into the mirror to adjust his tie before heading out the door.

A short man, Robert Patterson's 5'6" frame was best described simply as round. His near melon-like head sat atop a squatty round body. As if to accentuate his shape, Patterson wore oval shaped gold wire-rimmed glasses. The arms of the glasses made ridges in the sides of his head as small rolls of fat gathered around the wire going from the lenses to the ear. Several Members had bestowed upon him the nickname of Sgt. Bunsen Honeydew because he bore such a likeness to the lab-coat-wearing Muppet scientist of that name.

Despite his portly figure, Patterson was a precise man. He wore only custom-made suits with French-cuffed shirts highlighted by gold cuff links bearing the seal of the United States Congress. His silk ties always matched the silk handkerchief which protruded from his suit-coat pocket with exact folds. He dressed with studied style not to make up for his somewhat rotund figure (although it was a side-benefit). Instead, he did so because he felt the ceremonial duties he performed were of such historical importance that proper decorum demanded it.

As he walked to the House floor, Patterson noticed once again how quiet the Capitol was during these late night sessions. Only the soft clip-clop of his leather soles on the blue and sand colored tiles interrupted the quiet of the night. Patterson thought it appropriate each step sounded like the lonely cantor of an old horse walking the plains alone. He was an old war horse himself.

As he walked, Patterson turned his head each time he passed a window facing the National Mall. Pausing ever so briefly at one window, he silently mused about how much he loved the way the white stone of the Washington Monument looked when lit up against the black Washington sky. Washington is a beautiful city by day, but it is majestic at night. The view down the Mall confirmed Patterson's love of the nocturnal D.C.

It wasn't long before Patterson arrived at his favorite room in the Capitol, the Speaker's Lobby. Located just behind the floor of the House of Representatives, the lobby contains portraits of each man and woman to serve as Speaker of the House of Representatives. Its ornate walls and fresco-painted ceiling offer a bold entrance to the home of the world's greatest democratic body. While waiting for the last speech to end, Patterson made small-talk with a Capitol Hill police officer stationed at the door.

"Shoot anybody today?" Patterson asked the officer the same question he asked officers at the end of each day on the Hill.

"Not that I can remember," replied the officer jokingly, while silently patting the gun strapped to his hip.

"Oh well," he said as he always did, "maybe you'll get lucky tomorrow."

"Maybe," said the officer as he opened the door for Patterson. "Nice suit tonight, sir. Is that a new one?"

"Old suit," replied Patterson, smiling because the young man had noticed his attire. "New tie and handkerchief." He entered the floor of the House and stood to the side. Congressman Richard Thompson from Kentucky was finishing his speech. Patterson had met Thompson a year or so earlier after he had won a special election in Kentucky to gain a spot in the House. Although Thompson was absolutely last in seniority, Patterson genuinely liked him. He had a young family and an attractive wife who used to work on the Hill. With his small frame, sandy hair and horned-rimmed glasses, Thompson looked more like a Wall Street broker than a United States Congressman.

"Finally, Madame Speaker," said Thompson, removing his glasses, "while my friends are overseas toiling in the vineyards of Romanian democracy, I will be at the annual picnic in Fancy Farm, Kentucky. As you well know, Madame Speaker, Fancy Farm is the premiere political rally in the south. It harkens us back to a time when oratory mattered in the political discourse of our nation. My sincere desire for Romania is that someday they can have debate as free and open as we do at Fancy Farm, so they too can enjoy all of the benefits of a democratic nation."

Thompson gathered up his papers from the lectern.

"And with that, Madame Speaker, I yield back the balance of my time."

Patterson proceeded to the Speaker's rostrum while a wood gavel was brought down loudly on the podium. "The Gentleman from Kentucky yields back the balance of his time. There being no further business, the House stands adjourned until 10:00 a.m. on Thursday morning," the Speaker pro-tem announced. Patterson approached the Speaker's desk and removed the Mace of the House of Representatives from its holder. With that simple act, Congress was now formally adjourned.

Outside the floor of the House, in the Speaker's Lobby, Thompson approached Patterson, who was holding the Mace in his cotton-glove-covered hands. "Hey Sarge, got any plans for the break?"

"Nothing special for me," replied Patterson. "I'm just going to stick around the city. There's a new exhibit up at the Portrait Gallery I want to see. How about you? I can't believe you aren't gonna follow your staffer across the pond to Romania."

"God, no," said Thompson. "Josh, my Chief of Staff, is headed over. He still has that youthful idealism that makes him want to stay on a plane for ten or eleven hours in the name of liberty." He chuckled as he spoke. "Bob, remember the days when guys like us enjoyed that stuff?"

"That was longer ago for me than you," laughed Patterson. "I went there years ago to search out my roots on my mother's side. Her great-great, grand-something was from Romania. Though, at my age now, it would take me days to recover from the flight alone. Just about the time I got over the jet lag, it would be time to come home."

Thompson looked at his watch. "According to my calculation, they should be well on their way to Europe right now. I think they fly to Paris, have a layover, and then get the next flight into Romania. Youngsters like Josh can recover quickly, but I'm not too sure about Griff. He and I still have our boyish charm, but we're not getting any younger, you know."

"That's what I can't understand," said Patterson.

"What?"

"You and Griffith," said Patterson, referring to the well-known political consultant, Michael Griffith. Everyone on the Hill knew Griffith and Thompson had been joined at the hip since the time when they roomed together at the Phi Delta Theta house at Eastern Kentucky University. "I can't figure that one out. I have trouble picturing the two of you together. I know he's your friend, but he can get out there sometimes. And him, in Romania...wow."

"Aw, you've just seen his television persona. Griff is a lot smarter than he acts on TV," Thompson replied. He paused and smiled. "Of course, you may be right about sending him overseas to consult. Romania may never be the same again."

"Does he really run campaigns using scenes from *The Godfather*?" asked Patterson.

"All the time," replied Thompson. "When you finish a campaign with Griff, you feel like you've had Brando slap you on the cheek."

Patterson chuckled at the thought. "So, what are you doing besides Fancy Farm? I've always read about it, but I've never been."

"You ought to come down with me some year," encouraged Thompson in a tone which Patterson knew was sincere. "It's fun and they have great food. After the weekend, though, I'm going to have some down time with Ann and the kids."

"Good for you. She's a great gal. She was one of the few wives who ever made a special effort to meet me personally. This place can eat up relationships. When my wife was alive, she hated the late nights I had to put in here. Enjoy your time together and take advantage of it."

"Thanks, Bob," said Thompson. "Have a good break."

"You too, Congressman," Patterson said as he turned with the Mace and headed to his office.

As the Sergeant at Arms, Robert Patterson performed many tasks important to the daily operations of the United States House of Representatives. All of his chores, most repeated day in and day out, were duties that had been directed to his office by the House Speaker pursuant to a general order issued during the first session of the very first Congress. Patterson felt the general order so compelling and necessary to his very existence that he kept a framed copy of it on his leather-topped desk.

Patterson would pick up the framed copy of the order and reread it on a regular basis. Contemplating its words kept the lonely nights in perspective for him.

The orders of the Speaker stated the duties of the office would change "from time to time" and they had changed during the two hundred years the job had existed. It was far from a one-man job. The Sergeant and his large staff of deputies perform many ministerial duties which literally allow the House to operate on a daily basis. Everything from supervising the nightly custodial cleaning to aspects of law enforcement fall under the jurisdiction of the Sergeant's office.

Along with making sure the floors are waxed, the Sergeant's many jobs also include administering the protocol and ceremonies of the House.

While the administrative duties of the House are extremely important to the operations of the Congress, Patterson considered his ceremonial duties to be absolutely crucial.

Since the beginning of his appointment seven years previous, Patterson had taken these traditional duties quite seriously. He had led the President of the United States to the Speaker's rostrum for seven State of the Union Addresses. He had been the leader of formal Congressional delegations greeting foreign dignitaries on their visits to the Capitol. But he felt no duty was more important to his job than placing the Mace in its holder at the start of each session of the House and removing it at the end of the day. He rarely let his deputies perform this function.

When the United States House of Representatives organized at the First Federal Congress in 1786, it not only established the office of the Sergeant at Arms, but also approved the Mace as the appropriate symbol of that office. Since then, the Mace had become an integral symbol of order and decorum in each session of the House. Its presence at each session symbolizes that the power of the House does not rest in any one person, not even the Speaker. The Mace itself represents the power and presence of the Republic.

At the beginning of a session, the Sergeant at Arms takes the Mace from a cabinet in his office and proceeds to the Speaker's Lobby where he waits for the Speaker to arrive. Generally, before the Sergeant arrives, the lobby is abuzz with the excitement of Members readying themselves for the new legislative day. When the Sergeant arrives with the Mace, a hush falls over those gathered there. All of those who work on the Hill understand its significance. Even visitors, who are unfamiliar with the customs and traditions of the House, know something special is about to happen when the Sergeant at Arms enters the Speaker's Lobby from the North corridor, with the Mace held proudly in front of him.

The Sergeant at Arms then leads a procession onto the floor of the House and to the Speaker's rostrum and chair. The placement of the Mace into its green marble holder just to the right of the Speaker indicates the House is in session. If the House is meeting as a "Committee of the Whole House," a procedural device which allows for a smaller quorum and quicker votes, the Mace is placed in a holder next to the lower level desk. Members entering the floor for the first time on any given day look to the placement of the Mace to determine if the House is in session or if it is meeting as a Committee of the Whole.

The Mace is so significant no session of the United States House is brought to order until the Mace is properly placed in its holder on the floor, and no session is formally adjourned until it is removed.

The Mace itself is modeled on a regal Roman fasces, and measures nearly four feet from top to bottom. Its shaft contains thirteen ebony rods held together by two criss-crossing wraps of thin silver ribbon. Sitting atop the ebony rods is a cast silver globe, with a solid silver eagle perched on top—its wings spread wide.

The original Mace disappeared when the British burned the Capitol in 1814. No one knows for sure whether it was destroyed in the fire or stolen by a British soldier. The symbolism in the one that was commissioned to replace it is unmistakable. The 13 ebony rods represent the original 13 colonies in the Union. Taken by itself, any one of the rods is easily broken. When the rods are joined together, they possess a unified strength which makes them unbreakable. Much like the original colonies, as one functional unit the 13 are too strong to snap. The eagle which sits atop the globe is a statement of its time and represents the Manifest Destiny of America's westward expansion.

In the nineteenth century the replacement Mace was created for $400. Today, its value is literally priceless.

Patterson treated the Mace with great respect. He only handled it after putting on white cotton gloves in order to keep his oily fingerprints from the ebony shafts and silver ribbons.

After leaving Congressman Richard Thompson in the Speaker's Lobby, Patterson made the lonely, singular procession back to his portion of the Capitol. He entered his office and gently pushed the door closed with his foot. Patterson's office was large by Capitol Hill standards, but only because the volume of people he had to deal with on a daily basis demanded it. His desk sat near the Mace, a large marble pen and pencil set with his name on it being the only personal indulgence he allowed. A window with a beautiful view of the Mall was behind his desk.

Patterson had lied to Julie Bernstein when he said he had let his top deputy leave early so that she could get an early start on her family's summer vacation. True, she was leaving on vacation, but everyone in the House knew that he liked to be alone at night in his office. It was no problem for him to stay late. A widower, he liked the silence of the Capitol late in the evening.

As Patterson placed the Mace into its airtight, humidity-controlled case, he adjusted it so it stood perfectly square in the mahogany and glass cabinet. Once he was satisfied it was perfectly square, he leaned forward, inspecting it for smudges. Each time he would find an errant fingerprint on the silver, he would gently rub his cotton gloved fingers over it until the smudge disappeared.

Engrossed in inspecting and cleaning the Mace, Patterson did not notice the figure emerging from behind him in the darkness of the otherwise empty office. As he polished away a smudge on the silver wing of the eagle, the man made his way past Patterson's ten seat conference table. He reached around Patterson's neck from behind. A handkerchief soaked with chloroform was placed over Patterson's nose and mouth. Despite a brief initial struggle, Patterson made no movement other than slumping in a pudgy mass to the regal red carpet.

Patterson's silent attacker was dressed in a grey janitor's jumpsuit, with the seal of the United States Congress over his left pocket. A baseball cap bearing the same logo was pulled down low to his eyes, hiding his short black hair. He went to the glass case and looked briefly at the Mace. He knew its significance and, while his orders were to steal it, he had also been instructed to treat it with the utmost reverence.

The man was preparing to remove the Mace from its case, when he heard something behind him. He spun around just in time to have Robert Patterson hit him in the forehead with the heavy marble base of the desk pen and pencil holder.

"Sonofabitch," the man mumbled through clenched teeth as he dropped to his knees, one hand on his forehead, the other steadying his body as he hit the ground. He shook the cobwebs from his head only to see Patterson, still dazed from the chloroform, staggering towards the door. "Sonofabitch," he repeated.

He pulled himself up and sprung after Patterson, who was nearly to the door. He lunged forward and grabbed the roly-poly figure by the back collar of his finely appointed suit. Patterson twisted back in the man's direction and broke his grip by ducking under his arm. Unfortunately for Patterson, that put the intruder between him and the doorway.

Patterson lunged at the intruder and missed him with a roundhouse right hand. The swing was so violent it threw Patterson off balance. A smack to the back of the head sent the Sergeant at Arms to the floor. The man in the janitor's jump suit attempted to subdue Patterson, who quickly rolled from his grasp. He used a chair by the wall to pull himself up, and tried to swing it at the man. But by then, the intruder was upon him. Patterson dropped the chair and swung wildly at his attacker—his pudgy fist landing on the exact spot where, only moments ago, the block of solid marble had also landed.

Maybe it was the fact he had taken two blows to the head, but the intruder's instincts took over. He focused his eyes. Rage overcame caution. With a low groan, he grabbed Patterson and spun him around in a move similar to a "full-Nelson" in wrestling. Patterson started to shout for help. To silence him, the man grabbed Patterson's head and, in one quick movement, he snapped his neck. Patterson slumped to the floor.

This time Patterson would not get up.

The Sergeant at Arms of the United States House of Representatives, Robert Patterson, was dead.

"Sonofabitch."

Chapter 2

Michael Griffith sat in the first class comfort of the 767 jet and gently sipped on his second Maker's Mark bourbon of the young flight. He had already downed a quick one the flight attendant had poured for him while the flight crew had been loading other passengers. That first one had calmed his nerves enough to allow him to savor the second one a little more. It was still early in the flight from Washington to Paris, en route to Bucharest, Romania, but Griffith was about to spend hours on an intercontinental flight flying over nothing but water. A couple of quick shots of "Kentucky Champagne" would soothe his psyche. The third, and possibly fourth one, would make sleep inevitable.

Griffith slid his white snakeskin cowboy boots off his feet, pushed the button on the arm rest of his seat and leaned back in the dark blue leather chair. He was a type-A personality who was always fidgeting. The idea of spending several hours wrapped in a metal fuselage over nothing but water was nerve-racking. He looked out of the airplane window hoping to somehow see something which indicated ground below him. As he looked for the occasional light on the ground, he alternatively went from nervously rubbing his hands over his bald head to stroking his short pepper-colored beard.

He was not hiding his nerves very well.

Even the finest Kentucky bourbon could not calm Michael Griffith's uneasiness.

A nondescript, white three-ring binder seemed to stare at Griffith from the magazine holder on the back of the seat back in front of him. That binder was the briefing book for the Romanian presidential campaign. Inasmuch as Griffith was on his way to the small Eastern European Republic to consult in the final days for the campaign of the incumbent, Alexander Krasterich, he knew he should be studying it instead of drinking.

Griffith was well aware he should pick up the binder and study the campaign plan he was on his way to execute. He had looked at it only briefly in the days leading up to the flight. Each time he had picked it up, his attention had been diverted somewhere else. Every day there had been a new reason to toss it aside. The last time he cast it aside, he had done so with a pledge to himself he would read it on the plane. Now the time for study was at hand and he could not actually bring himself to open up the binder. Instead, he sipped on his Maker's and fidgeted in his seat.

Anyway, Griffith felt he really didn't need to study the binder. Romania, Bolivia or Alabama— it was all remarkably the same when you got down to the last couple of weeks of any campaign for top office. It was a routine he had repeated so many times in his career he hardly needed to study. When America's campaigns are completed, the political hacks of our nation head for the borders to consult in foreign elections. There may be a trade deficit of goods being exported from America, but political consulting is a one-sided growth export.

Michael Griffith was among the elite of America's political consultants. He was known in America for running campaigns using his Godfather Rules of Politics, basic lessons he had learned from watching the trilogy of movies about the fictional Corleone family of Little Italy, New York. Those lessons were a little harder to explain when he went overseas, but he always seemed to get by. And it really doesn't matter if the candidate understands the cinematic relevance of a reference like "don't hate your enemy, it effects your judgment." Griffith understood it and that was all that mattered.

As respected as Michael Griffith was in America for his political prowess, he was nearly a god on other continents. He had run successful campaigns for president in over a dozen countries. Foreign leaders seemed to love his appearance and persona. Blue jeans, snakeskin boots and rumpled shirts, as well as his shaved head and beard were all part of the American cowboy image he conveyed to them. For them, he was a steely-eyed, gun slinger straight out of a Clint Eastwood movie.

Griffith loved both that he was recognized worldwide as the best and he was paid so handsomely to consult. He just hated the overseas airplane flights the foreign campaigns required.

Celebrity, however, did have its benefits. Griffith had feigned embarrassment when the flight attendant in first class recognized him, a common occurrence in light of the numerous appearances he made on the twenty-four hour news networks. Griffith might have appeared uneasy with the extra consideration that came with being recognized, but he was not foolish enough to turn down the special attention. The young dishwater blond was attractive, treating him well and making sure his glass remained full.

"Another Maker's Mark, Mr. Griffith?" asked the American woman.

"Are you trying to get me loaded so you can take advantage of me?" Griffith replied.

"Why, no sir—not at all," said the woman with a sly smile.

"Too bad," laughed Griffith.

She giggled.

"That's the story of my life," he said, turning his attention to the twenty-something man sitting next to him. "Beautiful women don't realize that, when I'm drunk, they can take full advantage of me."

Griffith looked back at the woman. "Keep that in mind. It's a long flight, you know. Your chances of landing me for a date are better than 50/50."

"I'm sorry," the younger man in the adjacent seat interjected, with mock sincerity in his voice. "My father always acts this way after a couple of drinks."

The passenger sitting next to Griffith was actually his traveling companion for the next two weeks, Josh Barkman. Josh was fidgeting even more than Griffith. Unlike his older colleague, the young man's source of excitement stemmed from the fact he was flying first class to work on his first ever foreign campaign. Also, unlike Griffith, Josh had been studying his briefing binder with great intensity— underlining certain passages, highlighting others in yellow and making notes in the margin with a red pen.

Josh had also been studying the flight attendant, trying to figure out her age. She had that kind of look which cut in one of two directions and Josh couldn't tell whether she was a worn-out twenty-something, or a really hot forty-year-old.

"Oh, he's no bother," said the flight attendant, with a twinkle in her eye.

"Well, if he does bother you, I can have him thrown from the plane," said Josh.

"You go back to your studying," she laughed, smiling at Griffith and winking. "I can handle this one."

Josh Barkman smiled the boyish, charming smile of a young go-getter from Capitol Hill and looked over at Griffith. His intelligent blue eyes highlighted his curly blond hair. "I think she likes you. If you're sober enough by the time we land, I bet you can get her to go out to dinner with you."

"Mind your own business," Griffith replied. "And do not, repeat, do not tell people I am your father. I am by no means old enough to be your pappy."

"I don't know," said Josh. "Young women are turned on by that father-figure thing. She definitely has the potential to be the next ex-Mrs. Griffith, if you ask me."

"Well, I didn't ask you," said Griffith.

"I'm just trying to help," Josh replied.

"If you're so interested in match-making," Griffith instructed, "go find a date for my real ex-wife. I've got another 18 months of alimony until I'm off the hook." Griffith mumbled something under his breath and then looked at Josh.

"And what the hell do you know about dating anyway? You're pretty much married to the Hill."

"No, I'm not."

"Bullshit."

"Hey, I love my job," Josh replied defensively.

"Lovin' your job is one thing, boy," said Griffith. "You are fuckin' possessed."

"You were the one who told me to never forget where I worked," said Josh. "You told me I should come to work every day with the same excitement I had on day one."

"Yeah," Griffith replied, "but I never told you to enjoy the Hill to the exclusion of everything else in your life."

"I don't," Josh retorted.

"The hell you don't," Griffith shot back at the young man. "Hey, working on Capitol Hill is a great thing for a kid your age. You just need to realize it's not the only thing. When was the last time you were with a woman? And that does not include whacking away at porn on your laptop computer."

There was an uncomfortable pause.

"See," Griffith said. "That is exactly what I'm talking about. You are living in the nation's capitol, for sex as well as government, and you are spending the entirety of your weekends working at the Longworth House Office Building. You need to be gettin' out and havin' some fun."

"It's not all about sex," said Josh.

"God, Josh," replied Griffith. "You are so young and stupid. Washington is all about sex. Sex is the tension reliever that keeps the town running. Do you think Clinton screwed around because he was looking for a long-term relationship? Hell, no. Those women were tension relievers for him."

"And you think I'm too tense?" quizzed Josh.

"Hell, yes!" Griffith replied. "I've seen kids who have Potomac Fever and you have it bad. You're on a day long plane trip and you're dressed in khakis, a button-down and tie. You've got to loosen up. I've never seen a kid more in need of gettin' laid in my life."

"I thought the Congressman wanted you to be my mentor," said Josh a little sheepishly. "You're sounding more like Dr. Phil."

Josh went back to his briefing book. Griffith's style might have been a bit crass, but deep inside Josh felt the truthful cut of his words. He had been a workaholic since joining Congressman Richard Thompson's office as Chief of Staff. He was tired and stressed. But this trip to Europe—not anonymous political sex—was the kind of thing he was looking to for relief. The lecture had not helped.

When the flight attendant next came by, Josh asked her for a beer. "Make that a Maker's on the rocks," he recanted, in a tone that indicated maybe it was time for him to throw caution to the wind. He pulled his tie off and stuffed it in his pants pocket.

"That's my boy," said Griffith proudly, tussling at Josh's curly hair. "That's my boy. This is going to be a great trip."

To the flight attendant, the pair drinking Maker's in Row 2 looked as if they were unlikely traveling companions—the young Turk and the old warrior. In fact, they were as close as two could be in politics.

When Griffith ran the Congressional special-election campaign for his former college roommate, Richard Thompson, he had met Josh. Barkman was in his late twenties, but looked much younger. Blue eyes, curly blond hair and a baby face insured he was always asked for an I.D. when ordering a drink. Josh had been the political director in Thompson's campaign, and he had impressed both Griffith and Thompson with political savvy far beyond that which his youthful face had suggested. During the campaign, Griffith began entrusting Josh with more and more responsibilities. After the victory, Thompson hired Josh to run his Washington operation, and Griffith took the kid under his political wing to mentor him in the ways of politics.

In Griffith and Thompson's collective eyes, this trip was the next step in the mentoring process.

Congress was in Summer Recess and Congressman Thompson had given Josh permission to accompany Griffith on this international campaign escapade. Griffith was going as a paid political consultant. Josh was traveling as an observer of the campaign on behalf of one of the many government-sponsored institutes which monitor foreign elections.

When the flight attendant delivered the glass of Maker's Mark, Josh nearly spilled it.

Griffith laughed. Josh did not respond.

"And quit acting cute to the flight attendant," said Griffith. "I want you to get laid, but flight attendants are my specialty. Remember, I'm the rock star, not you. I get all the attention."

"The Congressman said you didn't travel overseas too well," Josh replied. "I'm beginning to understand what he meant."

"What the hell is that supposed to mean?" Griffith shot back in a gruff tone.

"He said you didn't like flying over water and that you would be pretty grumpy until the layover," Josh said. "He said you would hit on the flight attendant just like you did when you guys went to work on the first Romanian campaign, back when you were just out of college."

"Flight attendants love me," said Griffith.

"From the story I heard, that flight attendant and the Congressman had to help you off the plane," Josh said matter-of-factly.

"I was just hitting on her," Griffith replied.

"I guess it had nothing to do with the five or six Maker's you had on the flight," Josh laughed.

"Six or seven," said Griffith. "And I took that young lady out to dinner that night while your boss sat alone at the hotel piano bar."

"Well, whatever," said Josh as he pretended to turn his attention back to his briefing binder. "The Boss said this trip would be a great experience for me, but the flight would be one of the longest of my life."

"Don't look away from me like that, junior," said Griffith. "You may be a punk-kid, big dog Chief of Staff on Capitol Hill, but you're out of country now. You will need me to survive."

"What time is it?" asked Josh, ignoring Griffith's jovial threat.

"Who knows," said Griffith. "We've passed through so many time zones, I can't keep track any more. Why? Are you up past your normal bed time?"

"Naw," Josh replied. "Congressman Thompson told me to give you something exactly two hours into the first leg of the flight to calm you down. I don't think I can wait any longer."

"What is it? A valium?" asked Griffith.

"Nope, it's a special gift he bought just for you," Josh replied as he reached into his brief case and pulled out a brand new iPod, with a red bow taped to the front. He handed it to Griffith.

"He got me an iPod?" asked Griffith quizzically. "I don't even know how to work one of these damned things."

"Yeah, he figured you wouldn't know how to work it," laughed Josh. "That's why he pre-loaded it with music for you."

"He loaded it with music?" Griffith asked.

"Yeah," said Josh as he tried to turn his attention back to his briefing book.

"You mean he wants me to listen to John Prine, Warren Zevon, and Meat Loaf in a foreign land?"

"Apparently so," mumbled Josh.

"I had to listen to that shit every day we went to college," Griffith said to no one in particular. "I didn't like it then and I don't like his music now. There is no way in hell that listening to this crap will relax me on an overseas flight."

Josh reached back into his brief case and handed an envelope to his nervous flight mate. "Here—he told me to give you this note as soon as you started bitching."

"Gimme that," Griffith said as he snatched the note from Josh's hand.

"Looks like I lost," mumbled Josh.

"What's that supposed to mean?" asked Griffith.

"Five minutes was the over/under on how long it would take you to start bitching about a gift," said Josh. "I had the over."

Griffith frowned at Josh and opened up the note.

Dear Griff:

Thanks for taking the Kid with you on this trip. Although separated by distance, I'm expecting you to keep him out of trouble. That's a wild group of rebels on the other side. I don't think they're violent, but you never know. Be sure to bring him back in one piece.

I've told Josh you are a basket case on overseas flights and he'll need to be patient with you for the next couple of hours. I'm sure that by now you've told him about the last flight attendant in Romania.

"Fuck you," mumbled Griffith to himself as he continued to read.

Well, since you can't have a smoke until you land, I bought you and Josh each an iPod so you could get through the flight without killing each other. Enjoy the music. I've preloaded it with a lot of my music (which I know you liked so much in college).

Yours in the Bond,

Richard

"Great… your music," thought Griffith. "Just what I was afraid of. Like a Warren Zevon song about a headless mercenary is going to relax me now."

P.S.—I also preloaded the Marshall Tucker Band Anthology for you to listen to.

"All right, boy," smiled Griffith as he fumbled with the small silver and white box trying to figure out how to find the promised music.

Josh reached over and put his finger on the dial pad and showed Griffith how to find the music. "He bought one for me too," said Josh as he pulled another iPod out of his briefcase and attached the ear phones. "Except he loaded mine with the Drop Kick Murphys and Flogging Molly."

"Who's that?" asked Griffith.

"God, are you that old?" Josh laughed as he leaned back and stuck an ear bud in each ear. "That flight attendant is never going to hook up with an old man like you."

"Shut up and study your binder," said Griffith. He too leaned back in his seat and tried to relax while humming loudly to *Can't You See. Who the hell names a band Drop Kick Murphy or Flogging Molly anyway?* he thought to himself. He sipped on his bourbon, and then shuffled his shoulders around as if to shake the nerves from his bones. Then he took another sip, closed his eyes, and began quietly mouthing the words along with the song now surrounding him.

"Gonna take that south bound, ride it all the way to Georgia, 'til the train it run outta track ..."

Chapter 3

While the Mace of the United States House of Representatives is one of the oldest symbols of power in the U.S. Government, its origins are anything but American. The mace was a Roman symbol that became a part of the British parliamentary system. When settlements like Jamestown and Williamsburg were formed, they in turn used a mace to symbolize the authority of their councils and assemblies.

When the colonies began rising up against King George, the mace was often used as a symbol of opposition. Delegations of revolutionaries sometimes went to the homes of British governors led by a man carrying a makeshift mace.

After the Revolution, the mace became a central part of the daily decorum of the United States House of Representatives.

In the early years of the Republic, when the President would deliver the State of the Union address, the Congress would issue a formal reply. The reply would be taken directly to the residence of the President by a delegation from the Congress led on horseback by the Sergeant at Arms carrying the Mace. President John Adams was the last president to receive such a ceremonial response to his annual address. Thomas Jefferson quit issuing the State of the Union, and no one delivered it personally again until Woodrow Wilson.

The Mace has also been used throughout history to maintain order in the House of Representatives. Whenever there would be a dust-up on the floor of the House that could not be controlled by the Speaker's call for order, he would direct the Sergeant at Arms to "present the Mace" to the offending Member.

The Sergeant at Arms would then take the Mace and hold it high in the vicinity of the unruly act. For the most part, this was all that was needed to quell the melee.

In the mid-1800s, whenever the House debated any issue relating to slavery, fights and bloodshed frequently followed. The debate over Kansas statehood in 1858 (and whether it would enter the Union as a free state or a slave state) is a good example. It was not unheard of during those debates for actual fist fights to break out on the floor of the House. When order could not be restored by trying to gavel down the squabble, the Speaker would order the Mace be presented. The Sergeant at Arms would quickly retrieve the Mace from its holder and march it into the middle of the skirmish, holding it high so all could see it. Remarkably, that action alone would usually stop the fight and restore order.

As the plane carrying Griffith and Josh on their way to Romania winged its way through the black summer sky, a lone male figure in a grey janitor's jumpsuit and ball cap pushed a garbage cart through the halls of the United States Capitol.

The wheels on the bottom of the metal pipes that formed an X on either side of the thick canvas bag made high-pitched, squeaky noises as they coasted across the old tile floors of the undercroft of the Capitol. A drop cloth covered something poking out of one side. The bag was so filled it looked like it was ready to rip open at its seams. The weight in the bag caused the unwelcome squeak to be much louder than the man wanted.

The building was closed for business for the day, but business never really stops at the Capitol. Nighttime under the Capitol Dome just brings a new crew of workers to get the building ready for the next day. The nighttime crew of custodians and maintenance staff generally keep to themselves. It was easy to fit in. However, the man sure as hell did not need something like ultra squeaky wheels to draw attention to him.

The man made his way though the maze of hallways and tunnels to the dumpsters under the Cannon House Office

Building on the south side of the Capitol. When he reached the dumpster, he was met by a woman who had been standing in the shadows.

"You're late," said the woman. "Where the hell have you been?"

"We had some complications," he replied.

"I've been hiding here for over an hour," the woman replied. "The police around here aren't schooled in covert, but I was running out of tactics to stay out of their way."

"Sorry," he said. He removed the drop cloth, crumpled newspaper and other trash from the top of the canvas bag, revealing the lifeless body of Sergeant at Arms, Robert Patterson. "Like I said, we had some complications."

"What the fuck, Mark," said the woman. "This was supposed to be a clean mission."

"It was," said the man. "It couldn't be helped. And you are not supposed to say my name. I'm Shadow, remember."

"I know, I know," she replied anxiously. "But holy shit. This was not part of the operation. Get the football and get out. That was our mission. Remember? No blood."

"Yeah, I remember our instructions," said Mark.

"Then how do you explain this?" she said pointing at the dead body in the canvas bag.

"I thought I had knocked him out with the chloroform. He went down quickly … like a lump."

"So what went wrong?" asked the woman.

"Sonofabitch must have been faking it," he replied.

"Faking it?" she said.

"He wasn't out."

"You got outwitted by a fat bureaucrat," she replied in disgust.

"It got crazy," he said. "I'm looking at the football and composing myself to walk out the door when the fat little fucker comes up behind me and hits me on the head with a block of marble."

"So you killed him?" the woman asked with exasperation in her voice.

"Hey, he surprised me," said Mark. "Natural instincts took over. He tried to run and then hit me again. We struggled and I snapped his neck."

"Just like that," she said. "That's what I'm supposed to tell the boss. He smacked you in the head and you broke his neck."

"Hey, I'm not bragging about it," he mumbled.

"Good."

"But it happened," he said, "and now we have to deal with it."

"Fine. Let's deal with it and get the fuck out of here."

She leaned the so-called "football" in a corner and helped the man lift the entire bag and cart over the edge and into the dumpster. The mass of the contents in the canvas bag made a dull sound as it landed on the garbage inside the dumpster.

"I'll have a truck over here within an hour to pick up the garbage," Mark said.

"You do that," said the woman. "And try not to screw the pooch."

"Knock it off. I did not mean for this to happen."

"Just be on time tomorrow."

Chapter 4

The next morning, Richard Thompson was in his office early. When he arrived, his press secretary, Michelle Rainard, had already placed the morning press clippings on his desk. With Chief of Staff Josh Barkman in Romania, she was in charge. Unlike the other young political rookies in Thompson's office, Michelle was a Capitol Hill veteran. Pushing 40, the frumpy redhead liked the hustle and bustle of the Hill and had turned down many offers to go downtown to work with established public relations firms. Following the election, Michael Griffith had convinced her to work for one of the party's rising stars and that Thompson was her man.

Michelle was a good-natured woman who had put up with the quirks of many Members of Congress over the years...and Richard Thompson had some quirks. He constantly walked around the office singing songs. No Thompson moment was complete without him singing some song, off-tune, which—more often than not—perfectly fit the situation.

"Good morning, Boss," Michelle said cheerfully as Thompson sat down at his desk, humming to himself. "We got some press calls on your speech about Romania last night."

"Really?" asked Thompson with sincere surprise in his voice. "I didn't say anything all that interesting." He paused and smiled as he fumbled around with a pen on his desk. "Did I get press calls or did my uber-aggressive press secretary manufacture calls for me?"

Michelle smiled back. "Don't look a gift horse in the mouth, Boss. It doesn't matter how they became interested. They're interested. Let me know when you are ready to talk and I'll get them on the line."

"Great," Thompson replied. "Let's try to get them all in before we go into session at 10:00 this morning. It'll be a short session and there are no committee hearings today. I want to make sure I'm on the 2:20 flight home."

"Well, well, is someone a little anxious to start the recess?"

"Damn right," said Thompson. "And what do you care?"

"What do you mean?"

"You know what I mean. It'll be 'wheels up' early today. You forget I was a staffer back in the day. I know what it means when the boss leaves the office early. We'd be at the Capitol Hill Club as soon as someone called and said the plane was in the air. Our code was we were 'attending a Water Committee meeting.' What is it called these days?"

"Aw, Boss," smiled Michelle. "That's just all the other staffs who goof off when their Boss is out of town. We don't have any name for it because we want you here 24/7."

"You've been on the Hill too long, Michelle," said Thompson, looking over his horn-rimmed glasses. "I almost believe your bullshit." They both laughed. "Just get the calls lined up before three bells." He paused, and then began to sing. "Michelle, three bells. These are words that go together well…three bells Michelle."

Michelle rolled her eyes and turned to walk out of Thompson's office to get the list of calls.

The daily D.C. comings and goings of a United States Congressman are dictated by a series of bells, lights, and pagers. All across the office buildings on the Hill, a system is in use whereby bells sound in all the buildings to alert Members as to what is happening on the Floor. Clocks on the walls have lights around them to indicate the number of bells that have sounded. And if Members happen to miss the bells, they wear a pager which tells them audibly how many bells have sounded and what is being voted upon. Three bells indicate the House has ordered a quorum call.

"And one more thing, Boss," said Michelle, turning back at the doorway.

"What's that?"

"Josh and Griffith both told me you were no longer allowed to quote the Marquis de Lafayette in press interviews."

"Come on, Michelle," said Thompson. "This is the perfect chance. I was going to use Lafayette's quote about the birth of America. 'Humanity has won its battle. Liberty now has a country.' That's perfect for what's going on in Romania."

"Maybe," said Michelle. "But they both told me I would be fired if I let you sound that highbrow and geeky again."

"Highbrow and geeky?" asked Thompson.

"Yes, sir," she responded.

"Please remind the staff and Griff they work for me, not vice versa."

"Actually, geeky was your wife's word," she said referring to Thompson's wife, Ann.

Thompson glared at her over his glasses in mock anger. He purposely made the furrows in his forehead grow deep. Michelle knew that Thompson was kidding, but she also recognized his displeasure with the suggestion. "You're the Boss."

The United States Capitol stands against the blue sky of the District of Columbia as a modern-day temple to the legislative process envisioned by the Founding Fathers.

The center of it all is the United States House of Representatives. The "peoples' chamber" is the place where public opinion makes its way into the legislative process. Each and every item on the floor has a symbolic importance to representative government. One could conduct an entire college course on the symbolism of the floor. To sit on the floor, where some of the greatest debates in the world have occurred, is to understand that those symbols are as strong as the Republic itself.

When Richard Thompson became Kentucky's newest Member of the United States House of Representatives, the first thing he noticed on the House floor was the abundance of fasces. It's hard to miss them. On either side of the Speaker's chair there are two gold fasciae, each with a warrior's ax attached to its end. Fasces are also cast in bronze as handrails and painted fresco style around the Chamber and the Speaker's Lobby. Fasces are even used as frames for the portraits of General George Washington and the Marquis de Lafayette that are located on either side of the Speaker's rostrum.

Thompson loved the history of the House and made every effort to learn all he could about the symbolism portrayed on the floor.

Michelle came back into Thompson's office and handed him the list of calls she had lined up for him.

"This first one on the list is the most important," said Michelle. "Denise Hetzel is a D.C. reporter, but she is a stringer for a European policy rag out of London. They're following the Romanian elections because there has been a lot of talk about how well the former Communist republics are doing since joining the European Union."

"Romania joined around 2007, didn't they?" asked Thompson as he looked at the list. "From what I understand, it's pretty primitive in the countryside. What do the Brits have to say about it?"

"They're still leery of Romania," said Michelle. "They get unrestricted EU membership in 2014. I think the Prime Minister and some of the other foreign policy types in the U.K. would like to stretch that out another 10 years. Hopefully, Romania will have more political stability then."

"I doubt it," said Thompson. "When Griff and I were over there in the '90s, we could buy anything we wanted with Kent cigarettes and condoms. I showed some people at our hotel a Ziploc bag and they thought I was Howard Hughes."

"So, what did you buy with your cigarettes?" Michelle asked jokingly.

"None of your business," said Thompson. "Get Ms. Hetzel on the phone."

Just as Michelle was leaving the room, bells began to sound. Thompson looked at the clock. It was 8:17. With a puzzled look on his face, Thompson reached for his beeper and turned up the volume.

"Six bells, six bells at 8:17 to advise Members that today's session of the United States House of Representatives has been cancelled. Repeat, today's session has been cancelled. The bells indicate the House will stand in recess until further notice."

"What the hell does that mean?" quizzed Thompson. "Recess until further notice?"

"Odd," said Michelle. "They don't cancel many legislative days around here."

"Yeah, I know," Thompson replied.

"I'll call the Cloak Room and find out what's going on," Michelle replied. "If we really are cancelled, I'll see if I can get you on the 12:30 flight home."

Thompson got up from his desk and headed to the reception area of his office suite where other staffers were milling around. "You seem awfully anxious to get me out of here early," he announced so that everyone in the office could hear. As he walked out, he noticed a Capitol Hill police officer walking past his office door, down the building's main corridor. His police radio was buzzing with chatter.

"Hey, Radar," shouted Thompson. The officer was so familiar to Thompson that he called him by his nickname. "What's going on?"

Looking over his shoulder as he walked past, Radar replied, "It's a wild one today, Congressman. Someone's stolen the Mace and Bob Patterson is missing!"

Chapter 5

Occoquan, Virginia, is located about twenty-five miles south of the District of Columbia on Interstate 95. The small village is only a couple of narrow streets square and is closer to the Quantico Marine Base than to the nation's capital. The town sits on the Occoquan River, which leads out into the Chesapeake Bay. It's a quaint, historic little burg frequented on weekends by antique hunters and shoppers who reach the town by both car and boat.

Walking down the sidewalks of Occoquan visitors may think they are a million miles from the center of the nation's base of power. The old storefronts and small houses call back to a simpler time, when the nation didn't know every movement of its nation's leaders and, quite frankly, didn't much care.

On a wet and stormy day, Jane Kline made her way off the expressway exit and down the winding road to the small town, but shopping for antiques was the farthest thing from her mind. The freshly stolen domestic car, with even fresher stolen license plates, was not likely to draw the attention of any police. Nevertheless, she was not taking any chances. As the windshield wipers slapped back and forth, she slowly pulled up to a stop sign. Silently she counted to "three-Mississippi" with the rhythm of the wipers before removing her foot from the brake and accelerating forward. She couldn't risk even a routine traffic stop by some small-town Barney Fife.

Kline had encountered problems, like routine traffic stops, dozens of times in her career. When the problem couldn't be handled by the fake driver's license and other documents forged to establish her identity *du jour*, the Company had procedures in place to get her out.

This time, however, would be different. This time a traffic stop capture would be bad. To be more precise, this time a stop would be catastrophic. It wasn't the hot car or hotter plates. It was what she was carrying with her that mattered. The bounty in the trunk was masked to look like containers carrying fishing gear, but a curious cop could easily prove otherwise. Jane Kline was transporting the Mace, a stolen treasure of ebony rods and silver ribbon that had been code named simply "the football."

Kline parked her car in a small public parking lot that was normally occupied by vehicles carrying the masses of shoppers who visit the picturesque village. It was a weekday morning and she had no trouble locating an empty space. This weekend the town would be hopping with shoppers. Today it was quiet.

From the seat of the parked car, Kline looked out at the river and the boats docked up and down the public landing of the town. She pulled a small pair of binoculars out of her purse and checked out the registration numbers on each boat's hull. Spying a nondescript, white, twenty-three foot Crownline Cuddy Cabin, she focused her gaze. "279032VA," she mumbled to herself. "That's the one."

Kline turned off the engine and exited the car. Tight blue jeans and a khaki shirt covered her athletic 5'10" frame and a fishing vest covered her trim upper body. A long-billed fishing hat was pulled down low to her brown eyes and her short brown hair poked out from underneath the cap. The square jaw that jutted out from underneath the cap gave Jane Kline the stoic look of a woman who took charge. One stern look from Jane Kline could stop her male counterparts at the CIA in their tracks.

The trunk clicked open. From the back, Kline pulled a long cylinder, which looked like a tube filled with fishing poles to anyone who might be watching. With her other hand she grabbed a larger than usual tackle box. She flipped the keys in the trunk and closed the lid on top of them. As nonchalantly as possible, she removed a pair of thin latex gloves and shoved them in the pocket of her vest.

She made her way down the dock and handed the gear to the boat's captain. One steady foot at a time, she stepped on board.

"Ready for some fishing today, Mark?" she asked the captain.

"Looks like you brought the right gear to land the big one," he replied as he looked around to see if anyone was listening to the conversation. "It's a little rough out there today. I have some rain gear down there for you."

Kline went below deck and gently ditched her gear in the small cabin of the boat. She looked around until she located a couple of small bungee cords and secured the gear against the inside of the hull. She took her cap off and put the rain gear on, replaced the cap and pulled the hood of the jacket over her head. "I look as nondescript as the unabomber now," she mumbled as she added sunglasses to the ensemble.

Kline emerged from the cabin and stood on the deck. She carefully surveyed the shoreline, looking for anything abnormal. When she concluded it was time to go, she nodded at the captain, unhooked the mooring line from its cleat and pushed the boat back from the dock.

Both were quiet until the boat reached the channel. Mark spoke first. "So how bad was the reaction about the collateral damage?"

"Real bad," said Kline.

Kline was known to her colleagues as a loner who did not enjoy working with partners. Despite her vehement objection to the contrary, she had been ordered to work with a newbie, Mark Morrison, on this particular assignment. After meeting the tall muscular agent with short black hair and cool grey eyes, she knew from their first meeting she was not going to enjoy the partnership. He was full of himself and possessed an arrogant confidence which concerned, rather than amused, her. He was a pretty boy and she didn't like pretty boys. Her distrust of his instincts and abilities had been confirmed by his screw-up the night before in the offices of the Sergeant at Arms.

"I was afraid of that," he said, while sucking in air. They were just about out of the "No Wake" zone.

"The disposal division of the Company had to come by and pick up the garbage," she added. "They have your pen pal on ice up in Maryland until they can come up with an appropriate cover as to how he died. You are in deep shit, my friend."

"Sonofabitch," he said. "Like no one else in the Agency has ever killed anyone before."

"Well, he was a civilian," Kline replied, unable to comprehend how Morrison was taking absolutely no responsibility for the death of Robert Patterson.

"Yeah, I know," he said looking out at the open river ahead of them. He jammed the throttle down and the boat picked up speed. "I guess you're right. I *am* in deep shit now."

"Don't worry about it," Kline could think of nothing else to say other than the cliché. "We all have had a screw up sometime in our careers. This will not be your first and it certainly will not be your last." She paused and stared directly at Morrison. "Just don't let the next one happen on an operation where we are partners."

"Is this one biting you in the ass?" he asked.

"More than you could imagine," she said, not joking.

"Did the Director chew you out?"

"It's worse than that," Kline replied. "The Boss is behind this operation. He gave his personal approval."

"Sonofabitch," grunted Mark.

"Sonofabitch is damn right," she said. "The Director got his ass chewed by the Boss and he passed it down."

"Sorry," Mark said with some degree of sincerity. "Why the hell are we doing this anyway? I mean we stole some of our own country's shit. That doesn't make any sense to me."

"Don't ever ask that question again," Kline instructed,

glaring in disbelief at Morrison. "We just do. We don't ask why. We just do."

"You're right," he replied in a low tone, looking down. "Just like they all said at the office…you're always right."

Kline smiled, knowing that her reputation was preceding her with the young agent.

"And since you're always right," he added, "I need to figure out how to get this bull's eye off my back. I screwed the pooch royally last night."

"First off," replied Kline, "you have got to quit working this like it's a regular nine-to-five job."

"What do you mean by that?"

"Mark, you have got to start doing something to make yourself noticed at the Company. When I was new, language was the big thing. The more languages a new agent knew the better. Languages meant assignments back then. Hell, the first time I was assigned to Eastern Europe, it was because I knew more languages than the older agents. I am the lead on this assignment because I know Romanian." Kline's mind shot back to a day years ago in Romania that turned a girl from Southern California into a paid assassin.

"So, I need to learn Romanian?"

"No, Mark," Kline said with exasperation in her voice. "That was then. This is now. You need to figure out what the Agency needs right now and then excel in it. Back then the Company needed assassins that spoke Romanian. Today, we aren't supposed to kill people. Find out what we are allowed to do that you can do better."

"Got it," said Mark, although Kline was not quite sure he did, in fact, get it.

"And then, work 'em one at a time," said Kline. "And right now, our 'one at a time' is you getting me into Quantico unnoticed. Let's not follow up last night's fuck-up with another one. Keep your eyes open."

"I will," he said. "We look clean."

"Well, let's make sure," Kline replied.

"How?"

"By fishing."

"Fishing?" Morrison asked, puzzled.

"Fishing," Kline repeated. "If anyone is following us—land, water or air—stopping at some remote shore and doing some fishing will flush them out. We'll see 'em coming a mile away."

"Makes sense to me," Morrison said. "But I have to warn you, I'm not much of a fisherman."

"You, little boy, will not be fishing," she said. "I will."

"You will?"

"Yeah," she said. "Remember, our cover is that of a fishing charter and customer. I'm the customer. I fish. You watch."

"Aye, aye," he replied.

"Did you have the guys back at the Company dock pack some fishing gear?" she asked.

"Yeah," Morrison said. "They got a kick out of that request. I have never been to the Company warehouse before. It was fucking amazing. They have everything there, even fishing gear."

"I've been there before," said Kline. "Did some little old Irish-looking mug get you the boat?"

"Sure did," said Morrison. "He said everybody called him Kropper. He brought out the fishing gear and asked who it was for. When I told him it was for you, he took it back. He said he wanted to get you some good gear to work with. He said that you were always coming on to him and the two of you planned to get married some day. If he didn't get you some good gear, you would leave him."

Kline smiled. "I love that little old Mick. Treat him good, he'll get you anything you need. I just wish Kropper could have gotten me a clean car. Some poor schmuck is reporting his wheels missing from a D.C. parking garage right about now."

"They'll find it tomorrow as soon as the locals start towing cars out of the lot," said Morrison. "It will be the biggest crime wave to hit Occoquan in the last century. And you'll see Kropper as soon as we're done today. He's meeting us at the Company dock to pick up the boat."

Kline squinted her eyes, looking for a place to anchor. It had to be a place where they could easily spot anyone following them. More importantly, it had to be a spot where there were likely to be some fish. "Over there," said Kline, pointing to a small cove with a fallen tree sticking partially out of the water. "There will be some bass over there."

Kline pulled her gear from the steerage of the boat. A lightweight Shakespeare rod and reel were not what she would have chosen, but it was better than she had expected. Kropper had taken care of her—again. After attaching a frog lure, she cast her line toward the shore. While she was cranking the lure back in, Kline was scanning the woods in front of her. It was slightly overcast and a light mist was falling.

Only real fishermen are going to be out in this mess, she thought to herself. *If we have a trailer, they will stand out like a sore thumb.*

Kline took a deep breath as she reeled in the lure. The fresh river air winding its way leisurely up the valley reminded her of slow childhood walks with her grandmother in the small town where she had grown up. With her service in the CIA, Kline's life had become a lot more hectic and she relished those times when a fresh breeze brought back such youthful recollections. She would have to dive back into the reality of a blown mission soon enough. She smiled as the smell of the river offered her a mental repose, however brief.

After about fifteen minutes, Morrison broke the silence. "I think we're clean. Are you ready to go?"

"We still have some time and I'm not leaving until I actually catch a fish," Kline said. She changed out her frog lure for a shiny rapalla minnow which she cast toward the fallen tree by the shore.

On her fourth cast with the new lure, something hit. A smile broke out on her face as she yanked on the rod to set the lure. The rod whipped from side to side as she quickly cranked the fish closer and closer to the boat. "Ohhh, this is a big buster, Marko. Quick. Grab the net," she shouted.

"What?"

"Grab the net, dumb ass," she repeated. "I've got him close."

Morrison looked around quickly and found the net. He leaned over the starboard side of the boat as Kline pulled the fish close enough for him to scoop it up.

"Got him!" he shouted.

Kline reached into the open net and grabbed the bass by its large lower lip. She removed the lure and held him high, looking at him from side to side in admiration. Then she leaned over the side and gently released the fish back into the river. "Another day, pal … I'll see you on another day."

"Now, Mark," she told her undercover skipper, "we can go."

Chapter 6

It was approaching evening as Michael Griffith, Josh Barkman, and Sue Myers, the attractive flight attendant, approached the baggage claim in the Henri Coanda International Airport in Bucharest, Romania. Griffith had built an extra day into the schedule to overcome the jet lag he knew would come with the long flight. Although the President of Romania, Alexander Krasterich, was sending a car to pick them up at the airport, meetings with the campaign team were not starting for another day.

Before they even landed in Paris, Griffith had convinced Sue to fly to Bucharest with him for dinner on his bonus day in Romania, before he and Josh had to start working. Josh was amazed at how smooth Griffith had been in his interaction with Sue. Josh had a certain boyish charm about him which endeared him to women, but socially he was a bit awkward. As confident he was with his political skills, he lacked the same self-assurance with the opposite sex. He was that kid whom parents love and want their daughters to date, but the daughters often found little interest in him.

"All right, boy," Griffith said to Josh as they disembarked from the plane. "Welcome to Romania. Remember we are in-country now. It's not like any place you have ever been before. This isn't D.C. New rules apply."

"I know, I know," said Josh. "I read the briefing book."

"Fuck the briefing book, man," said Griffith shaking his head negatively as they entered the terminal where the bags would be staged before going through customs. There were several stations and Griffith scanned the room looking for the bags from their flight from Paris. "You are just like your boss."

"Who's his boss?" asked Sue.

"Josh works for Congressman Richard Thompson from Kentucky," replied Griffith.

"Kentucky?" inquired Sue looking at Josh. "I love it there. Early in my career, I used to fly in and out of there a lot." She then looked back at Griffith who had found the conveyor delivering their bags and had begun walking towards them. Sue and Josh followed Griffith as their travel-weary leader. "So, how do you know his boss?"

"Thompson and I roomed together in college before we moved to D.C. many years ago. We did everything together, including working on a lot of campaigns. Right after they killed Nicolae Ceausescu, I got assigned to come over here to advise the Romanians on how to set up political parties and run elections. Thompson came with me as an official observer. Thompson was all by the book then, too." Griffith paused and punched Josh playfully in the arm. "It looks like his Chief of Staff is following in his footsteps. You're an official chip off the stick-up-the-ass block."

"I still can't believe you were over here then," said Sue.

"Yeah," Griffith replied. "I was on one of three teams of advisors sent in by the American government in January of 1990, a couple of weeks after the Romanian army executed the old man and his wife, Elena. They executed him on Christmas Day, so it took a week or so to get a team together over the holidays."

"That must have been one helluva trip," said Sue.

"It was a helluva trip," said Griffith. "This place was a fucking rat hole. The water was so salty it tasted like Alka Seltzer. The more you drank it, the thirstier you became. The assignment was fun, but I hated the country."

"I told you on the plane, it's changed," said Sue.

"You better be right about what you said about the food," said Griffith, referring to an earlier comment Sue had made on the plane about restaurants in Romania. "Back then even the best restaurant in town served some sort of gray mystery meat covered in anonymous white gravy."

"Don't worry," said Sue. "Like I tried to tell you on the plane, this is not the place you came to years ago. I fly here all the time now. Bucharest is actually a fun place." She moved in closer to him and smiled. "We'll have a good time tonight."

"Oh, we'll have a good time," Griffith replied. "But I doubt that it will be because of Bucharest. This town was the most depressing place I'd ever been in my life."

"You'll be surprised," said Sue. "A lot has changed."

"I really doubt it," said Griffith in a tone that suddenly seemed more sour than normal. "Don't go anywhere by yourself, Josh. This fucking place is scary. Don't go anywhere alone."

Sue looked at Josh, made a face and shook her head no. The trio grabbed their luggage and headed to customs. Accustomed to the heavy scrutiny given to baggage security in America, Josh was surprised at the lack of review as they went through Romanian customs. A few bags were opened randomly, but most were just allowed into the country without as much as a question about what was in them. Josh was through first and waited as Griffith and Sue explained to the immigration officer they were not a couple and needed to fill out separate forms. They got their passports stamped and headed to the main terminal.

"So, do you think we were with him or against him?" asked Josh, intentionally changing the subject as they walked.

"Who?" Griffith replied blankly. He wasn't ignoring Josh, but seemed to be distracted by Sue's charm.

"Nicolae Ceausescu," replied Josh. "There's always been some question about whether we supported Ceausescu or opposed him. No one has ever cleared it up."

"You think we were behind a Communist?" asked Sue.

"I've read a lot about Ceausescu in preparation for this trip. He didn't always follow the dictates of the Kremlin," Josh replied. "So, some people thought because he thumbed his nose occasionally at Russia we were propping him up. Ceausescu liked playing both sides and received backing from both us and Moscow. That's why it took so long for the Romanian people to finally overthrow him."

"We were behind Ceausescu?" asked Sue. "Come on."

"Seriously. A lot of people said we were secretly backing him. But, you're right. He was an evil guy. Critics claim we were on the wrong side … you know, from a moral standpoint. What about it, Griff? What do you think?"

"Hard telling," said Griffith. "Josh, you know I'm not a policy wonk like you and your boss. I'm the political guy. I don't follow the policy that closely. And I'm sure as hell not moral." He winked at Sue. "But, I'll tell you this much. He was a class-A nut job."

"Really?" interjected Sue. "How so?"

"Obsessive Compulsive Disorder," Griffith replied. "He was scared shitless of germs. He used to have staff carry a bottle of alcohol solution with him. He'd shake hands and then have the staff spray his hands. Apparently, he did it in front of the Queen one day in London."

"I bet that went over well," said Sue.

"Yeah," Griffith continued. "And he was old-world, old-school."

"What do you mean by that?" Josh asked.

"He was superstitious as hell," said Griffith. "Romania may be the most superstitious country in the world. Ceausescu bought into all that gypsy hex and evil eye shit."

"Evil eye?" asked Sue.

"Evil eye, baby," repeated Griffith raising one eyebrow higher than the other. "If you believe in it, you believe that someone can pass along a curse or a hex by a simple gaze." He looked at Josh. "Blue eyes have the power. We couldn't have put you on the team back then. You would have scared the shit out of everyday Romanians."

"Yeah, right," said Josh skeptically.

"Seriously, boy," said Griffith. "Your baby blues would have them crappin' their pants."

"Fine. Now, quit avoiding the question. Were we behind Ceausescu or the opposition?"

Griffith looked seriously at Josh for a moment. "Straight up. I think we were behind Ceausescu. We were so anxious to defeat Russia in those days that we backed anyone who looked like they might be open to market reforms. Hell, Nixon came over here and gave him a damn car."

"So Chomsky was right," said Josh referring to Romanian dissident Noam Chomsky. "He thinks we propped the Communist government up until the final days."

"All I can tell you is when we got over here in '90, it was a cluster-fuck of the first-degree. People were afraid their neighbors would turn them in as enemies of the state. I'm talking serious repression. The secret police, the Securitate, were still organized, even though they had no real leader. But they went ahead and followed us everywhere and bugged our rooms anyway. And they were bad at it. You could pick out your tail, from a block away. It was pretty surreal."

"That must have been wild," Josh said. "Is it true what the boss said … they put you two in a room where someone had just been assassinated?"

Griffith laughed out loud and nodded his head affirmatively. "We show up in the room on the 3rd floor of the Intercontinental and it's cold as hell. I open the drapes, looking for the room heater, and we've got this great view of the town square. Then I notice the plate glass to the window is just leaning in place."

"No shit?" Josh replied.

"I ask Thompson to toss me the comforter on the bed, so I can tuck it around the window to stop the draft coming in. He peels it back off the bed and freaks out. There's blood spatters all over the damn bed."

"Yuk," said Sue.

"It turns out some rebel from the mountains, opposed to Ceausescu, had been staying in the room. He opens the drapes to admire the view of the square, and some Securitate sniper pops him through the window."

"And they just leaned the new window in place?" Sue asked.

"Hell, they didn't even change the sheets," replied Griffith. "The dude's blood was all over the place."

"What did you do?" asked Josh.

"We slept in our clothes a lot," laughed Griffith.

"Well, I hope you don't have that room tonight," Sue said, reaching for Griffith's arm as they neared the baggage claim area. "How much did you get paid back then?"

"Aw, hell," said Griffith. "We were kids back then. We did it for damn near nothing. Officially, we were just observers. We did it for a per diem. Just like Josh today. I'm getting paid big bucks by the President's campaign, but Josh is over here as a volunteer observing for the U.S. Government. The truth is, when you're his age, you'd pay them for the experience."

The three entered the main lobby and looked around. Josh was amazed that all of the signs and store advertisements were written in English and Romanian. "We need to find our interpreter. The President is sending over a car and we're supposed to look for them out front."

"Don't talk to gypsies," warned Griffith.

"Where did that come from?" asked Josh.

"Just listen to me," said Griff. "Don't talk to them. They'll pick your pocket."

"How do I know they are gypsies?" asked Josh.

"Easy," said Griffith. "They speak the best English."

As the trio walked from the airport lobby to the curb, it was hard to miss who they were supposed to meet. Three dark blue SUVs were lined up along the street with their motors running, each with a small U.S. flag attached to one front fender, a Romanian flag to the other. A Romanian military officer stood at parade rest by the rear door of the middle car, a small red carpet leading the way to the back seat.

There was a smaller, older man standing next to a soldier. The pale, gaunt figure wore an old gray herringbone suit, crumpled white shirt and narrow black tie. The black and white check hat he wore— which reminded Griffith of the kind "Bear" Bryant always wore— made his pencil-thin mustache stand out. He carried a cane in one hand and an old tattered paperback book in the other. As they approached with their luggage, the little man recognized them as the people he was looking for in the crowd. He shouted instructions to several of the other men in uniform who quickly made their way to the Americans and relieved them of their baggage.

"Good afternoon," said the man in broken English as he approached them. "My name is Yorgi and I will be accompanying you as your Romanian guide and interpreter for your time in our country."

He eyeballed the three Americans and stuck out his hand to Josh first. "You must be Yoshuua Barackemenn."

"Josh Barkman, but close enough."

"Weelcome to Romania Yoshuua," said the man. He then looked at Griffith's boots and bald head. "Which makes you Mickeel Greffeth."

"Just call me Griff and we'll be fine."

"Greef," said the man, trying to please his guest. "Very well."

The man then looked at Sue with a puzzled look on his face. He had obviously been informed he was meeting two people, not three, at the airport. "She's with me," informed Griffith.

"Your," the man fumbled through the book looking for the right word to translate from Soþia, the Romanian word for spouse, "wife?"

"No," replied Griffith. "She's not my wife."

"Ahhhh," the man smiled. "She's your ballet dancer."

"Ballet dancer?" asked Josh puzzled.

"Yeah," said Sue. "They refer to call girls over here as ballet dancers. And, no, I am not his ballet dancer. My name is Sue Myers, and I am his guest for the evening." She turned to Griffith and quietly said to him, "Sonofabitch doesn't know the English word for wife, but he sure as hell knows how to call someone a whore."

"My sincerest apologies, Mees Sue," said Yorgi sincerely while bowing to her and tipping his hat. Sue nodded an acceptance of his apology.

"Wow, ballet dancer. I've never had quite such an appreciation for the arts before," Josh said, with what he intended as a humorously leering up-and-down look at Sue. Since landing, he had decided Sue was a hot 40-something, not a worn out 20-something. She scowled back at him in a mock frown.

"Watch yourself, Josh," laughed Griffith. "I think she can take you."

The soldier who had been standing next to the car motioned the trio to enter the back seat as Yorgi jumped into the front with the military driver. Griffith looked around as he settled into the car. "What the hell is a Dacia Logan," he asked, referring to the make and model emblem on the side of the car.

"Romanian-made cars," said Yorgi in a slow and deliberate fashion to keep his English as proper as possible. "They are made at a factory in Mioveni—about an hour or so out of Bucharest in the Fagaris Mountains. We are quite proud of them."

"You should be," said Sue. "They are very nice."

"Great," muttered Griffith just loud enough so that only Sue could hear. "Mountain made Romanian cars ... I hope the wheels don't fall off."

"Shhh," whispered Sue, placing her finger to Griffith's lips.

As the cars made their way from the airport to the Intercontinental in downtown Bucharest, Josh made small-talk with Yorgi. Griffith, however, looked out the window at a town much more vibrant than his old memories recalled.

It's not the incredibly dark place it was back then, Griffith thought. *Everything looks brighter. The roads ... the cars ... hell, even the people. Back then a 30-year-old looked a hundred. Look at them now, you can't define the generations.*

People are smiling, Griffith thought to himself as he watched the people passing by. Smiling. *God, no one smiled back in '90. Everyone had the frown of an old man or woman. There was no happiness to be found. Everyone was afraid.*

The cars passed a vehicle traveling slower than the quick pace they were making. When the Romanian motorcade passed the car, the driver recognized the American flag and placed the fingers of his right hand under his chin and flipped them forward—the Romanian version of flipping the bird.

"Look at that," said Griffith. "They flipped us off because we're Americans. Back in the 90s, these people thought we were gods. They were thirsty for freedom, and they thought that we were going to bring it to them—in prepackaged boxes with the special prize inside being American Democracy." He smiled at the memory of an old woman scattering flowers in front of him and Thompson as they walked through the streets of a small village in the northern part of the country.

"And now they flip us the bird. I guess things have changed. I wonder if they remember what a prick Ceausescu was.

"They have probably forgotten the lessons we taught them. Just like Americans tend to forget. Maybe we taught them our ways too well."

Chapter 7

Outside the barbed-wire security fences that define the borders of Quantico Marine Base, there is a small town of the same name. Most people living in and around Washington, D.C. have no idea the town itself actually exists. And even those who know it exists have a damn hard time finding it. To get to the City of Quantico, Virginia, one has to navigate through various twists and turns within the Marine base before leaving the base on the river side. The entire town is no more than about a dozen city blocks, but that is more than enough room for its thriving population of 561 residents.

The town of Quantico supports the military base. It has its own stop on the Amtrack line, but when the train from D.C. stops there in the morning, everyone walks to the base rather than to the tiny city. The one thriving business in the town is the Army Navy Store on Potomac Street.

If a visitor can't find Quantico via car, they can always visit via boat. Quantico sits right on a bend in the Potomac River. A small dock at the end of Potomac Street makes the town easily accessible by water. And that's exactly how Jane Kline and Mark Morrison arrived.

Kline looked at her watch as Morrison maneuvered the boat to the dock. They were right on time. Morrison noticed Kline's athletic body made her look younger than her 35 years as she jumped from the deck of the boat onto the dock and bent over to tie a line to the mooring cleat. Even in her fishing gear, she looked good. She jumped back onto the boat and made her way down under to retrieve the tube and tackle box.

"Wait here," Kline said to Morrison as she headed towards the city. "This shouldn't take long."

"Aye, aye, Captain," replied Morrison as he saluted a reply which had more than just a hint of sarcasm in it.

Kline thought about going back to her young mentee and explaining how the meeting she was about to have was not going to be a pleasant one—all because of his screw-up. Only her training kept her stride moving forward. An argument would only draw attention to the pair and possibly make her late for the meeting. A lecture on insubordination could wait for later. She kept walking.

Kline proceeded up Potomac Street toward the Army Navy store. As she did so, she was carefully observing the people mingling around on either side of the street, all of whom seemed to be young jar-heads waiting for the start of their next shifts.

The conversation on the boat had reminded Kline of her very first "hit" for the Company. She was sent to Romania to "dispatch" a political leader in the north part of the country. The leader, along with being the head of a rising political party, was also actively involved with the drug trade in Eastern Europe. She was given the assignment precisely because she had taken a crash course in the difficult language of Romanian. As she had spoken to Morrison about his future with the Agency, she remembered the fear in the target's eyes as she lowered her gun and pointed it between his eyes. More remarkably, Kline remembered the emotionless determination she had displayed when she had pulled the trigger.

Kline continued her walk. Outside the store, a tall, slim, silver-haired man in blue jeans, a button down blue shirt and a rain jacket sat on a bench with that day's edition of *The Washington Post* in front of his long weathered face. As he read the paper through dark sun glasses, he rolled a large Churchill cigar from side to side in his mouth. Benny Vesper was one of those guys who had been around Washington politics all of his adult life. He knew government better than any career bureaucrat and inside-the-beltway politics far better than most other hacks. He had advised many presidents over the years, formally and informally. He was Chief of Staff to President Jack Mocker and was in Quantico on the President's direct orders.

"Good morning, Jane," said Vesper, in his normal drone-like, deep monotone. "Welcome to Quantico." Kline wasn't surprised when he didn't stick out his hand to shake. "Let's walk around to the side of the building."

"Mr. Vesper," replied Kline as they walked. She wanted to keep the tone as cordial as possible. "Thanks for the welcome, but I've been here before. You forget, we do a lot of our training here."

"Yeah," said Vesper. "How'd that training work out for you last night?"

Normally, Vesper's tone never indicated whether a comment was a joke, sarcasm, or a compliment. This time, however, Kline could tell Vesper was angry. Vesper stopped walking and leaned up against the side of the building taking a deep drag on the cigar. As he slowly puffed out the smoke, Kline could see the anger emanating from twitching muscles in Vesper's jaw.

Jane Kline was career CIA and had worked under a couple of presidential administrations. She and Vesper had clashed before. An early accomplishment in her career had placed her on a select covert team of agents that interacted directly with the President. Over the years, she got along with most administrations. They understood her role. But she didn't like Vesper, or his boss Mocker and it wasn't their politics. She was trained not to question politics. She just didn't like their holier-than-thou attitude when it came to covert operations. Vesper had made it clear in their meeting that he and the President didn't like her or the CIA. The feeling was mutual.

She winced at having given Vesper such an easy opening to smack her, and the Agency, down.

"We had a problem," said Kline.

"Problem … is that what you call murder now?" replied Vesper. "You murdered the Sergeant at Arms of the House of Representatives."

"I didn't murder anybody," Kline said.

"No, but some dumb shit on your team sure as hell killed him."

"It couldn't be helped. Sometimes things happen in covert operations."

"Yeah," said Vesper. "We've been over that before, haven't we? But you aren't in some third-world hell hole this time with some illiterate villager's balls strapped to a live electrical cord. You fucking killed an American."

"I know what happened," said Kline. Vesper's baritone voice had a tendency to carry, so Kline looked over her shoulder to make sure no one from the street was listening.

"You know what happened," said Vesper, "but you can't even begin to understand the implications. You're just like every other trigger-happy puke over at the Agency who gets their rocks off at playing 'secret agent man.' The implications for the President right now are history altering."

"I get that," replied Kline.

"Good, because you sure fucked this one up," Vesper wouldn't relent. "We'll have to leak a story that Patterson is a suspect in the theft. He was a good man. I hate to do it, but you people left us no choice."

"It's a good thing he had no family," replied Kline.

"It's amazing to me how you people actually won the Cold War. The Russians must have been real fuck-ups back then." Vesper's sarcasm got even thicker. "Got any one car parades we can assign you to organize? Or would that be too complicated for your crack team of covert operatives?"

Kline didn't respond.

"You would probably kill the fucking driver," said Vesper.

"Look," Kline had had just about enough from Vesper. "This was your mission, not ours. I'm not sure why you need this goddamn thing, but we got it for you. You, of all people, know there is collateral damage in covert operations and sometimes we can't stop them from happening. Patterson was the collateral damage this time and I take full responsibility.

But you remember one thing, Mr. Vesper. This was your mission, not ours."

"Don't take that tone of voice with me, Agent Kline," responded Vesper. "You still work for the President, and I'm here on his direct orders."

"Fine," Kline responded. "We both have orders from the President. Well, they are fulfilled. Here it is." Kline placed the tube, containing the fasciae, and the tackle box, with the silver globe and eagle in it, on the ground. Vesper looked down, momentarily confused.

"What the hell is this?" he asked.

"It's your football."

"You took it apart?"

"I had to," replied Kline. Now it was her turn for sarcasm. "I had to figure out a way to get it to you. I couldn't just parade up Potomac Street in Quantico carrying the Mace, now could I? It might attract a wee bit of attention."

"Yes, it would," responded a tight-lipped Vesper.

"And you're putting it on a plane on Sunday night with a bunch of observers. Right?"

Vesper nodded affirmatively.

"So, it's disassembled and packed tight in the tube and tackle box. Toss it in the belly of the plane and reassemble it when it gets to wherever it's going. The tools you need are taped to the top of the tackle box."

"Clever."

"Thanks. That's why they call us covert."

Chapter 8

The name of the Carpathian Mountains is derived from a root word meaning "to turn" or "change." The locals call them the Transylvanian Alps. Only a few curvy roads cut through the rough but beautiful terrain. At many points, the range is so high that snow caps the peaks even in the summer.

In a remote location just outside of the Romanian town of Brasov in the Southern Carpathian Mountains, a group of men gathered in a diminutive, three-room shack. The shack was nearly on top of the road, but there wasn't another house around it for more than a half mile in either direction. The road outside the shack was so curvy and twisty, and the terrain of the valley so hilly, that no one would actually see the house until nearly on top of it.

Adding to the cover for the house was the dense, green forest which began just twenty or thirty yards behind the back of the building. To find this location someone either had to be looking for it, or lost. And that obscurity of the location was just fine for the people inside.

On this day, as on most days, heavy dew kept the dark smoke from the chimney low to the ground and filled the countryside with the smell of wet, burnt wood. The musty smell stuck to the clothes of anyone in the vicinity like gum to a shoe on a hot day. A rusty, beat-up, 1970's-era black four-door Buick Electra was parked in front of the cottage.

Inside the house, several men sat near the fire, discussing politics and the upcoming Romanian presidential elections. The man leading the discussion, General Gheorghe Alexandro, was the oldest in the room and the owner of the small house. Alexandro's daughter, Noua, a beautiful brunette with high cheekbones and brown eyes, served the men coffee as they spoke.

All but one of the men around the table had a gritty, old-world look to them. It was Abel Bogdan who stood out amongst them. His face was clean shaven and he did not have the weathered look of the others. His clothes, while not elaborate or expensive, were not wrinkled or stained. The clothes Bogdan wore hung on his six-foot frame with a distinction recognized by the others as someone from the city. They knew the strapping politician as a local leader from Brasov but did not know why the dark eyed Bogdan had joined them on this day.

The men also knew Gheorghe Alexandro had led Securitate forces in Romania under Nicolae Ceausescu. He had a reputation in those days as a ruthless man, often led to act by his own personal superstitions. Even today, he made sure all the men in the room, and Noua, wore a *comicello*, a white curved amulet believed to ward off the curse of the "evil eye," on chains around their necks.

In his prime, Alexandro had been known for taking aggressive actions against political opponents of the state. In November 1987, he led the government forces that put down the Brasov Rebellion, a strike in which 20,000 people left work and marched on Communist Party Headquarters in Brasov to protest pending job layoffs at the factories. The workers occupied the headquarters and threw portraits of Ceausescu into a fire on the town square. Alexandro's forces surrounded the city and viciously put down the rebellion. Those who led the rebellion were either jailed or "relocated" to other regions of Romania.

Neither Alexandro nor Nicolae Ceausescu realized the actions taken by the government to quell the Brasov Rebellion were the beginning of the end for Communism in Romania. The people began to rise up. Two years after the rebellion, Ceausescu would be executed by a firing squad and General Alexandro would instantly become a general without an army to command. Alexandro himself had barely escaped with his life, leaving the presidential palace in an automobile that had been given to Ceausescu by the American president, Richard Nixon. It was the same vehicle that today was parked outside his small mountain home.

In those days, Alexandro was a striking figure—his black hair and muscular body making a lasting (albeit devilish) impression. Today, he was a mere shadow of his former self. Gray streaked through his hair and his once straight frame now slumped at the shoulders. A slight limp on his left side kept his gait a bit uneven and you could count his years by the lines in his wrinkled face.

Noua had been born to the Alexandros shortly after the fall of Communism in Romania, late in her father's life. Noua's mother had died at her birth from complications that were untreatable by the midwife who had delivered her. General Alexandro found the lack of proper medical care just another reason to despise the democratic reform which had come to Romania. "A Communist country would have never let my wife die," he often said.

After his wife's death, Alexandro forsook public schooling for his daughter and educated Noua himself. Under his strict and physically disciplined tutelage, Noua learned to speak English, appreciate Romanian culture, and hate Westerners. The hate was derived partly from the lessons and partly from her father's brutal personality itself. It was not unusual for Alexandro to punctuate his lessons on democratic reform with a leather strap to Noua's backside. Scars and welts were the vestiges of his lessons.

Once, Noua had questioned a tenet of Communist ideology. Her father beat her so badly that she required stitches in the back of her head from a fall she took following a vicious slap to her face. She was raised in hate … physically and philosophically. But there were compensations. Even though she was a woman, General Alexandro considered her his most trusted lieutenant.

Noua poured another round of coffee to the men in the room as her father continued to speak.

"If Nicolae would have let me kill them all in '87," Alexandro told the men, "Romania, and maybe all of Eastern Europe, would be Communist today. We'd be free of these American devils."

He paused for effect as all eyes in the room focused on him.

"But alas, he did not and Nicolae, like our party, is dead. So, it is up to us to ensure that the Party rises from the ashes. We alone hold the destiny of Romanian Communism in our hands."

"But how do we do that, General?" asked one of the men. "We only have small pockets of support throughout the farmland and the rural villages. Our followers are poor and uneducated. We have no support in the larger cities."

"That, Comrade," said Alexandro, "is where you are wrong. The rural farm people are not our weakness. They are our strength. Democracy has made the people living in the cities soft and vulnerable. They don't even realize it, but they are weaker today than they were twenty years ago. Democracy has done nothing for them. They have cars and phones, but they have no future. People like us ... who live in the mountains ... we have time to think and to realize that we are worse off. The rural towns and villages, they also yearn for change ... for leadership. They can be led back to the ways of the Party."

"What party?" asked another man. "The Communist Party is banned in Romania. We have no party."

"True, true," Alexandro replied. "But there are nearly 200 political parties in the country. Many of them espouse Communist principles; they just call themselves by some populist name. With them, and our friend Abel Gustov at the helm of the Parliament, we shall form a coalition to recapture the government. Then, when we are again in control, we can call ourselves whatever we choose." Alexandro nodded toward Bogdan which was accepted by those around the table to be a glowing endorsement.

"But there is so little time before the election," the man

insisted. "There is no time to build such a coalition. It cannot be done."

"Forces within the Kremlin are with *us* this time," Alexandro quickly replied. "Many of our old friends remain in high office and do not like Russia's cozy relationship with the West. They assure me the Americans will not interfere with our plans. In fact, they are helping. They are dealing with the Americans. With the help of the Russians, we shall put out a singular message so strong that all the common people of Romania will follow us."

"You keep speaking of this message, General. Tell us. Tell us what it is."

"In time," replied Alexandro. "I cannot tell you right now. I will in time."

"The Americans, General?" said one of the other men with anger in his voice. "Your friends at the Kremlin cannot assure that the Americans will not become involved. They will do what they did last time. They said they backed you and Nicolae, but where were they when the revolt came? Nowhere! We cannot trust them!"

"Our friends are talking to their secret police," interjected Bogdan. Alexandro let him speak, but his facial expression indicated that he was clearly irritated at the fact Bogdan had interjected his thoughts into the discussion. "I have been assured these negotiations are being held at the highest of levels."

"They talk to us through their police, but they send one of their best operatives to Bucharest to run the President's campaign." The man at the table mocked a spit on the floor to show his disgust. "The Americans talk out of both sides of their mouth."

"I have a back up plan to deal with him." Alexandro looked at his attractive daughter, rubbed the amulet on the necklace around his neck and smiled. "I will take care of the operative. The American operative, the one they call Michael Griffith, will never give that traitor, President Krasterich, the first word of political advice."

Chapter 9

Griffith, Sue, and Josh sat at the bar in the lobby of the InterContinental Hotel enjoying a nightcap following dinner. The hotel piano bar was bustling with young Romanians chain-smoking Marlboro cigarettes, drinking American vodka, and wearing designer clothes about two or three seasons out of style. The piano player was singing Elton John and Billy Joel tunes in Romanian-accented English.

The lobby of the InterContinental is made entirely of marble. The floor is brown and tan polished stone in geometric patterns. The columns rising up from the floor are green marble. While the use of stone makes for an interesting visual, its acoustics are horrible. The stone causes the piano and the murmur of the crowd to echo. Even with a small crowd, the piano bar can be loud.

Tonight the bar was more crowded than normal. Word was out around Bucharest the Westerners had arrived earlier that day for the upcoming election and were staying at the hotel. The three outsiders at the bar seemed to be the center of attention for all of the young people. It was clear that everyone knew the trio was from America. They had instant celebrity status. The points, whispers and looks were all very apparent. Occasionally, someone would take a picture of them with a cell phone camera.

Josh listened at the mahogany bar as Griffith told war stories of the foreign political trips he had made over the years. Normally, Josh loved listening to Griff's stories, but this trip was different. Josh was longing to have some war stories of his own to tell. His mind was drifting as Griffith spoke.

"Sooooo ..." interjected Sue, herself also tiring of Griffith's war stories. "How did you like dinner? Admit it. It was better than you expected, wasn't it?"

"It was good," replied Griffith. "Surprisingly, it was great. I never thought I'd get a decent meal over here. I can't believe that I actually ordered a steak from this hotel. It was a lot better than anything I ever remember eating back in '90. Hell, when we were over here the last time, we were so afraid of the food we smuggled in a suitcase filled with enough Vienna sausages and Pop Tarts to live on for two weeks."

"And you went from town to town on horseback," smirked Josh.

"Shut the fuck up, boy."

"Griff, you're living in the past," Josh chuckled. "You just can't admit the fact Romania has changed."

"He's right, you know," said Sue. "Right … with cute blue eyes, a full head of curly blond hair." Sue kissed Josh on the cheek and laughed. "Oh, if you were only ten years older or I was ten years younger."

Griffith sulked at Sue's suggestive remark towards Josh. He liked being the center of attention, especially when there was a woman involved. Not knowing what else to do, he simply smacked Josh on the back of the head.

"Come on, Griff, admit it," said Josh in response to the tap Griffith had given to him. "Say it. Just like this …I was wr-wr-wr-wrong." Josh stuttered the word for comedic emphasis.

Josh and Sue's laughter forced a smile to Griffith's face. It took a second, but he mouthed the word "wrong" before he leaned over to kiss Sue. As he leaned back, a young Romanian woman in a tight white leather skirt with a gauze midriff top approached the Americans. Griffith was instantly mesmerized by her natural beauty. If she was twenty, it wasn't by much. Her dark eyes were mysterious and danced to the tune of a devil's fiddle.

"Hi, are you Michael Griffith?" she said in perfect English with only the hint of an accent.

"I am," said Griffith, as he lit up a cigarette. "And who are you? More importantly, why in the hell are you not my interpreter? You speak better English and are a helluva lot prettier than that Yorgi fella."

"My name is Noua," said the young woman, as she stuck out her hand while simultaneously squeezing herself in between Griffith and Sue. "It is a pleasure to meet an American as famous as you. You are even more handsome in person than you are on the television shows I have watched."

Griffith smiled ruefully as he exhaled smoke. "Aw, I'm really not all that famous. I am handsome, though."

"And, you are busy for the evening," interjected Sue, moving back in between Noua and Griffith.

"Are you his ballet dancer?" asked Noua.

Josh was taking a drink of his watered down bourbon and nearly spit it out when he heard the question. Sue noticed Josh's reaction, and she found it so amusing that she turned away from Noua long enough to give Josh a playful smack on the back of his head. "I take back what I just said about being 10 years younger. I'll keep my age, boy, and kick your ass."

"You guys have got to quit this head-smacking thing," said Josh.

"I read you are here to run the President's campaign," Noua said. "You are the one who is going to take his message to the people. That must be a very important position."

Griffith laughed and smiled a little sinister grin. "Oh, now I understand. You want to meet the famous Americans here to run the campaign."

"Yes. I am quite interested in politics. I follow the American elections on the television. I could talk about it all night long."

"Well, I'm not the one you want to meet."

"Yes, you are," said Noua. "You are the one. Aren't you Michael Griffith?"

"I am. I am. But I work for him," Griffith said pointing to a stunned Josh.

"Him?"

"Oh, yeah," said Griffith. "You've never heard of Josh Barkman?"

"No," said Noua. "Who is Josh Barkman?" She looked at Josh's bright blue eyes and quickly rubbed the amulet hanging from the necklace around her neck.

"That's him," Griffith said, pointing to a now smiling Josh. "He runs the political show for the Americans in Romania."

"Really?"

"Of course," interjected Sue. "He's the brains behind Michael Griffith."

"The brains behind Griffith? Him? Josh Barkman?"

"Yes," reiterated Sue. "Everyone in America knows Michael Griffith is nothing without Josh Barkman."

Griffith shot Sue a knowing smile. "This young man is a superstar in America. Have you never heard of the *Lehrer News Hour*?"

"No."

"Good," said Griffith. "Well, it's the biggest news show in America. We all watch it. Jim Lehrer calls him every day to ask what they should report."

Noua looked at Josh and smiled a soft facial introduction. Josh's face was beet red, but he smiled back.

"Honey, you don't want Michael Griffith," said Sue. "He's a has-been."

"Careful," Griffith murmured to Sue as Noua sized up Josh. "Don't oversell this."

"I'm not," whispered Sue in return.

"What's a has-been?" asked Noua.

"That's someone who is going home with me tonight," said Sue, as she grabbed Griffith's ass from behind. "You know, a has-been is an old man who is way past his prime."

"He's the brains behind all of this," said Griffith. "In fact, that's what we call him back home ... 'America's Brain.' We all do what he says."

"Really?" Noua sounded convinced. "America's Brain."

"Oh yeah, America's Brain." Griffith kissed Noua on the cheek, looked at Josh and winked. "I'm going to my room now with my … ballet dancer. Enjoy your time with 'America's Brain.'" He paused and pointed at Josh. When Noua looked away from Griffith, he blew Josh a kiss. "Have fun," he mouthed.

As Griffith and Sue walked away they heard Noua ask: "So … they call you 'America's Brain?'"

"Were we just cruel to that girl?" asked Sue as she and Griffith waited for the elevator.

"Hell no," said Griffith. "She's just some Romanian power-fucker who gets off on banging some visiting dignitary. Did you see that white leather skirt? There's no panty line underneath. We just helped her zero in on the right target. In the morning, Josh won't be able to walk upright or wipe the smile off his face. She's liable to rip his dick off tonight."

They stepped onto the elevator.

"Then are we being cruel to Josh?"

"Don't worry about Josh right now." Another patron of the hotel tried to step onto the elevator with the pair. Griffith held up his hand stopping the woman in her tracks as the doors closed in her face. "Sorry, this elevator is taken."

Griffith pushed Sue against the back wall of the elevator, pulled her left leg up around his waist and kissed her hard. His tongue parted Sue's lips and slipped its way into her mouth. As their tongues met, Sue felt her other leg buckle slightly from the power in his kiss. She started to wrap her leg tighter around Griffith and return the kiss when he pulled back.

"What?" asked Sue.

"Nothing," said Griffith with a sly smile. "But, how's that for a has-been?"

Chapter 10

The hour was growing late as Josh and Noua sat at the bar. The crowd mingling in the piano bar had thinned. The energy flowing from the perceived celebrity of the young American had waned as patrons of the establishment paired up and went their separate ways.

Since Griffith and Sue had left, Josh had been doing most of the talking. Bold in politics, Josh was an introvert around women. Griffith's buildup had given Josh the ability to role play and be someone he wasn't—a man confident around a beautiful woman. He was afraid that if he quit talking, Noua might see the real Josh and walk out of the bar. Remarkably, the more he talked, the more interested she became. And the more interested she became, the more intimate she seemed to become.

Josh was contemplating how to initiate physical contact that would inspire her to go to his room when, seemingly out of nowhere, Noua spun him around on the bar stool and forced his legs open with a swift invasion of her hips. She leaned forward and kissed him, her tongue gently sliding up the side of his face to his ear. Noua sucked on Josh's ear lobe, then pulled back, smiled seductively at him and leaned forward to kiss him again. As they kissed, Josh cautiously slid his hands around to the small of her back. He moved his hand under her top to touch her soft skin. When Noua didn't object, he moved his hand lower along the outside of her leather skirt until it rested on her ass.

Holy shit, she's not wearing panties, Josh thought with excitement.

As Josh's hand gently massaged Noua's ass, she ran her hands along the inside of his thighs. She gently brushed her hands along the front of his pants. The touch was slight but clearly intentional. Josh shifted in his chair to try to hide his quickly hardening desire for Noua.

"It's okay," said Noua as she pulled back and put her hand firmly on his crotch. "That's exactly how I want you."

Josh was speechless.

"I want you inside of me. All night long. I want to fall asleep with you inside of me and wake up the same way. When you're not inside of me, I'm going to run my tongue up your …"

"Check please," said Josh as he stood up and fumbled for the paper card that the hotel clerk had given him for charging incidentals to his room.

After paying for the evening's tab, Josh started to walk with Noua to the elevator. She grabbed his hand and pulled him towards the front door. "No," she insisted. "Not here."

"Come on," said Josh. "My room is right upstairs."

"I am no ballet dancer," she replied.

"I didn't say you were," Josh replied.

"Only ballet dancers go to hotel rooms with strangers to make love. Let's go to my apartment. I only live a couple of blocks away."

"I'm not supposed to leave the building," mumbled Josh.

"What?"

"Griffith told me I should never leave the hotel alone."

"Griffith? I thought he said you were the brains?"

"I don't know …."

Noua kissed Josh. It was demanding—hard and very thorough—and sent chills down Josh's spine. "Come. I know the city well. You'll be safe with me."

What the hell does Griff know? It's a new Romania. Times have changed. Sue even sees it. It's time for me to create my own stories. He set this up for me. Hell, Griff would do it. Josh grabbed Noua's hand. "Let's go."

As the happy couple walked out the revolving door of the InterContinental, Josh put his arm around Noua's waist.

No man can deny the excitement of placing his arm around a woman's waist for the first time. He slid his hand under her blouse and touched her bare waist. The feel of Noua's body as Josh wrapped his hand around her, the smell of her hair as he leaned over to nuzzle her neck, and the anticipation building on the walk to her apartment had Josh's entire body on testosterone overdrive. His mind was racing with the expectation of the night's delights rushing through him.

As they rounded a corner about three blocks from the hotel, a beat-up, late era black Buick approached from a side street. The car pulled up to the curb, and the passenger in the car asked Noua a question in Romanian.

"They need directions," Noua said to Josh. "Let me tell them how to get to the main motorway." She then turned and began pointing in various directions while talking to the man. The passenger got out of the car and returned the conversation while visually following the points and jabs she was making with her fingers.

Josh was so enthralled with Noua he didn't hear the footsteps of the two men who walked up behind him on the street. He was temporarily stunned as each grabbed an arm. The passenger opened the back door of the car and the two men tried to force him into the back of the rusty Buick. "What the fuck ..." were the only words Josh could get out of his mouth.

Josh pulled his right hand free, swung and hit the large man holding his left arm. The punch landed on the man's right cheek and he fell to the ground.

Josh tried to run, but the passenger who had been asking for directions grabbed Josh's right arm. The other man reestablished his grip on Josh and held him upright as the man whom Josh had punched stood up and smashed his fist into Josh's stomach, knocking the wind out of him. The only thing keeping Josh from doubling over was the fact that the two other men continued to hold him up. The man who had punched Josh in the stomach wiped his lip to reveal blood.

He became enraged. He said something to the other two men in Romanian and hit Josh squarely in the jaw.

Josh's knees buckled, but this time the men let Josh fall to the ground. Stunned and on his knees, someone pushed him full to the ground from behind. While one man placed his knee on Josh's back pinning his face to the pavement, another man moved to grab Josh's arms. He quickly wrapped duct tape around Josh's wrists. While still on his stomach, someone used tape to bind Josh's ankles.

The same person who had pushed Josh to the ground grabbed him by his belt and pulled him up. Realizing what was happening, Josh tried to shake the cobwebs from his head. His thoughts focused.

Shit. I shouldn't have left the hotel. Secret police. Don't let them get you or Noua into the car. Don't let them get you or Noua into the car.

Josh couldn't see who was behind him pushing him into the car. In a swift motion, he swung his head backwards hitting the person holding him by the belt on the nose with the back of his head. To his shock, Noua screamed in pain. He stopped momentarily and turned at the thought of having hit the woman he was trying to seduce. As Josh turned, the last thing he saw was Noua sending a punch his way that landed squarely between his eyes.

Lights out.

The Romanians placed a blindfold over Josh's eyes, duct tape over his bloody mouth and tossed the unconscious American into the now open trunk of the old black Buick.

Unfortunately for the Romanians, Noua's loud scream had attracted the attention of two young men who came running in their direction. Noua pulled an old Makarov PM semiautomatic pistol from her purse, squared her shoulders on the men and fired. One man fell in his tracks and the other quickly ducked behind a car. As he scurried under the frame of the parked car he was using for cover, he pulled a cell phone from his pants pocket and began snapping pictures.

"Let's go," said the driver of the car.

"But, the other one," said Noua.

"No. Leave him. We must get out of here. Now!"

As the car sped past the man under the car, he stuck his arm out into the street and snapped several more pictures.

Josh awoke slowly. Blindfolded and bound, he called on his other senses to try to determine his situation. The sounds and bumpy ride, coupled with the smell of old rubber, oil and his fetal position in a contained small area, led him quickly to the conclusion that he was in the trunk of the car that had been driven by the men asking for directions. He tried to recall details.

How many were there? What did they look like?

Josh tried to remember, but it was all still quite fuzzy. Then, suddenly, it all came crashing back.

Noua. God, Noua was part of this. The beautiful woman I just picked up in a bar set me up. Noua kidnapped me.

What at first appeared to be nothing more than a bad dream had abruptly morphed into his unfortunate truth. Darkness was more than what he was seeing with the cloth over his eyes. Darkness suddenly was his reality.

Chapter 11

Richard Thompson moved around his bedroom in an aimless manner—grabbing miscellaneous clothing and tossing each item indiscriminately into a small travel bag. His wife, Ann, was sitting on a backless short stool in front of her small secretary desk checking e-mails on a desktop computer. He looked over at her blond hair just touching the collar of her tight, low-cut, knit shirt. He was sure that she looked different than she had in the days when they first met as fellow staffers on Capitol Hill—he just could not figure out quite how.

Thompson silently chuckled as he remembered that, in those days, he looked as awkward as he acted. When they had first met, he was a newbie staffer for his mentor—Kentucky Congressman Garrett Jackson. He was so intimidated by Ann's beauty that, after they had been introduced, he could barely bring himself to speak to her. Her blond hair, blue green eyes and stellar body left him speechless. If not for the prodding of his roommate and best friend, Michael Griffith, he might never have asked her out.

When Thompson finally got up the nerve to ask Ann for a date, he had already determined she was the woman he wanted to marry. After only one date, Ann became the total focus of his life. Everything revolved around her. Likewise, Ann became Richard Thompson's biggest fan. Their passionate relationship soon became the talk of Capitol Hill staffers and K Street lobbyists. When they were married a year or so later, Griffith stood by their side as the best man.

But to Thompson on this day, young love on Capitol Hill seemed both a lifetime and an instant ago. Three kids later, she looked the same in his eyes. For him, the passion remained strong.

On the other hand, he caught his own reflection in a mirror from across the room and noticed he had definitely changed. It was painfully obvious he was no longer the baby-faced staffer just out of college. His face was fuller. Light touches of grey were now visible in his sandy brown hair. And, the beltline ... well ... he couldn't deny the belt had been loosened more than a notch or two. The mirror reflected his self-image. Richard Thompson sometimes found it hard to understand how his wife still had the same passion for him.

It was more than the expanding belly. Life with a Member of Congress is not easy. Spouses spend many nights alone and kids often go to bed with one parent a long way from home. Relationships get strained by the stress from the focus of the public's eye. There is no normality to everyday life. Time spent together is very precious.

Their marriage had been tested several times since Thompson had entered public life and it seemed that the couple was constantly working on their relationship. For Thompson, the stress of his job and a hectic schedule left little time for intimacy with his wife. For Ann, women who constantly wanted to be close to powerful men gnawed at her faith in the marital bond she had with her husband. Now, for a brief time anyway, they were alone together.

It was time for Thompson to bring up the elephant in the room. "I really wish you would go to Fancy Farm with me," he pleaded with his wife.

"Richard," she said as she looked around from the stool in front of her computer screen, "let's not go over this again ... pleeaasse."

"I know, I know," Thompson replied.

"Apparently you do not know," said Ann. "We have been over this a million times."

"Well, let's make it a million and one."

"We've been asking our families to watch the kids too much lately. Every time we have a black-tie dinner to go to, we ask them to step up. I just don't want to do it for a two-day trip to Western Kentucky."

"Babe, you don't understand," replied Thompson. "I've been in D.C. so much lately and, now, as soon as I'm home on recess, I have to leave."

"I just can't, Richard. Not this time."

"I'm not going to change your mind, am I?"

"Not for Fancy Farm. It will be hot as hell there and all politics. It's just too much like work. Let's save the overnight babysitters for a real trip, not a political rally."

Thompson paused his assault on his suitcase long enough to gently touch his wife on her shoulders from behind.

"Don't try to tempt me on this with sex," said Ann. "I'm horny, but not that horny. I said 'no' on this and that's final. Anyway, Joey is driving you down. Go to Fancy Farm. Spend a day on your friend's boat. Go fishing with Joe and I'll see you Sunday night."

He touched her again. "I don't want to wait until Sunday night."

"Well, I don't want to go to Kentucky Lake," replied Ann. "That place ... that boat ... has some really bad memories for me. If I never see your friend's boat again, it will be too soon."

"The best way to overcome your fears is to confront them," said Thompson.

"Sunday night," Ann firmly replied. "Then we'll have the whole recess together."

He leaned forward and gently ran his tongue up her spine, by the base of her neck. When he came to those little sensitive hairs on the back of her neck, he bit at them, pulling back on them as he bit. She squeezed her legs together and shivered.

"No fair," Ann literally squealed. "Don't do this to me when I'm already horny and we're talking about you leaving."

"I want to make you horny and come with me," replied Thompson, as he rubbed Ann's sides, "... in more ways than one."

"Look, Joey is going to be here in an hour to pick you up to go to Fancy Farm."

"Which at least gives me an hour," he said as he slid his hands inside her blouse and cupped her large breasts. He gently pinched her nipples through her thin bra.

Ann leaned her torso backwards and rubbed her back against Thompson's crotch. "You're as hard as times in '29," she laughed. "This ain't gonna take an hour."

Chapter 12

Drive to Western Kentucky, take a right at the end of the earth and you can see Fancy Farm from there.

Fancy Farm, Kentucky, is a small unincorporated community in the western-most portion of the state, an area known as the Jackson Purchase. It was established by Catholic settlers in 1829 only a decade after President Andrew Jackson purchased the region from the Chickasaw Indians. From the standpoint of terrain and weather, the area is less like the rest of Kentucky and more like the Mississippi Delta.

The small community of Fancy Farm grew up around St. Jerome's Catholic Church. According to church legend, the village got its name when, in 1845, local residents applied for a permit to open a post office. When the Inspector was sent to investigate the request, he met with the residents at a well kept farm near the church. The Inspector approved the post office. When he was asked what to name it, the Inspector supposedly named it Fancy Farm out of respect for the place where he had met with the locals.

In August of 1880, the church held a picnic, barn dance, and "gander pulling," (a frontier sport played by men on horseback.) A live goose was hung upside down from the branch of a tree. After the neck had been sufficiently greased or soaped, men rode past the goose at full speed. The man who could snatch the goose's head from its body won the competition.

The grand picnic continued as an annual event which was attended by local families in and around Graves County, Kentucky. At some point in time, local elected officials—and those who wanted their jobs—began showing up at the picnic. Lard-necked geese hanging upside down from trees were replaced by a flatbed wagon and politicians. Normally used for hauling hay, on the day of the picnic, the wagon was decorated in red, white, and blue bunting. One-by-one the politicians took turns mounting the wagon and speaking to the local electorate.

Much like the frontier sport of "gander pulling," the speeches had a rough and tumble element to them. Candidates would verbally attack each other with direct gusto. The crowd was usually just as raucous. Cheers, boos, whistles and hisses were common when the politicians spoke.

The political speeches were mostly local until 1931. In that year, a legendary Kentucky politician, A. B. "Happy" Chandler, was running for statewide office for the first time. He needed a base from which to launch his western Kentucky campaign. He picked the Fancy Farm picnic as the place.

After that, the prestige of Fancy Farm grew. Today, it is recognized as the "official" kickoff to Kentucky's political campaign season.

And today, it's not always just about the speeches. College kids roam the crowd in costumes handing out props as politicians speak. In 2003, Republicans mocked the Democratic candidate for governor by having the Seven Dwarfs roam the crowd, each with his own message to hand out on paper. For instance, Sleepy handed out a paper on how the Democratic candidate had slept through his 8 years as Attorney General. Not to be outdone, the Democrats had an Arnold Schwarzenegger-style "Terminator" show up handing out "pink slips" signifying the termination of jobs that would arguably happen if the Republican won office.

Currently, there are only about 500 residents of Fancy Farm. Yet, over 15,000 attend the picnic, which is a fundraiser for the St. Jerome parish. The crowd raises nearly a quarter of a million dollars annually. The speeches are the central point of the political gathering, and it's been recognized by the *Guinness Book of World Records* as the largest picnic in the world.

Congressman Thompson's driver for the weekend was James Joseph Bradley who, because of his rotund figure, was known to most, simply as The Fat Man. He had been Thompson's law partner before Thompson had gotten elected to Congress. Through a common love of baseball, politics, and obscure movie trivia, the two had become inseparable at the law firm. Their friendship had only strengthened following Thompson's election.

The Fat Man's pear shape and scruffy graying beard made his nickname quite appropriate.

As The Fat Man drove the car down the road leading to the church, Thompson looked out the window at the quaint rural scenery. He had been explaining the history of the picnic to The Fat Man for almost an hour.

"They actually pulled the head off a goose at the neck?" asked The Fat Man.

"Yup," said Thompson.

"Damn," replied The Fat Man. "And I thought that 'corn hole' was a useless game."

"Remember," said Thompson. "This was all new frontier back then. Hell, Lincoln did it."

"Abraham Lincoln? President Abraham Lincoln played gander pull?" asked The Fat Man. "Get out."

"No shit," said Thompson. "There's a great painting in the Illinois state library showing Abraham Lincoln umpiring a 'gander pull.'"

"I guess he wasn't worrying in 1860 about getting an endorsement from People for the Ethical Treatment of Animals," The Fat Man observed.

"Guess not," laughed Thompson. "I think that even Ducks Unlimited would disapprove of that contest today."

There was a pause as the car came to one of the few stop signs along the road. Thompson pointed straight ahead, indicating that The Fat Man should continue along the same road.

"It's going to be hotter than hell out there today," said The Fat Man as they continued along their way.

"It's always hot at Fancy Farm," replied Thompson. "You never know what's gonna be hotter at Fancy Farm—the temperature or the rhetoric."

"I hope it's the mutton," The Fat Man replied. "How much do they make again?"

"18,000 pounds of lamb, pork, and chicken," said Thompson.

"That's nine tons of food," exclaimed The Fat Man.

"Bet your sweet ass," Thompson replied. "Am I even going to see you after we park?"

"Doubtful," pondered The Fat Man. "Very doubtful. I want to get a case of their barbecue sauce to take back with us."

"Well, try not to miss my speech," instructed Thompson.

"Why?" asked The Fat Man. "Are you afraid that I'll be the only one cheering for you?"

"Well, there's that," pondered Thompson. "But I need you to actually listen to it."

"I've got to listen to your speech when Catholics are cooking up nine tons of barbecue?" asked The Fat Man. "I'm not sure I can be that focused. That's asking a lot. I love you like a brother, but I am not sure I love you that much."

"Seriously," replied Thompson. "I need a favor and I need you to listen to my speech today to understand what I'm doing."

"Fine," the Fat Man replied in a tone of mock depression. "I'll do it. Pull me away from barbecue mutton, but I'll do it."

"Thanks," Thompson replied. "You are a pal. Have you been following the stories about how the House Mace was stolen right before we broke for recess?"

"Yeah," said The Fat Man. "Apparently the Sergeant at Arms went missing right along with the Mace. According to what I saw on the news before we left, he's the number one suspect in the theft."

"That's bullcrap," said Thompson. "I heard that too, but I don't buy it. I know Bob Patterson. He's a mild mannered guy who wouldn't say 'shit' if he had a mouth full of it. I can't see him stealing the Mace."

"The news said there is a national manhunt on for him," said The Fat Man.

"I actually saw him that night on the floor. He seemed normal. And he always treated the Mace like it was a baby."

"Maybe he snapped," replied The Fat Man. "Washington does weird things to normal people."

"Not this guy. It just doesn't fit."

"In any event, Patterson and the Mace are both missing right now."

"Yeah, back to that," said Thompson. "I'm going to wrap my whole speech today around the Mace."

"That sounds interesting," The Fat Man said. "It's certainly current. What's the theme?"

"When a Member of the House gets out of hand," said Thompson, "the Speaker orders the Sergeant at Arms to present the Mace to that Congressman to bring him under control. They literally walk the Mace along side of the Member to calm him or her down. I'm going to explain that process today in my speech."

"I think I see where you are headed," said The Fat Man. "You are going to present the Mace."

"Right," confirmed Thompson. "I'm going to present the Mace to all of Kentucky's problems that are out of control."

"Actually, that's not bad. Do you want me to find some props?" asked The Fat Man.

"I'm one step ahead of you," said Thompson. "I've got a bunch of college kids who stayed up all night making Maces out of cardboard tubes and tin foil. When I present a Mace, they are going to walk around the crowd with one that has the name of the issue on it."

"You're probably going to get a headline tomorrow with this one, Rick," The Fat Man declared.

"That's what I think," Thompson replied with confidence. "And that's where I need your help. I want to write an article for *Roll Call* with the same idea behind it, except I want to use national issues."

"That would be cool," said The Fat Man. "What do you want from me?"

"I need some research assistance," said Thompson.

"Sure," said The Fat Man. "What do you need?"

"I need more research about the history of the original Mace," Thompson replied.

"What do you mean 'original' Mace?" asked The Fat Man. "The one that was stolen the other night is not the original Mace?"

"No," said Thompson. "The original Mace was commissioned for the very first Congress. It was used until the British occupied Washington during the War of 1812. The British took the Capitol in 1814 and the original Mace disappeared. Historians say it was burned when the Brits set fire to the building."

"But … " The Fat Man prompted.

"But," repeated Thompson, "at the time, it was rumored that it was actually stolen by a British officer and smuggled back to England."

"Okay," said The Fat Man. "So what?"

"So, I want you to research the history of that rumor and, if it's out there, find the Mace."

Chapter 13

Wearing only a complimentary white terry cloth robe with a gold hotel insignia, Griffith pushed a cart of food and drinks into the bedroom of the two-room suite at the InterContinental. The manner in which the red curtains had been draped and the designs in the red carpet gave the room somewhat of an old European elegance. Of course, much of that regal feel was ruined by the presence of the standard television bureau and dark-stained wood tables and chairs found in almost every hotel room worldwide.

Still, the room was nicer than those Griffith remembered from his last visit. The room was not all that had Griffith in a good mood. Sue had provided Griffith with a night of sexual companionship which had previously been unmatched in his many years of political travel. The crusty old hack was happily whistling *Can't Ya See* as he pushed the food cart from the sitting area into the bedroom.

Sue lay in the bed, naked under the sheets. The room service porter's knock at the door had awakened her. Now, the smells of the food and the coffee were causing her to sit up in bed. She held the sheets, in false modesty, in front of her breasts.

"Good morning, my pretty little ballet dancer," said Griffith cheerfully. "Your morning nourishment awaits you. After last night, I am going to assume that you do need some nourishment."

Sue smiled at Griffith. She flipped her hair around from side-to-side to try and make it look somewhat presentable.

"Don't worry," said Griffith, doing his very best to make the uncomfortable morning-after feel as comfortable as possible. "You look great. I need a good shot of Vitamin B & E, but you look great."

Griffith began raising the lids off the various plates on the cart. "Scrambled eggs," said Griffith, "that actually look yellow ... fried potatoes ... something that resembles bacon or ham."

Sue giggled.

"Coffee."

Griffith saved the best for last and smiled at Sue.

"And, of course," Griffith said revealing a glass filled with red juice and a celery stick, "Bloody Marys filled with Vodka strong enough to kill the germs in all the other food. That's the first rule of foreign campaigns, you know. Drink enough alcohol to kill any local disease."

Sue took the glass from Griffith and took a sip. "Mmmm … that hits the spot."

"Speaking of hitting the spot," Griffith said. "You're a noisy one."

"Sorry," she replied. "I do tend to get a little loud."

"Don't apologize," said Griffith. "I liked it."

Griffith took a sip of his Bloody Mary. "Here's to killing whatever Romania has to offer."

"Michael Griffith, you're impossible. You just refuse to admit Romania has changed."

"No, my lady," said Griffith. "I admitted it once last night. One is my limit. I won't do it twice."

Sue got up from the bed and walked around looking for her clothes, which had been indiscriminately tossed around the room the night before. She knew she had experienced intense sexual pleasure like last night some time in her life, but she just couldn't remember when. She found her red panties on top of a lamp. As she bent over to put them on, she noticed Griffith looking at her.

"What are you looking at?" said Sue.

"Something special," said Griffith as he lay down on the bed. He placed his drink on the table and patted the sheets in a silent invitation for Sue to join him in bed.

"Last night you were too old to go one more time."

“That was last night and this is this morning. Besides, celery has natural Viagra in it.”

“No it doesn’t,” said Sue.

Griffith smiled. “Last night was good.”

“Good,” exclaimed Sue. “You better do fucking better than that.”

Griffith laughed out loud. “All right, last night was great. You were … are great.”

In her panties and nothing else, Sue walked over to the tray of food and grabbed some bacon. “Goddamn right I was great. Maybe the best you’ve ever had.” Sue paused. “How do you think Josh is feeling this morning?”

“My guess,” said Griffith, “is that Josh won’t be able to wipe the smile off his face for a week.”

“You may be right. He’s a cute kid, but he just seems so shy around women. I hope he had fun last night. You think a lot of him, don’t you?”

“Josh is something special,” said Griffith. “I’ve been around a lot of young kids in politics and so many of them are driven by their own desire to succeed. This kid is just like his boss. He believes. He thinks that he can change the world.”

“Maybe he can,” said Sue. “Did you ever think about that?”

“Forget Josh for a minute,” said Griffith. “I’ve got a question for you.”

“What?”

“So, when do you have to be back?”

“What do you mean?” asked Sue.

“It’s a pretty simple question,” said Griffith. “When do you have to be back to work?

“Why?”

“Well, my job over here isn’t all that tough,” said Griffith, “and, um, I’ve got this great suite for a couple of weeks.”

“Michael, what are you trying to say?”

“Well,” Griffith replied, “it’s just that we had a great

time yesterday and, um, I think we could have some fun, and, um … ."

"You aren't very good at this are you?"

"No goddamnit, I'm not," said Griffith, as he stood up and grabbed Sue around the waist before rolling her back onto the bed with him. "And you're going to make me work for it, aren't you?"

"You're damn right I am," laughed Sue. "Michael, if you want me to stay around a couple of days, you're going to have to ask. And don't expect me to say yes just because you're good in bed."

"I just thought that, um ... " The phone rang. "Saved by the bell," Griffith said as he answered it. "Empty Arms Hotel, Griffith here." He smiled at Sue. "Yorgi boy, I told you to call me Griff." As Griffith listened, he got up from the bed. His smile dropped into a frown and his face went instantly pale. His body jerked as he steadied himself with one arm against the wall. "I'll be right down."

He looked at Sue, shock etched in his face.

"Michael … Michael what's wrong?"

"It's Josh … he's been kidnapped."

Chapter 14

The picnic at Fancy Farm does not look quite like it did in Happy Chandler's day.

The old hay wagon covered in bunting has been replaced by a wooden stage. It's on the site of where the 'old lyin' tree' used to stand. The tree was another place where they used to give speeches. A large concrete patio in front of the stage was covered with a tin roof a few years ago in order to provide some relief from the sun to the participants and audience.

As The Fat Man pulled the car into the parking lot behind the stage, Thompson pointed over to a tree where some local politician was giving an interview to a local radio station reporter. "See that tree?" asked Thompson.

"Yeah," said The Fat Man. "What about it?"

"That's the Happy Chandler tree," said Thompson. "That's where everyone gives interviews … right under a tree dedicated to Happy."

"Is that the old lyin' tree?" asked The Fat Man.

"Naw, that stage is where the old lyin' tree used to stand. They say it got hit by lightning. But the year after it went down, Governor Louie Nunn was speaking and said that the politicians killed it. Louie said too much … umm … fertilizer will kill anything."

"Well, try not to kill any trees today with your bullshit," said The Fat Man.

"Thanks," Thompson replied. "The band plays until 2:00. That means you've got about an hour until the speeches start. I'm fifth up."

"And where, may I ask, do they serve the mutton?" asked The Fat Man, twiddling his fingers together.

"Right down that little hill by the smokehouse."

"And you don't need me until you speak?"

"Nope," said Thompson. "But if you need to find me, I'll be hanging out on the right side of the stage talking to the folks."

"And listening to the music?"

"You know me too well," Thompson replied. "You get some mutton and I'll be singing along to *Fox on the Run*."

"At least we both know our vices," said The Fat Man. "I'll see you in about an hour."

Thompson hung around the stage for the next hour or so soaking in the scene of southern politics as it was meant to be. Teamsters had parked big rigs here and there with large banners on the sides proclaiming pro-union themes. Staffers gave out hand-fans with their bosses' names and elected offices on them. Candidates shook hands and asked for votes.

When the speeches started, Thompson made his way to his seat on the stage. Every time someone spoke, one side of the crowd cheered while the other side jeered. Then it came time for Thompson to take the microphone.

"Ladies and Gentlemen, please welcome to the Fancy Farm stage, from up in Northern Kentucky's Fourth Congressional District ... Congressman Richard Thompson."

Thompson took off his blue blazer and tossed it over his chair for effect. As he approached the podium, he rolled up his sleeves and loosened his tie.

"Thank you, ladies and gentlemen," said Thompson. "You know, I've been here many times before, but it's always been as a part of the crowd."

"And you should have stayed there," shouted a guy in the fourth row.

"But today, I get to talk to you as an elected official from our great Commonwealth of Kentucky," Thompson continued, undeterred by the heckler. After some brief introductory comments about the church and the crowd, Thompson got to the meat of his speech.

"The biggest news in Washington is that someone stole the Mace from the House of Representatives this week. That is a big problem for us in Washington, because the Mace is a very important part of the pomp and circumstance of Congress. Whenever an elected Member of the House gets out of line on the floor, the Speaker presents the Mace to him or her in order to get them back in regular order.

"Well, there have been a lot of elected officials in Kentucky who have been out of order lately."

Students carrying the cardboard replicas of the Mace began entering the crowd from an opening by the front of the stage as Thompson shouted: "Lo and behold, I've found the Mace. I found it right here in Western Kentucky. To all of you who need to get in line … I present the Mace."

Hoops and hollers went up from one side of the crowd. The other side booed just as loud. The press corps scribbled in their notebooks.

"To those who voted for the governor's tax and spend budget … I present the Mace."

"To all those in the state capitol who have forgotten that the American free enterprise system is the backbone of this country and voted against tax simplification … I present the Mace."

The Fat Man stood on the side of the stage eating a barbecued mutton sandwich while listening to his friend. He was as good on the stump today as The Fat Man had ever seen him.

"And to my colleagues on Capitol Hill in Washington who have laid a tax burden on our children and grandchildren so large that they may never pay them off … I present the Mace."

Thompson continued to present the Mace to group after group during his three minutes, until the Bluegrass band began playing, signaling that his time was up. Thompson went back to his seat on the stage to the handshakes and backslaps of those on his side of the stage.

When he had settled back into his seat, he looked over to the side of the stage where The Fat Man was standing. Thompson smiled and nodded in his direction. The Fat Man returned the smile and tipped his barbecue mutton sandwich in a sticky toast to a job well done.

Chapter 15

Not far from Fancy Farm are Kentucky Lake and Lake Barkley. Due to the Tennessee Valley Authority projects from the New Deal era, the two interconnecting lakes form more man-made shoreline than any other lakes in the south. Kentucky Lake connects to the Tennessee River before flowing into the Mississippi River. Thompson had learned to sail there on a forty-three foot sail boat owned by a client while he was practicing law. Whenever he was in the vicinity, the friend let him sleep on it. The gentle rocking of the boat at night gave Thompson a sense of tranquility he often seemed to lack on land.

Thompson and The Fat Man had driven straight to where the sail boat was moored following the speech at Fancy Farm. Filled with barbecued mutton, The Fat Man had decided to call it an early night and was fast asleep in one of the cabins on the boat. Alone, Thompson sat on the deck smoking a cigar, drinking a Makers' Mark Manhattan and listening to one of his favorite CDs, *Preludes* by Warren Zevon. The music is a compilation of songs recorded throughout Zevon's career, but never released. As one of his favorite songs, *The Rosarita Beach Café*, played low over the iPod speakers in front of him, Thompson became wrapped up in silent thoughts as thick as the cigar smoke coming from his lips.

Tennessee sour mash whiskey on my breath,
Rosalie, Suzy and Lucy on my mind,
Drove my old car down the dusty streets of this old border town,
But, I never thought I'd be stuck here for such a long, long time.

Thompson took a puff on his cigar as he listened and relaxed. The place itself held conflicting memories for him. It was lovely, especially at night. But it was also the spot where one of the most traumatic events of his life had occurred. His first term in office had been marred by a foiled plot by a deranged man to kill him and his wife on the boat over Thompson's involvement in a Congressional investigation into steroid abuse in professional baseball. The plot had barely been thwarted by the FBI, but had resulted in Thompson being shot while protecting Ann from the gunman.

I can understand why Ann doesn't like this place anymore. Hell, we both nearly died here when that whack-job tried to shoot us. I should have the same feelings, but I don't. I get it with Ann. What I don't get is why I like coming back so much. I should have the same feelings. I should be afraid here.

Thompson leaned back and placed the hand holding his cigar over the back of the deck bench as if he was actually putting his arm around his wife Ann.

Right down there in the galley, we stared death in the face. We looked down the barrel of a gun and we came out on the right side of the dirt. I should hate this place but I don't. In fact, this boat is one of the few places in my life where I feel eminently safe. This is my territory. It's like I'm looking down the barrel from the safe side, hammer cocked and ready to fire.

Thompson took a sip of his Manhattan and looked to the horizon as Zevon sung.

...I've got a million dollar bill, but they can't change it,
And, they won't let me leave until my tab is paid,
So, I might as well settle down,
And buy the house another round,
Send my mail to the Rosarita Beach Café.

Maybe that's it, Thompson thought while blowing smoke rings for his own enjoyment. *Everyone wants to be immortal. I am.*

On this deck, I am immortal. I won here. If I beat back a crazy who was trying to kill me here, I can beat back anything.

Well, I soon fell in with thugs and thieves and gamblers from the beach,
And the devil himself suggested an all-night game,
But the night winds came along, like some dark-eyed senorita's song,
And blew my straight-flush out across the waves.

Bring the devil on, Thompson challenged the Lord in a silent prayer, influenced in large part by vermouth-sweetened bourbon. *This is the one place where I will play him in an all-night game. Fuck it. Let him deal the cards. Life is good. Send my mail to the Kentucky Lake boat dock!*

The next morning Thompson had The Fat Man up early so they could get ready for their fishing charter out on the lake. The Fat Man was not much of a sportsman, so Thompson had to insist he come along on the charter. Thompson knew that one of The Fat Man's many phobias would kick in prior to the time of departure. True to form, The Fat Man had spent breakfast worrying over the depth of the lake and expressing his fear, that the fishing boat they were going to be on would sink.

They were sitting on the benches on the stern of the sail boat, discussing the situation when Thompson spotted a small bass boat entering the harbor. "Our ride is here," said Thompson.

"You kidding me?" asked The Fat Man. "We're going out on that big lake in that little boat?"

Thompson just laughed. “Mornin’ Ira!” he shouted, waving at the old man approaching in his small bass boat.

The Fat Man peeked around the main mast peering at the old codger slowly idling his bass boat past the “No Wake” sign poking out of the water and moving in their general direction. Ira looked small and frail. His long grey hair was pulled back in a pony tail and flowed down his back from under a green John Deere ball cap. A cigarette peeked out from his full white beard, which was stained with chewing tobacco juice.

A white and brown brittle-haired old dog was balancing himself at the bow of the boat.

“What the hell is that?” asked The Fat Man.

“What?” replied Thompson.

“That mangy old lump of fleas on the boat,” said The Fat Man.

“That’s Ira’s dog, Waldo,” said Thompson.

The Fat Man grumbled. “I was talkin’ about Ira,” he said under his breath.

“Bitch all you want, my friend,” said Thompson continuing his wave, “but Ira is the number one fishing guide on Kentucky Lake. He doesn’t go anywhere without Waldo.”

“Really?” asked The Fat Man sarcastically. “I would have never pictured the two as a couple.”

“Yeah,” Thompson replied. “Remember that little joint we passed yesterday on our way to the boat?”

“The one you said had the good omelets?” asked The Fat Man.

“That’s the one,” said Thompson.

“What about it?” The Fat Man asked.

“Well, Ira’s a fixture up there,” said Thompson. “He shows up every morning after fishing to get breakfast. Waldo comes with him every day but usually stays in the bed of the pickup truck until Ira comes out with food. One morning it’s raining and Ira’s fishing charter cancels. He shows up at the diner and walks in with Waldo at his side. The owner tells him that Waldo has to leave. It gets heated and Ira jumps over the counter and grabs the owner by his string tie and explained the law to him."

"What law?" asked The Fat Man.

"No one's quite sure," Thompson laughed, "but since that day, if Waldo wants to come in, he comes in."

"Swell," said The Fat Man. "*The Old Man and the Sea* meets *Deliverance*. I'm spending the morning on a lake in a little skiff with a psychotic fisherman and his dog."

"And whatever you do," instructed Thompson, "do not, I repeat, do not question his veteran credentials."

"My dad was a veteran," replied The Fat Man, offended. "I'd never question someone's record. Is there a problem?"

"Everyone around here knows he served, but he claims to have been at Iwo Jima and Tet," said Thompson.

The Fat Man paused. "That's impossible. He can't be more than 65."

"You want Ira to grab you by the neck and explain it to you?" interjected Thompson.

The Fat Man shook his head no.

"Good call," laughed Thompson. "Then, as far as you're concerned, Ira's last name might as well be Hayes and he raised the flag at Iwo Jima."

Ira had moored the boat and was walking up the dock with Waldo at his side when he shouted a greeting at Thompson. "How ya doin,' Congressman? Are you ready to catch some fish?"

"Never better, my friend," replied Thompson as he handed the fishing gear over the port rail of the sail boat to the old man. "And you better believe that I am ready to catch some fish. Are they biting?"

"You bet 'cha," replied Ira as he grabbed the tackle box from Thompson and pointed his arm out to the lake in no particular direction. "Right up by the pass through. Yesterday, the biguns was hittin' on little spinners."

"I'm sure you will explain to me what that means," The Fat Man said as they walked up the dock to the bass boat.

"Ira, this is my friend I was telling you about," Thompson said to Ira. "His name is Joe. He and I were law partners before I got elected to Congress."

"Howdy, Joe," said Ira, while he took his hat off with his left hand and stuck his right hand out to shake with The Fat Man. "Pleased to make your acquaintance."

"Likewise," said The Fat Man as he placed one foot into the boat and then the other, awkwardly boarding the small vessel. He balanced from side-to-side as if to steady himself. He tightened the bright orange, triple XL life vest he had purchased specially for the occasion.

"You're a lawyer, huh?" asked Ira of The Fat Man, who nodded an affirmative response. "Just like the Congressman … I know a little somethin' 'bout the law now. Had an uncle who was a judge. He got me outta world of hurt over the years."

"How's your back been feelin'?" Thompson asked Ira, hoping to change the subject.

"Pretty sore these days," said Ira. "But hell, my back has been hurtin' ever since I had part of it shot off at Iwo Jima. I joined the Navy at six foot three inches and came home after Tet at just under six feet."

Thompson looked at The Fat Man with a smiling stare that commanded him to remain quiet on the topic.

"How deep is this lake?" asked The Fat Man as he sat down next to Ira.

"Worried 'bout fallin' in, are ya?" asked Ira. Thompson laughed as he pushed the fishing boat away from the dock. All remained quiet as the boat slowly moved out of the dock area. Once the boat was out of the zone in which wakes were regulated, Ira shoved the throttle down and the bow of the boat kicked up a bit. Thompson silently smiled as The Fat Man white knuckled the arm of his chair.

As the boat rocked over wave after wave, Thompson

leaned back and let all his cares slip from his mind.

Damn this air smells good, Thompson thought to himself as fresh water spray dampened his face. He tilted his head backwards and filled his lungs with air as full as they could possibly get. *What a great way to start a recess. I hit it out of the park at Fancy Farm. And now I'm about to catch a big ol' bass.*

Thompson started singing a Robert Earl Keene, Jr. song out loud:

...Up in the morning,
Before the sun,
Fixed me some coffee and a honey bun,
Jumped in my pickup
Gave her some gas,
Lord, I'm goin' out to catch a five pound bass.

I wonder how many of the other Members of the House like to fish?

There's probably not too many. That may be what's wrong with Congress. Fishing takes patience. You've got to sit around for hours trying to find the right bait ... looking for options.

There's no patience in the Halls of Congress. Everyone knows the answers and wants results right away. They need a day of learning from an old guy like Ira.

The bow of the boat sank down as Ira throttled the motor down to idle. "We're here, boys," said Ira. "Congressman, over by those logs is my private honey hole. If we don't catch any big bass over there, ain't no big bass out here to be caught."

"I'm all in," said Thompson. He paused and looked up as a sea plane flew a couple of hundred yards behind them, obviously preparing to put down on the lake somewhere near the main dock.

"Well, let's go then," smiled a semi-toothless Ira.

Chapter 16

Josh Barkman was pulled roughly from the back of the trunk and stood up outside the small shack owned by General Alexandro. When he tried to stand on his own, Josh's legs immediately cramped up and he fell to the ground. The men all laughed at his plight. Even from the ground, it felt better than being shoved in the trunk of a car. The air around him was clean. He could smell a fire burning somewhere close.

His brief respite of fresh air was short-lived. With several men talking in Romanian at the same time, he was picked up and carried. Still blindfolded, he was not able to tell where he was being taken. When they entered the house, the sound of the men's boots on the wood floor indicated to Josh he had been moved inside a structure of some kind. He was carried into a side room and placed in a chair.

Josh tried to take a physical inventory of his pains, but he was so sore he hardly knew where to begin. His wrists and ankles hurt, but that probably was due to the fact they were still taped together. His stomach muscles hurt from the punch he had taken there. He breathed deeply and moved slightly from side to side before determining he probably didn't have any broken ribs.

But, his head … God, his head was killing him. The tension from the blindfold he was still wearing kept pressure on the places he had been hit. He was pretty sure his left eye was swollen shut from the punch delivered by Noua. Although his jaw was sore and taped shut, he was able to move it from side to side. No broken bones there.

As Josh finished his personal body inventory he could hear a loud argument in the next room. For the past several minutes or so, a voice he recognized as Noua's had been arguing with some man in Romanian.

"You idiot woman," Alexandro shouted at Noua as he threw a pan across the room in anger. "Your instructions were very clear ... precise."

"I know, Father," Noua replied. "Please let me explain."

"There is nothing for you to explain. You were supposed to capture Michael Griffith. This is not Michael Griffith. This is just some boy."

"But, Father, I met Michael Griffith. The boy is the one he calls America's Brain."

"You have been tricked," Alexandro shouted.

"No, I have not been tricked. He is the important one. He is the one who was sent to run everything. Michael Griffith himself told me so."

"And you believed him. You believed an American."

"Yes, Father," Noua said lowering her head.

He got up from his chair and slapped her hard across the face. "I trained you better. You disappoint me."

"I am sorry," Noua said, afraid that touching the red spot on her face where she had just been slapped would be seen as a sign of disrespect. The men standing around Noua looked at her, afraid to show any emotion.

General Alexandro stormed out of the house and slammed the door. Noua sat in place until she heard the rickety old car start up and pull away. Only then, she put her hand to her face. Despite the pain and humiliation, she refused to cry. She got up and stormed into the adjacent room where Josh was sitting. She slammed the door to the room behind her so the men remaining in the room could not see what was about to happen. She stormed to where Josh was seated and ripped the duct tape from his mouth.

The sting of the tape being pulled from over Josh's mouth caused him to wince. When the blindfold was removed with similar violence, he was able to see Noua through his one good eye. She was still wearing the same clothes from the night before, the white leather skirt and revealing top.

"Who are you?" she screamed at Josh in English.

"You know my name. It's Josh."

"You lied to me and you tricked me. You are no one. Just a boy." Noua swung and slapped Josh across the face with the same intensity her father had done to her only moments earlier. Josh fell out of the chair onto the floor. The pain caused by her slap to a portion of his face that was still tender from the earlier punches was severe.

From his prone position on the floor, he could see Noua go to her purse and get her Russian revolver. She walked over to him on the floor and placed it in front of his face.

"I will shoot you for bringing me shame. You will die for what you have done to me."

Josh froze. Preparing to die, he looked directly at her, his one good blue eye looking squarely at her. She reached to touch the amulet around her neck. It was gone. Somehow in the scuffle in Bucharest, it had broken and fallen. Now, in her home, blue eyes … the evil eye … stared directly at her.

Noua stepped back in horror and then ran from the room, leaving Josh lying on the floor.

Chapter 17

The Fat Man had warned Thompson before the trip he wasn't much of a fisherman. As Thompson looked to the stern of the bass boat, Ira was coaching The Fat Man on how to cast towards the shore. When a fish finally hit, The Fat Man had a look of panic on his face.

"Start cranking," instructed Ira, as he grabbed the net. "Easy, easy. Don't let him go under the boat."

"How the hell am I supposed to do that?" asked The Fat Man as he continued to crank, "Call his mom?"

"Just work him to your left," said Ira calmly. "Just a little more." Ira dipped the net into the water and pulled the hooked fish onto the boat. "Got 'em. First fish of the day goes to Joe. And he's a keeper."

As Ira tossed the fish into the locker, Thompson looked at The Fat Man. The look on his face had gone from panic to triumph. He was even taking his life vest off to be better able to cast out.

Thompson had gone back to his own fishing chores, when Waldo began barking at an approaching bass boat. The boat was clearly headed in the direction of Ira.

"That lousy fucker," said Ira as the boat approached.

"What?" asked The Fat Man.

"It's that damned Hatter boy," said Ira. "He's always tryin' to horn in on my honey-hole. Now, he's got a boat load of folks and he wants to fish at my private spot."

"I really don't think it's your private spot," said The Fat Man, trying to calm Ira down.

"The hell it isn't," said Ira as he reached for his shotgun.

"Whoa," said Thompson. "Hold on now, Ira. No one's pullin' a gun here."

"But he's trying to invade my hole."

"Let's see what he wants," said Thompson, as the other boat cut its engine and began to idle towards the trio. "Besides, one of those guys looks familiar."

"Is that Leo Argo?" asked The Fat Man.

"I think so," replied Thompson. "I wonder what the hell he wants."

Thompson didn't say it out loud, but he knew that Argo's presence on the lake was not a good sign. *He was probably on the sea plane that flew over a half hour or so ago,* thought Thompson. *I know one damn thing for sure. He is not here to fish. This can't be good news.*

"Who's Argo?" asked Ira.

"FBI Agent out of Washington," said Thompson. Thompson tried to explain more, but the letters FBI were all Ira had to hear. He reached around and tried to start the engine.

"God damn FBI," shouted Ira as he looked around nervously for a place to hide. "They've been chasin' me since Tupelo in '72. You bastards set me up."

"Calm down, Ira," said Thompson. "He's a friend of mine. He's here for me, not you."

"Are you sure?" asked Ira. "He may know about Tupelo."

"He doesn't," Thompson replied. "Take my word for it. Play it cool and you'll be fine."

"Take the word of a politician, and play it cool with a Fed," Ira said to Waldo as he nervously petted the dog on the head. "If this ain't one helluva morning. Damn Tupelo."

Richard Thompson had met Leo Argo during Thompson's run for Congress. The FBI had involved Thompson in its investigation of a high-ranking and corrupt Member of Congress. Argo had been the lead agent on the operation. He was a big, burly, light-skinned Cuban with a bald head and large smile. However, as the boats idled side by side, Argo was not smiling.

Thompson looked at The Fat Man. He was not covering his emotions well. The Fat Man's face was drawn and his posture was stiff. He showed the concern that Thompson was feeling, but outwardly hiding.

The Hatter boy shouted a conditioned greeting at Ira. "Don't shoot. We're not here to fish. This guy is just lookin' for someone."

"Why are you out here, Leo?" asked Thompson of the large man. "The look on your face leaves me with the distinct impression that you're not out here to catch fish."

"I'm not, Congressman," replied Argo. "I'm afraid that I have some bad news for you. I called your house late last night and Ann said you were here."

"You spoke to Ann? She never called us last night."

"When I told her what was happening," said Argo, "we agreed that I should fly in and tell you in person."

The Fat Man moved to the middle of the boat, nodded a greeting at Argo and listened to the conversation.

"What is it, Leo?" asked Thompson. "What's wrong?"

"It's Josh Barkman, Congressman."

"Josh? What's wrong with Josh?"

"I hate to be the one to tell you this," Argo continued, "but Josh has been kidnapped."

Thompson's heart seemed to stop in place. He sat down in a fishing chair on the boat and placed his head in his hands.

"What happened, Leo?" The Fat Man asked.

"It's still pretty sketchy," said Argo. "But the last time anyone saw him, he was leaving a bar at his hotel with a pretty young Romanian girl."

"Sounds to me like he's shacked up," said Ira.

"I wish he was," said Argo. "There were some witnesses who saw a fight, and then saw a young blond American male being duct-taped and thrown into the trunk of a car. The woman shot and killed the guy's friend."

"My God," said Thompson. "This isn't happening. That kid is like a son to me. Oh fuck, this isn't happening." The Fat Man waddled over towards Thompson and put his hand on Thompson's back. There was a long silence. Thompson took a deep breath to focus. "Okay. Has anyone taken responsibility for the kidnapping?"

"Not yet," replied Argo. "Our best shot at finding him is to keep it from the press. Once word gets out, every looney in Eastern Europe will claim responsibility." Argo paused. "I know this is a big shock to you, Rick, I mean Congressman. Ann didn't want you to hear this over the phone. That's why I flew in."

Thompson nodded while he took in several deep breaths. "So, what do we do now … and please, right now it's Rick."

"Well," said Argo. "You're headed back on the sea plane with me to D.C."

"I can't," said Thompson. "I need to head home to Ann first."

"Ann is at home packing for both of you. She's going to meet you tonight at Quantico Marine Base."

"Quantico? Why?"

"Because there's a plane leaving Quantico tomorrow headed to Romania filled with observers."

"So?"

"You and Ann are on that plane."

Chapter 18

Presidential Chief of Staff, Benny Vesper, stood up as President Jack Mocker entered the Oval Office carrying his morning Diet Coke. It was Saturday and the President was dressed in jeans, tennis shoes, and a red golf shirt. As he entered the room, Vesper couldn't help but notice how much the President had aged during his six years in office. He had come to office as a tall, dark-haired, square jawed leader of the people. Midway through his second term, his hair had grayed on the temples and his tight face and jaw seemed to have drooped from the stress of being the leader of the free world.

It happens to all of them, Vesper thought. *They all come in looking like young men and leave looking like old geezers. Thank God I looked like shit when I got here.*

"Good morning, Mr. President."

"Good morning, Benny. I didn't expect to see you in here on a Saturday morning." The President shook hands with Benny and moved to the couch as he spoke. Vesper waited until Mocker was seated before he sat down in a chair opposite the couch and continued.

"Well, I had to come by and talk to you. We had some problems last night in Romania."

"Aw, fuck," replied Mocker. "What now?"

"One of our U.S. election observers was kidnapped." President Mocker flopped his head back against the couch and closed his eyes. A deep sigh indicated he was ready for Vesper to continue. "Some kid from the Hill." Vesper paused and looked at his briefing folder to recall the name. "Josh Barkman—he was out with some broad late last night and got tossed in the back of a car."

"The Hill. Great. Congress will get involved. Who does he work for?"

"Richard Thompson, from Kentucky's Fourth District," replied Vesper. "That's the district right across the Ohio River from Cincinnati."

"Thompson," said Mocker as he took a drink from his soft drink. "Isn't he the guy who won the special?"

"Yeah," Vesper said assuringly. "That will help us. Not many folks on the Hill know him that well yet."

"So, what do we know?"

"Well," said Vesper, "we don't know a whole lot yet. Our feet on the ground tell us it could be any one of a hundred fringe groups. They are interviewing people right now to see if we can get a positive identification on the Romanian girl."

"Have we made official contact with the government in Romania yet?" asked the President.

"Yes, sir," replied Vesper. "All channels are open and communicating. We sent our concern. The President of Romania sent his regrets. All the standard stuff is flying back and forth. And one more thing, sir."

"What?" There was a pause. When Vesper didn't respond, the President looked directly at him. "What?"

"You won't like this, sir … ."

"What?" said Mocker. "Go ahead and tell me. It can't get any worse."

"The person with the best description of the kidnapper is Michael Griffith."

"You've got to be kidding me," said a surprised Mocker. "What the hell is he doing there?"

"The incumbent hired him to consult in the presidential elections," said Vesper. "He's there running President Krasterich's reelection campaign. Apparently, Griffith and this new Congressman … Thompson … went there in '90 when they worked on the Hill as staffers. This Josh kid is someone who was traveling with Griffith as an observer."

"I can't get that bastard Griffith out of my life. He killed us in the last midterm elections and now he's against me in Romania."

"Well, Mr. President, formally, sir, he's with us in Romania."

"Yeah, yeah. Whatever." Mocker paused to gather his thoughts. "How about our friends over in the Kremlin? What do they know?"

"They're telling me that they're not involved and they know nothing," said Vesper.

"And you trust them?"

"Sir, I've never trusted them," said Vesper. "But I tend to think they are telling the truth. I don't think they are behind this. They have as much at stake here as we do. Maybe more."

"All right," said Mocker. "So, what do we do now?"

"First," said Vesper. "I've got the FBI informing the Congressman about the incident. They have some sort of relationship with the guy and someone is in Kentucky right now briefing him about it. They are going to fly him to D.C. and put him on the plane we have leaving Quantico for Romania."

"Are you nuts?" asked Mocker. "You're putting a United States Congressman on a military transport carrying the football in its belly?"

"Yeah," replied Vesper. "There's a method to my madness. We may be able to use him. He'll probably do anything to get this kid back. If we play it right, we might even be able to use him to move the football for us."

"I don't like this," said Mocker.

"It's already in motion, Mr. President," said Vesper.

"This is fucked up," Mocker replied, pausing to think. "Then I want Kline and her boy on the plane, too."

"I don't think that's a good idea," replied Vesper, more out of dislike for Kline than for the plan itself. "No, I don't like that at all."

"This is an order, Benny," said Mocker. "We've already stolen the Mace and the Sergeant at Arms is dead. Now, a staffer's been kidnapped and you are sending a Member of Congress over to unknowingly run interference for us. No, I want Kline involved. She knows Romania from her past missions. I've read her dossier. Dress her up as an observer if you want, but I want Jane Kline on that flight."

"But, Mr. President…"

"No buts. That's an order."

"Yes, sir."

"That's all, Benny."

"Thank you, Mr. President."

Chapter 19

No matter what the circumstance, music always seemed to be the one of two constants in Richard Thompson's life. His office had a Nietzsche quote framed on the wall: "Without music, life would be a mistake." Music usually reflected his mood or set the tone for the mood he desired.

Thompson had his iPod buds in his ears as the small eight-seat jet carrying him and FBI Agent Leo Argo made the final leg of its approach to the landing strip at Quantico. He had tried to close his eyes and relax in the luxurious, tan leather seats of the plane, but the somber and gloomy nature of his thoughts made sleep impossible. He and Argo had spoken very little the entire flight. When they spoke, the exchanges were short.

"Where are my kids?"

"Ann said she was sending them to her sister's house, I think."

"When can I speak to Griffith?"

"Not until you get there. We can't get a secured line."

"Does the President know?"

"Yes."

Thompson was thinking thoughts as dark as the cold water of Kentucky Lake and there was no chance of changing his mood. So, he just listened as Warren Zevon lyrically reflected his deep melancholy.

...Everybody's restless,
And they've got no place to go,
Someone's always trying to tell them,
Something they already know,
So their anger and resentment show.

Leo Argo interrupted the song by tapping Thompson on the arm and telling him to turn off his iPod for the landing. When the wheels hit the ground, they set the stage for what Thompson really wanted … Ann, his wife, his life's other constant. According to Argo, she was already waiting for him in a holding room at the base. He desperately needed to see her. Music couldn't change his mood. Maybe she could. She was the one person who could add some hope to his despair.

Thompson thanked the pilot for the flight and he and Argo started the walk to the small building connected to the main hangar. From a distance, he could see Ann looking out the window, gently waving a sad greeting. As he got closer, he could see her eyes were red from crying.

As Thompson walked through the door, Ann ran to his side and hugged him hard. The couple didn't speak for a long time. They just held each other as tears welled up in their eyes.

Leo Argo finally spoke. "I'm sorry, you two, but there's really no place private for you to go. Why don't we step out front where we can talk?"

Thompson suddenly realized the room was filled with about 20 people. All were awaiting the departure of the military flight to Romania. As none of them had any idea that a kidnapping had taken place, they were all staring quizzically at Thompson and Ann. Argo led them outside to the sidewalk. The three of them sat on a bench along the sidewalk about 15 yards away. Ann took hold of Thompson's hand. As she did, Thompson lost all of his composure.

"Oh dear God, Ann," Thompson said as he held Ann tightly. "What have they done to Josh?"

"It's going to be fine, Richard," Ann responded with more confidence in her voice than in her heart. "We're going to find him. He's going to be fine."

"Why in the hell did I let him go in the first place?"

"This is not your fault, babe," Ann again comforted. "You, no one, could have predicted this would have happened."

"When he asked, I should have said no," said Thompson. "I should not have let him go. If anything happens to him, I'll never forgive myself."

"Come on, Richard. You know he would have talked you into going anyway."

"But I could have said no."

"It's not your fault."

"And where the hell was Griff?" asked Thompson rhetorically. "He should have told him not to go out at night alone."

"That's a question I want to know as well," said Ann, turning to Argo. "Where was Michael Griffith when this happened?"

"Let's just say he had already gone to bed for the night," Argo replied. Ann rolled her eyes, conscious of Argo's attempt to be discreet.

Thompson looked over at Argo. "Has anyone called Josh's parents? They need to know what is going on."

"We're not going to do that right now," said Argo. "This is all out of the press right now. It's better for Josh's safety if we keep this as quiet as possible."

"That's just wrong, Leo," said Ann. "His mom and dad deserve to know what's going on.

"I agree with Ann on this one," interjected Thompson. "I should call them."

"Do what you want to do, Congressman, but I can tell you that would be a bad call to make. If this leaks out in any way, it could put Josh's life in danger. His mom and dad would tell folks who might end up telling the press. My advice is to stay cool until you get on the ground in Romania."

"All right," said Thompson. "We won't call."

"In fact," said Argo, "those folks back in the building are all going with you to Romania as election observers. You'll need to compose yourself before you go back in. You can't give them any hint that anything is wrong."

"And you, Leo," asked Ann, "Are you going with us?"

"I can't, Mrs. Thompson," replied Argo. "I'm FBI. I don't have any jurisdiction outside the country."

"So, if you're not with us, who do we look for when we get there?" asked Thompson.

"When you land, the U.S. Embassy will have someone there at the plane to pick you up. Don't go to the hotel with the rest of the gang in there. Go straight to the Embassy. Someone will get in touch with you there."

"All right," replied Thompson, as he tried to compose himself. He looked at Ann. "Are you ready to go inside and meet everyone?"

Chapter 20

In the days leading up to Thompson's election to United States Congress, The Fat Man had been extremely active in his friend's campaign. In doing so, he had learned a lot about politics. The Fat Man was a movie geek and Griffith's style of teaching politics by using scenes and lines from the *Godfather* trilogy of movies suited his persona perfectly.

In the months following the election, the key Griffith lesson that stuck with The Fat Man the most was the one regarding loyalty. Griffith reminded everyone throughout the campaign that loyalty was a campaign worker's number one asset. He punctuated the lesson by reminding everyone who would listen that in the original *Godfather* movie, Vito Corleone's top Button Man, Luca Brazi, had died after pledging his loyalty to the Don.

The Fat Man was a loyal Button Man for his friend Richard Thompson. Just like Luca, all Thompson had to do was "push a button" and The Fat Man would follow through on the order. As he drove home, he realized that was also the most enduring trait of Josh Barkman. The Fat Man didn't know the young man as well as the others, but he admired and appreciated the loyalty Josh had displayed to Thompson.

Moreover, The Fat Man knew that Thompson and his wife, Ann, repaid Josh's loyalty with similar personal allegiance. Both of them thought of the kid as if he was one of their own children. He knew at the moment the lives of all three were a living hell.

Armed with all that knowledge, in the first hour of the six-hour drive back from the lake, The Fat Man had been thinking a lot about Josh's kidnapping. What had been most frustrating to him was that, despite his concern, there was absolutely nothing he could do from Kentucky to assist. So as he drove, he made a conscious choice to spend the rest of the trip home in a productive manner—getting to work on the project Thompson assigned to him. As he rolled along the Western Kentucky Parkway, he placed multiple calls back to the law office and asked a young female associate to start on general research about the original Mace.

When he arrived home, The Fat Man went straight to his law office. Now he sat alone in a conference room assembling his thoughts in a diagram he was crafting on a large white board in the room. It was getting late, but he knew if he went home he wasn't going to sleep. He was known around the law office for pulling all-nighters.

Looks like tonight's a night to add to the stories they tell about me, The Fat Man thought to himself as he pushed a black leather chair back from the glass-covered conference table. He tossed a memo the associate had prepared for him on the table. *What's another late night at the office?*

About five hours into the all-nighter, The Fat Man stood up and stretched his arms towards the ceiling, forcing his shirt to ride up his belly. He let out a crude growl-like noise in order to focus his attention on the white board at the end of the conference room. He walked to the end of the room, picked up a marker and drew a crude dome and mace on the white board.

The Mace had clearly been in the Capitol when the British occupied it in 1814, The Fat Man silently mused. *All right, bright boy, that wasn't tough. What happened to it next?*

The Fat Man drew a line out from the left of the Capitol. He picked up a red marker and drew a flame. *Option one—it burned in the fire.* "Gone," he wrote in black under the flame and then underlined it twice with red.

The Fat Man walked around the room for a minute tossing the marker in the air from hand-to-hand as he sauntered over to the conference table. He picked up a printout of a page he found on an internet site containing U.K. military papers. It contained the personal notes of Admiral George

Cockburn of the British Navy. He looked at the paper intently for nearly a minute before he walked back to the white board.

According to Admiral Cockburn's notes on the burning of the Capitol, there was a young British subordinate officer who loved the building and didn't want it to be burned. The Fat Man looked again at the paper, tapping it as he thought. *Kevin Matthews—that's his name. He pulled up another paper. Matthews was also the one in charge of the three boats sent back to London filled with American bounty.*

Walking back to the white board, The Fat Man then drew a line out from the right side of the Capitol. Next to the line he drew a smiley face. Under the face he wrote the name "Kevin Matthews." He paced again before going back to the board where he drew two lines down from the smiley face. Under one line he put an X and wrote "Sunk—Gone." Under the other line he wrote "London."

He was staring at the white board when Stephanie, a tall brunette with a runner's body, walked into the room. "What are you doing, Mr. Bradley?"

"Pondering all of the research you did for me yesterday," he replied. "If the Mace made it out of the Capitol it landed in London."

She looked at the board. "Maybe not. You've left one important possibility off your diagram. There's a distinct possibility the original Mace never left America."

As instructed by an earlier voice message, Benny Vesper left his office to meet the President in the Situation Room in the basement of the White House. He showed his credentials to the Marine officer standing guard outside the door and entered the tightly secured, 5,000-square-foot complex of windowless rooms. Vesper sat down at the large conference table in the middle of the room and looked at the six flat screen panel televisions waiting for his secure video conference to appear on one of them. He looked at his watch.

He still had a few minutes.

Built by President John F. Kennedy following the failed Bay of Pigs invasion of Cuba, the room was stripped down to the brick following 9/11. It was rebuilt with the most up-to-date communications technology in the world. Far more nondescript than depicted in movies and television, the room and the technology it contains allow the President and his national security team to have protected communications with United States intelligence teams and leaders worldwide.

Today, Vesper would be placing a personal call to the Number Two man at the Kremlin. The leader of neither country would dare talk on the phone to the other directly on the subject of Romania, but it went without saying that both of them would be listening to, if not directing, their top advisors on the call.

Vesper carried a yellow legal pad outlining the very clear points President Mocker wanted him to make during the call:

If the Russians were found to be behind the kidnapping the deal was off. Period. Balance of power be damned.

If they were not behind the kidnapping they were to offer all assistance in finding the missing American.

Most important, this unfortunate incident would affect the price per barrel.

Vesper had arrived in the Situation Room ahead of President Mocker. Only a single technician was in the room, there to establish the link and then leave. He was nervously shifting around in his chair when the President entered the situation room. Vesper stood up.

"Good afternoon, Mr. President," said Vesper and the technician simultaneously.

The President sat down. Talking to Vesper, the technician said: "The secure line to the Kremlin is awaiting your presence."

Griffith paced nervously in a waiting room at the Palace of the Parliament in Bucharest. Sue and Yorgi sat patiently, but the stress of the situation was showing on them as well. The Romanian President was late for their meeting. As each minute passed, Griffith became more agitated.

The Palace is recognized as the largest civilian administrative building in the world. Only the Pentagon is larger, but it contains military administration. The building was started by Nicolae Ceausescu, but never fully completed following his execution. It is an opulent structure, containing over one million cubic meters of marble. It took 3,500 tons of crystal to make the nearly 500 chandeliers that adorn the ceilings.

Griff, unimpressed by the structure itself, began to mumble to himself.

"Mr. Greef, you need to calm down," said Yorgi. "President Krasterich is an important man. He is known to be late for meetings. To be agitated when he arrives will show disrespect."

"I don't give a goddamn how important he thinks he is. Every minute we wait is another minute we lose in finding Josh."

"Baby, you've got to calm down," interjected Sue. "You're going to have a stroke."

"Theeese keednappings happen all the time over here, Mr. Greef. They all show up a day or so later. Yoshua weel show up."

Richard Thompson was sitting on the plane next to Ann. The trip was agonizing for both of them. Per Argo's instructions, they were doing their best acting jobs, trying to remain calm and anonymous. It was difficult. Every time they tried to talk, the conversation seemed to return to Josh. There would be a story about one time when he had done something funny or a reflection about another time he had performed a task in his usual stellar fashion. The stories inevitably would lead to welling eyes, suppressing tears of concern about Josh's well-being, and they would have to stop. Occasionally, they communicated to each other by passing notes. There was less emotion that way.

When all seemed to be asleep on the plane, Thompson leaned over and whispered in Ann's ear. "So, what do we do when we get to Romania? Do we call Josh's parents?"

Almost immediately, a woman got up from her seat and approached the Thompsons.

"I'm sorry," said Ann. "Were we being too loud?"

"No. You're fine. I just wanted to introduce myself. I'm Jane Kline."

Noua was sitting by the fire when she heard her father's car pull up in front of the house. Alexandro's men were long gone and Noua was alone. When her father entered the room, she could smell the alcohol on his breath.

"You have ruined it all," shouted Alexandro as he lunged at Noua. He raised his hand and attempted to strike her face, but the alcohol caused him to stumble. The blow glanced off her arm. "You are nothing to me," he shouted in frustration at his drunken lack of coordination.

Noua was glad he was drunk. The assault tonight would just be verbal. Her father was way too drunk to hurt her physically. Still Alexandro's verbal assault on Noua would continue well into the night.

Josh walked a young blond girl home from a sophomore dance. Hand in hand, they passed hedge row after hedge row along the small city street until they came to a break in one which led to the entrance to the girl's house. He walked her to the door and turned to face her. Nervous, with sweaty palms, he gently put his hands on her hips and leaned forward. Both closed their eyes. Josh kissed the girl on the lips. She kissed him back in an awkward first kiss for both. The nervousness turned to pleasure—the pleasure to bliss.

Suddenly, as Alexandro screamed at Noua, Josh awoke from his congenial dream of teenage innocence. In the blink of an eye, he suddenly remembered that his reality was as harsh as the floor he was sleeping on—and that he was sore, hungry, cold and in darkness.

Chapter 21

"What do you mean, there's a possibility the original Mace never left America?" The Fat Man looked quizzically at Stephanie as he stood up and walked to the glass-covered counter in the conference room which was stocked with ice and seemingly enough Mountain Dew to keep an army of soldiers awake and wired for a week-long battle. He popped one open, sniffed the Dew as if it were some fine port wine and listened intently to Stephanie's response.

"Just what I said," replied Stephanie matter-of-factly as she walked to the white board and picked up a red marker. "You're trying to come up with all of the possibilities, right?"

"Right."

"But all of your possibilities on the white board start with the Mace either being burned or going over the pond to the U.K.," said Stephanie.

"That's because I am only looking at possibilities that have some factual basis for their inclusion," said The Fat Man.

"Okay," said Stephanie. "So we both agree on that point. We're on the same page."

"I've read all of the research you pulled for me and there are only two possibilities. Everything indicates the Mace was either burned by Admiral Cockburn who led the British troops, or was stolen by a lower ranking officer named Matthews and taken to England."

"That's where I think you're wrong," interjected Stephanie.

"Why do you think I am wrong?"

"Let me rephrase. That's where I think that you haven't considered all of the possibilities."

"Better," said The Fat Man. He gulped a mouthful of his drink and sniffed the air above the mouth of the plastic bottle, simultaneously enjoying the bouquet and savoring the nectar of the caffeine gods on his taste buds. "You may proceed."

"All right," said Stephanie. "If Cockburn left it at the Capitol, it's gone. It went up in the fire. It melted into the pores of the marble floor."

"Right," replied The Fat Man. "And if it went on the boat with Matthews, then odds are it's also gone. Three boats headed back to England. Only one of the three boats made it across the Atlantic Ocean. Two of them sank in a storm just off the British Isles."

"I've checked English military records," said Stephanie. "Matthews was on one of the boats that went down."

"Which means it's gone," said The Fat Man. "Matthews probably would have made sure that something as valuable as the Mace was in his quarters. If he went down the Mace went down with him."

"Unless," said Stephanie, "he was concerned that someone would steal it from him on the voyage back to England."

"Maybe," said The Fat Man. "But chances are he didn't show it to anyone anyway."

"Right. But what did he plan to do with the Mace once he got it back to England? Wouldn't he be concerned that the British government would never allow him to keep it when he got home?"

"He'd be concerned, of course."

"So, start with that basic premise," said Stephanie. She paused and looked at The Fat Man seeking his approval to proceed.

"I'm listening…"

"Seriously, stick with me on this one," said Stephanie. "I need you to suspend disbelief a bit. Take a big gulp of Dew."

"I don't know," replied The Fat Man. "I just don't want to go anywhere without a foundation."

"Humor me," replied Stephanie. "I've got a foundation. It's slim, but I've got one."

"Great," said The Fat Man. "There is nothing slim in what I do."

"What other options do you have?" Stephanie said. "Your white board has the Mace laying somewhere on the bottom of the Irish Sea. Unless you're planning on becoming the next Mel Fisher you're not going to find it."

"It could happen," said The Fat Man.

"While you're getting certified in scuba, follow my lead."

"All right," said The Fat Man. "What's your hypothesis?"

"Well," Stephanie continued, "according to Cockburn's notes, Matthews was very impressed with the architecture of the Capitol and he didn't want the British troops to set it on fire. When they did, maybe he saved the Mace from destruction."

"That's your theory," replied The Fat Man.

"But if he wanted to save the Mace, why would he take it on a boat where it might get stolen?" she asked. "And he would know that if it was discovered on the boat, it would be appropriated by the government."

She again looked at The Fat Man. "Keep going," he said.

"Wouldn't Matthews instead have the Mace sent to someone who could insure its safety?"

"Great theory," said The Fat Man. He pondered the possibility for a moment while taking another gulp. "It even makes some degree of sense. But, where would Matthews send it?"

"I haven't figured that out yet..."

Chapter 22

Prior to the final approach to Bucharest Airport Jane Kline quietly instructed Thompson and Ann to be the final couple off of the plane. For the entire flight, they managed to remain somewhat anonymous to the other passengers. Now that they were in-country, the three of them, along with Kline's partner, Mark Morrison, were to quietly disconnect themselves from the rest of the group. As instructed, while the others aboard disembarked, Thompson stayed behind fumbling through his briefcase.

When everyone but the pilots had left the plane, Thompson quit his charade and sat back down with Ann. Both had an edgy look of anxious anticipation on their faces. They were finally in Romania. The ridges in Thompson's forehead looked like they were carved in granite. Neither spoke to the other, but both were thinking similar dark thoughts about Josh's safety.

"I want the others to all clear immigration first," Kline said as she walked back along the aisle of the large military transport toward the Thompsons. "I don't want the real observers to know your real purpose here. When they head to the hotel, we're headed straight to the embassy."

"I understand," replied Thompson nervously.

"We'll give them about ten minutes and then head in."

"That's all it will take for them to get through immigration?" asked Ann.

"This is Romania, Mrs. Thompson," said Kline. "Bucharest isn't exactly the home of crack security technology."

"I guess not," mused Ann. "I know that my tone may sound a little short. Please understand—we are just anxious and want to get to the Embassy as quickly as possible. We really want to find out what's going on with the efforts to locate Josh."

"She's right," interjected Thompson. "I need to know what's going on here."

"Don't worry, Congressman," said Kline. "The State Department knows we're coming. I've been assured we'll get a briefing as soon as we arrive. You'll get first class attention. Just sit tight and we'll be out of here soon."

Kline turned and went back to the front of the plane where she began to talk quietly with her partner.

"How are they holding up?" whispered Morrison.

"Pretty well, I think. I mean how would you be holding up if some kid who you treated like your own son was missing in a foreign country?" replied Kline.

"You're right—not nearly as good as they are right now," replied Morrison as he looked back at the couple. Kline noticed that he seemed to be studying them closely.

Kline gave Morrison a questioning look as if to say "What?"

Morrison responded to the unspoken question. "She's pretty hot for an older lady."

"You're a real puke," said Kline as she shook her head. "You know that, Shadow? You're a 100%, class-A, certified puke."

"Hey," said Morrison. "I may be covert, but I'm not dead. I'm just sayin' she's a good looking' babe for her age."

"Just shut up," said Kline. "and whatever you do, don't say that around anyone. Her husband is a Congressman. You think you're in deep shit now. Just imagine if he hears you and calls the director."

"Sonofabitch," replied Morrison, looking away and suddenly self-conscious. "I don't need that kind of heat on me right now."

He paused for a few seconds and then looked back at Kline. "Do you think we'll find the kid?"

"No one has taken responsibility yet," said Kline. "And

that bothers me. Usually by now, the kidnapper would have contacted someone for a ransom or made some political demand. No one has demanded anything."

"This is going to be a tough assignment."

"Just remember," said Kline, "the whereabouts of Josh Barkman is not your number one assignment. You're responsible for the football. You need to get that thing past the goal line. If you can help me out with the Barkman kidnapping, then fine. But your job is the football. We'll be getting delivery instructions after we get into the Embassy in Bucharest."

"I know," said Morrison. "I'm ready for my assignment."

"Anyway, for all we know, the kid may be dead by now."

"Whoa. Sonofabitch."

As Kline walked to the front of the plane, Ann turned to Thompson. "She doesn't look like a CIA agent. He does, but she doesn't."

"She's probably out of the public affairs office," replied Thompson.

"That sounds pretty chauvinistic."

"What? She's a pretty woman. You said it yourself just a minute ago," Thompson replied.

"I said she didn't look like a CIA type," Ann retorted. "You said she was pretty."

"She's an attractive woman. I just don't envision her as being one of the blood and guts CIA types. She's probably been sent over here to keep an eye on us."

"And the man is in charge, I guess," said Ann. "… the one who keeps looking back here at me."

"He's not looking at you," said Thompson.

"The hell he isn't," snapped Ann.

"Look," Thompson said. "Let's not fight. I really can't deal with a fight right now. Yes, I think Kline is attractive and the guy may be looking at you. Okay? It's been a long flight under very tough circumstances. We're tired, and we're probably about to get a very difficult briefing. Let's not make it any worse than it already is."

"You're right," said Ann, relaxing her shoulders. "I'm sorry for snapping at you. This is just a weird circumstance for both of us. We've got to focus on Josh. That's what's important now."

"I can't get him out of my head. If something has happened to that kid I'll never forgive myself for letting him go," said Thompson.

"You can't do this to yourself, Richard. What happened wasn't your fault. It wasn't anyone's fault."

"I encouraged him to go. I said it would be good for him."

"And who could have expected this kind of an outcome? Come on. No one could have predicted this."

"I guess," replied Thompson, as he exhaled to calm his nerves. "But it's more than that right now."

"What?"

"I still have to face Griff," said Thompson.

"You can't blame him either," Ann said.

"Maybe. But where the hell was he when Josh was getting kidnapped?"

"I'm telling you, babe. You can't blame Griff. Josh is a grown man."

"I know. I know. But Griff should have been watching out for him."

Up in the front of the plane Kline looked at her watch and stood up. "All right, gang, it's time to head to the Embassy."

Chapter 23

The opening scene from the television show *WKRP in Cincinnati* used to show a panoramic view of the Queen City shot from Devou Park in Northern Kentucky. The location is only a couple of miles or so from Congressman Richard Thompson's home. In the river valley below the location where that intro was recorded there are nearly a dozen church steeples within eyesight, standing testament to the faith of the community.

One of the grand steeples of Northern Kentucky belongs to Trinity Episcopal Church. An old style English church, Trinity is known, in part, for its ornate stained glass windows and massive pipe organ. Its rich history dates back to 1842. Plaques containing the family names of community leaders from the late-1800s and early-1900s adorn the walls.

The stained glass windows are some of the most beautiful in the community, and they draw visitors and tourists who visit the sanctuary just to view the sun beaming through their multicolored images. The windows were made by craftsmen who were among some of the most famous stained glass window makers in the world at the time.

A devout Catholic, The Fat Man nevertheless often attended Trinity Episcopal Church for the special community events they regularly sponsored. He had an old world personality and he enjoyed the atmosphere of the church's surroundings. Of all the church's special events, The Fat Man tried to go to all of the lunchtime concerts featuring the 1,928 pipes protruding from the church's majestic pipe organ.

As for the windows, The Fat Man's favorite was installed in 1902. It portrayed Michael, the leader of the archangels and the guardian of the souls of men, in military armor. In the window, the golden figure of Michael is surrounded by the columns of Heaven as viewed through the surrounding clouds. Wings protrude from Michael's armor and a white flag with a red cross is behind him. When the noon sun shines through it, it exudes an inspirational brilliance.

The trip to Fancy Farm, followed by the all-nighter at the office, had taken a toll on The Fat Man. When he was fresh out of law school it seemed he could go for days on little, if any, sleep. After the conversation with Stephanie, he realized that he was very tired. So he had gone home to grab a quick nap and a shower. As he headed back into the office, just before noon, he remembered Trinity was having one of its special concerts that day. Hoping the music would clear his head, he diverted his car from his regular route to the office and headed for Covington. Now, as he sat in the first pew, waiting for the music to begin, he gazed aimlessly at the fan vaulted ceiling of the transept.

Joe Pennington, the Rector of Trinity, was used to seeing The Fat Man at the church and often referred to him as his "favorite Catholic" because he always left something in the collection plate following each concert. When Father Pennington saw him sitting in the first pew he walked up and sat down beside him.

"Good morning, counselor," said Father Pennington, slapping The Fat Man on the knee as he sat down. "Good to see you, as always, but I've got to say, you look horrible. Are you working too hard again?"

"Thanks, Padre," replied The Fat Man. "I stayed pretty late at the office last night. I only look bad because I feel that way too. What about you? You've got your robes on today. What's up with that?"

"I'm working at this concert," replied Father Pennington. "I've got a reading during the second song."

The pair got quiet as the organist came out and began the first song. The Fat Man and Father Pennington both tapped their right feet in time with the music. When it ended, Father Pennington leaned over and whispered: "I've got to go to work."

As the music proceeded into its second progression Father Pennington rose and stood behind the wooden eagle lectern holding the *Bible*. The eagle lectern, with its wings spread wide and its head looking over its right side as a sign of peace, had been given to the church by Kentucky Governor John White Stevenson in 1881. The symbolism of the lectern relates to the preaching of St. John, whose word was said to carry as far as an eagle could fly.

At various points in the second progression of the song the music would stop and Father Pennington would read a verse from the *Bible*. The Fat Man listened to each verse and let his mind wander as he contemplated the meaning. During the third reading, Father Pennington read a verse from Ecclesiastes. "A wise man's heart directs him toward the right, but the foolish man's heart directs him toward the left," he proclaimed.

The Fat Man was contemplating Father Pennington's words while listening to the music and alternatively changing his visual attention back and forth between the eagle lectern and the stained-glass image of unforgiving eyes of Michael the Archangel.

The words rattled around in The Fat Man's head.

A wise man's heart directs him toward the right, but the foolish man's heart directs him toward the left.

The Fat Man looked at the steely eyes of Michael. The music rang. He looked at Joe and the eagle.

A wise man's heart directs him toward the right, but the foolish man's heart directs him toward the left.

Suddenly, The Fat Man jumped up from his pew with a start. He felt as if his breath had literally been taken away from him. Father Pennington looked down from the eagle lectern startled by the frantic motions of his "favorite Catholic."

The Fat Man looked back at Father Pennington and mouthed the words: "I'm sorry. I've got to go." He rushed out of the church.

Chapter 24

When Stephanie walked into the conference room The Fat Man was busily erasing his graphic of 1814 international intrigue from the white board. Hearing her enter the room he turned. Thrusting his arms in the air he shouted, "You were right. You were right."

"Thank you," she replied. "About what?"

"Matthews … Cockburn … the Navy …," replied The Fat Man. "You were right. It never left the country."

"Slow down," Stephanie instructed. "Slow down and speak in a language I can understand."

"The Mace," The Fat Man said in a slow deliberate manner. "You were right about the Mace. It was stolen by Matthews, but it never left the country. He was worried someone would steal it or the government would appropriate it. It wasn't on the ship with him when he left America."

"That's quite a swing for you," Stephanie said. "How did you come up with this revelation?"

"Not Revelations … Ecclesiastes."

"I'm lost," said Stephanie. "Who gave you the foundation?"

"Michael gave me the foundation," he said.

"Okay, now we're getting somewhere," said Stephanie. "Michael gave you a foundation. Michael who?"

"Michael the Archangel."

"Michael the Archangel told you all of this," said Stephanie, trying to suppress a laugh. "I didn't know that you were pals with the guy who decides who gets into Heaven on Judgment Day."

"Well, I've never met him personally," replied The Fat Man.

"I kind of figured that," said Stephanie. "Just start at the beginning. And please use small words."

"On the way into the office today, I remembered that Trinity was having a noon concert and I decided to drop by and listen," said the Fat Man. "It was a good concert by the way. And the third song had a place in it where Father Pennington read verses in the song."

"Thank you," said Stephanie. "The words all have meaning. I'm following you so far, but I have absolutely no idea where you are going."

"One of the verses he read was from Ecclesiastes. It was a confusing one."

"Isn't every verse from Ecclesiastes confusing?" asked Stephanie.

"Yeah," replied The Fat Man. "Kind of. This one was about looking right and left. And I was staring at the stained-glass window of Michael trying to figure out what the verse meant when something dawned on me."

"What, that you're totally wacked?"

"No …well, that too … but you were right," said The Fat Man. "Matthews sent it somewhere in America, and I think I know where he sent it."

"Again, Michael the Archangel told you this…"

"I humored you yesterday," said The Fat Man. "You put the whole thing in my head."

"I am truly sorry."

"Anyhow," said The Fat Man, "after the original Mace was stolen the House commissioned a new one…right?"

"Right," Stephanie replied. "That was the one that was stolen the other night."

"When it was presented to the House there was a big ceremony," said The Fat Man, "I read the speeches. All the Members commented in the Congressional Record on what a great likeness it was to the original one. But Michael got me thinking about that. How would the maker of the new one have known what the old one looked like? There were not any cameras back then."

"So," said Stephanie, "it could have been described to him."

"Yeah, I know, but there's something else."

"What?" asked Stephanie.

"The eagle," he replied.

"What about it?"

"It is supposed to represent manifest destiny, right?"

"That's what the history says," she replied. "So what?"

"When Father Joe was reading the scripture, he did it from this really cool podium that has a life-sized, wood carving of an eagle on it. The eagle on Father Joe's podium is looking over his right wing." The Fat Man sat back, crossed his arms and smiled a great big grin as if he had just given Stephanie the missing piece of a jigsaw puzzle.

Stephanie looked at The Fat Man with a quizzical look on her face. When he didn't respond to her look, she spoke: "I don't get it."

"Trinity's eagle is looking over its right wing. If it were sitting on a globe like on the Mace it should be looking over its right wing. Eagles representing manifest destiny look west. But the eagle on top of the globe on the Mace looks over his left wing…east."

"An eagle facing east is also symbolic of war."

"It's more than just the facing east thing," said The Fat Man. "I saw a C-Span documentary on television one time about the renovation of the Mace. They mentioned the name of the company that made it, but I couldn't remember the name."

Just as The Fat Man was about to finish his thought, the phone rang.

"I already called the FBI," said The Fat Man, as he looked at the number on the caller ID. "This is a guy we know up in D.C. named Leo Argo." He hit the connect button. "Hey Leo. You're on speaker with my colleague Stephanie. What'd you find out?"

"Well, you were right," said Argo. "The Smithsonian did a renovation of the Mace about two years or so ago. They took it apart, polished it and put it back together. The name of the silversmith was printed on the inside of the silver cast globe. It was a company called Shaw Silver Company of New York. I did a quick search and it turns out they were the leading silversmiths in New York at the time."

"Did you track them down?"

"Sure did," said Argo. "The family immigrated from Aston under Layne in the UK, just outside of Manchester in the late 1700s. They were a typical immigrant family, except for having more than usual to start with. The family owned the silver company and a couple of bars."

"Anything else about them?" asked The Fat Man.

"Yup."

"Before Shaw came to America he was married to a young lady from Manchester."

"Was her maiden name Matthews?"

"How'd you guess?"

"Just a hunch," replied the Fat Man. "It was just a hunch."

Chapter 25

Thompson's heartbeat accelerated as the motorcade drove through the gate of the wrought iron fence surrounding the white Victorian building housing the American Embassy in Romania. Noticing that her husband took an enormous deep breath as the gate closed behind them, Ann grabbed Thompson's hand and squeezed it. He immediately turned his head and looked deep into her eyes. She nodded at him in a silent affirmation of her faith in his judgment at handling the forthcoming meeting.

Thompson and Michael Griffith had been friends since they had roamed the campus of Eastern Kentucky University in search of women and beer. When they moved to Washington to seek their fame and fortune in politics, they were inseparable. Griffith had introduced Thompson to Ann and stood up at their wedding as the best man. Griffith ran Thompson's special election campaign for Congress.

In Washington, a Member of Congress has numerous acquaintances and very few true friends. Griffith was Thompson's closest and truest friend.

On any given day, Griffith could likely be found hanging out in Thompson's Congressional office in the Longworth House office building, rather than in his own office in Old Town Alexandria. Since Thompson's family generally remained in the district when he was off in Washington doing the people's work, Griffith and Thompson had dinner together during the week as often as they could.

Over dinner, they frequently discussed the future of Thompson's Chief of Staff, Josh Barkman. Thompson brought Josh into the campaign over Griffith's initial objection. However, during the election, Griffith watched Josh handle the campaign with the political gut of a seasoned veteran.

Griffith went from being Josh's greatest critic to his biggest fan.

When Griffith and Thompson discussed Josh, they each reinforced the other's conclusion that he was more than just another bright young man with a future in government. They agreed that Josh had the personality and instincts that pointed to a future leadership role. In fact, they truly believed that Josh was in that elite top level of young people who someday would be running the country. Thompson took pride in helping to shape such a person. Griffith thought Josh could be that style of leader who would eventually define Griffith's political legacy. Both believed it to be their role to mentor him in his life and career.

Griffith and Thompson concluded that it was important for Josh to experience politics outside of the United States. Both of them had done it as young men and each felt he had grown personally and politically from the experience. The trip Josh and Griffith had taken to Romania was supposed to be that journey of political matriculation. Griffith had already signed on to advise in the reelection campaign of the incumbent President and it had been easy to get Josh on board as an official election observer with one of the Washington think tanks.

The trip had the added benefit of being to a foreign country which Griffith and Thompson had visited together early in their political careers. It would give them some ability to compare and contrast their own youthful experiences with Josh's.

It had been a joint decision that Thompson would not accompany Josh and Griffith on the trip. The election in Romania was going to be held during what is known in Congress as the "District Work Period" when Members get time off from being in D.C. Members generally use that time either to join trips to foreign countries or head home and visit with constituents in their districts. Thompson, like most Members, decided to spend the time back home in Kentucky.

There was some constituent work to be done and Thompson needed some down time with Ann and his family. Thompson, therefore, charged Griffith with the well-being of Josh during the trip to Romania. Now that Josh had gone missing Thompson felt extremely guilty that he was not "in-country" when Josh was kidnapped. Moreover, he could not shake his gut feeling that somehow Griffith bore some responsibility for Josh's disappearance.

Balancing his anger on one hand with his guilt on the other left Thompson dreading the reunion with Griffith.

The United States *chargé d'affaire*, Shelley Stephenson, met Thompson, Ann, and the CIA agents at the front door of the embassy. "Hello Congressman...Mrs. Thompson, welcome to Romania," she said extending a hand to Thompson. She looked at Kline and Morrison as they began to walk into the lobby of the building. "And, you must be the two special observers I was told would be staying with us."

"We are," said Kline.

The short blond woman did not question Kline further. Stephenson knew Kline and Morrison were not election observers. She knew that a cache of smuggled guns had been left in their rooms. Also, neither Kline nor Morrison had the look of wide-eyed idealists, joyous at the mere thought of spreading democracy across the globe. Those folks were staying over at the InterContinental and Stephenson would be meeting with them later. She was certain these two "observers" were CIA, but did not dare say it out loud.

"Well, this will be your home away from home," said Stephenson. "If there is anything we can do to make your stay more comfortable just let me know. We'll take care of it for you. There's an American restaurant in the basement that's open late into the night. After midnight, you can find some food in the restaurant's fridge."

"Thank you," said Ann. "We really appreciate the hospitality."

"Mr. Morrison. Can I have those tubes taken to your room for you?"

"No, thank you. I'll take care of these personally."

"Very well then," Stephenson replied. "I think that you'll find your room with all of the accompaniments you requested."

"Very good," replied Kline, knowing that accompaniments meant guns.

"The Bucharest Chief of Police wanted me to call him as soon as you got here so he could brief all of you on the situation with Mr. Barkman. His office is only a couple of blocks away. I'll go ahead and give him a call."

"Good," replied Thompson. "I'd like to meet with him as quickly as possible."

"Understood," replied Stephenson. "Until then, Mr. Griffith and his friend are waiting for you in the conference room." She gestured to a set of double doors. "Let me know if you need anything. I'll be in my office."

"Friend?" asked Ann rhetorically as Thompson led his wife, Kline and Morrison to the conference room. Ann silently reflected that it was remarkable how much the room looked like any government conference room located on American soil. It contained the same standard issue black leather sofa, dark-stained wood tables and gold metal lamps with heavy cardboard lamp shades that can be found in just about any space owned and operated by the United States government.

As the four Americans entered the room, Griffith and Sue stood up and walked toward them.

"Who the hell is this?" asked Thompson abruptly.

"Hi to you, too," replied Griffith. "And I was just about to ask you the same thing."

"Congressman Thompson, her name is Sue," said Kline as she walked to the conference table and opened her brief case. "And everyone please sit down. Give me a minute while I get my files together." She pulled several file folders out of her case and placed them on the table. After digging for a minute, she located a small black metal device and turned it on. She started walking around the perimeter of the room holding the small device in front of her face while she walked.

"Excuse me," said Sue. "How do you know my name?"

"So how goes the President's reelection campaign?" asked Morrison, deliberately making small talk while Kline continued to walk around the room searching for listening devices.

Griffith, knowing what was happening, looked at Sue and placed a finger to his lips. "Fine," replied Griffith. "The countryside towns and villages are opposed to the President. But, as long as the cities turn out on election day, we'll win."

"We're clean," said Kline as she turned off the device. "Sorry for the impersonal introduction, but we need to know who's listening to us."

"Don't they sweep the embassies on a weekly basis?" asked Thompson.

"Yeah, but they're not very good at it," replied Morrison. "We need to make sure."

Kline approached Griffith and Sue and stuck out her hand. "Hi. My name is Jane Kline. This is my associate Mark Morrison. We're formally here as election observers, but our mission is to find Josh Barkman and return him to U.S. soil alive."

"You're CIA," said Griffith.

"I'm an election observer," replied Kline.

"Holy shit," said Sue. "Is one of those files about me?"

"Yes, it is," said Kline. "But don't worry, you're not a suspect. We've already cleared you."

"Cleared her," asked Ann. "Of what?"

"Of having any involvement in Josh's kidnapping," replied Kline. "Apparently, she was Mr. Griffith's companion the night the boy was kidnapped."

"I'm not sure I'm following you," said Thompson.

"On the night in question the two of them went to dinner with Josh," Kline said as she opened up one of the file folders and read from a report in it. “They had dinner and headed to the piano bar at the InterContinental Hotel. That’s where the kidnapper approached Josh. Am I right thus far?”

“Dead on,” replied Griffith.

“How do you know all of this?” asked Sue.

“That’s my job,” replied Kline. “Now, Mr. Griffith, tell me about how the kidnapper approached you. Tell me about the meeting.”

Griffith hung his head and then made direct eye contact with Kline. “Why are you asking?” he said in a low voice. “Your file has already told you what you want to know.”

Thompson looked at Griffith who was locked in a stare down with Kline. “What?” asked Thompson. “What does the file say, Griff?”

“She knows exactly what it says. I’m surprised she hasn’t told you yet. That the whole fucking thing was my fault.”

Chapter 26

Josh had lost all track of time as he shivered on the damp, wood floor of General Alexandro's old house. He had been trying to stay alert by using techniques he had read about in college and a few tricks he had learned on the campaign trail. Nothing seemed to be working. He could feel himself fading.

Part of Josh's black mood came from sheer exhaustion. Deep sleep had been nearly impossible for many reasons. The blanket his captors had given to him was insufficient to keep the cold draft circulating through the house off of his sore and weakened body. Also, escape was always on his mind and he did not want to miss any opportunity. Time and time again he played and replayed scenes in his mind in which he would escape and make his way to freedom.

As often as Josh thought of escape, he also thought of death. The contemplation of imminent demise at the hands of his captors was uppermost on his mind.

So Josh slept intermittently on the floor of the house. He grabbed naps at intervals which were sometimes as short as 10 minutes or so. While he felt that this gave him a better chance of escaping at some opportune moment, it also made it difficult for him to track days and nights. He was already unsure of exactly how many days he had been a captive. The stubble of his beard was the closest thing he had to a personal sun dial.

While awake, Josh busied his mind with mental exercises. He read once that an American soldier held captive during the Viet Nam War played a round of golf every day in his mind in order to stay mentally sharp. Josh did not play golf, so he replayed the video game Halo over and over in his head.

When he was not playing a virtual computer game in his

brain, Josh used his waking hours to inventory his dismal surroundings. The kidnappers kept his legs duct taped together, but they had untaped his wrists to allow him enough mobility to move himself into sitting and lying positions. As he moved, he could look out a window in a small adjacent room at the back of the house. The sunlight was welcome but also helped to accentuate the incredible amount of dirt that had accumulated on the floor. Josh had speculated that the floor had not been swept or mopped in years. The corners had so much dirt packed into them that the places where the walls and floor met were rounded with cement-like mud.

Occasionally, Josh would allow his mind to wander back to childhood memories of growing up in a small town in Kansas. At first those images had been pleasant and they had brought him some relief. Soon, however, those thoughts started a chain reaction of negativity that wore on his psyche. How were his mom and dad reacting to the news he had been kidnapped? Uncle Barry had a bad heart. Josh hoped the news had not worsened his condition. If he died in this old house who would come to his funeral? The mental and emotional pressure was building.

A guard sat in the room with Josh at all times. The faces changed, but each constantly rubbed the amulet around their neck in order to ward off the young American's evil blue eyes. There had been three guards that rotated in and out of the room on a regular basis. He heard other voices in the house, but they never entered the room where Josh was being held. Josh silently nicknamed the guards he had seen according to their hair and body styles. The nicknames helped him keep track of their shifts and added a very small touch of humor to his humorless situation.

On the first shift, Josh had been guarded by a young muscular man with brown curly hair who resembled a guy who worked the door at Josh's favorite bar in Georgetown. Josh had nicknamed him "Bouncer." The other male guard had a shaved head. He was much smaller than Bouncer and he was the one who had punched Josh in the stomach the night he was kidnapped. He reminded Josh of a wrestler he had watched on television as a kid. So Josh named him after the wrestler and thought of him as "Honeycat."

The third guard was Noua, the beautiful Romanian woman who had set him up at the InterContinental. She was beautiful but, unfortunately for Josh, she was also the meanest and most brutal of the guards. Noua spoke fluent English. Yet she didn't seem interested in sharing her language skills with Josh. On the rare occasion when Noua did speak to Josh, it had been in a sharp demeaning tone, and it usually had been followed by a sharp kick somewhere to Josh's body.

Still remembering Griffith's Godfather Rule #8—keep your friends close and your enemies closer—Josh had tried repeatedly to engage her in conversation. The first time Josh had tried to speak directly to Noua, his words had resulted in a charging woman who kicked him repeatedly while yelling at him in half-English and half-Romanian to shut up. With his arms unbound he had been able to block the kicks to his upper body and face. However, one or two had connected with his already sore legs.

Nevertheless, Josh had not let the first attack dissuade him from talking. His relentless research prior to the trip on Romania and its political structure had given him something to talk about. At first he spent his time alone with Noua simply reciting out loud to himself basic facts and figures about the Parliament, political parties, and mountain geography.

It had dawned on Josh that, since Noua's original target was Griff, she must be part of one of the many political parties who opposed the reelection of President Krasterich. So during one session when Noua had been guarding Josh, he talked out loud to himself about the election research the think tank had done on the president.

According to the research, Krasterich was a heavy drinker and known womanizer. So Josh started talking about the President's less than stellar personal character. His musings on the immorality of Romania's current leader had gotten a rise out of Noua. "He is a pig," she had said. "Just like you, Mr. America's Brain. You tried to sleep with me at the bar. Krasterich is a pig and so are you." She had accentuated her comments with spit on the floor. "Now, shut-up."

For once Noua had spoken to him without striking him.

Progress is progress, he thought to himself as he drifted into a nap. *And at this point, I'll take whatever progress I can get.*

When Josh awoke, Noua was gone and Honeycat stared at him from the guard's chair. Knowing that Honeycat spoke no English, Josh spoke freely. "You know what, Honeycat? You're one ugly motherfucker." Josh smiled at Honeycat as if he was paying him some sort of ultimate compliment. Honeycat stared back emotionless. "The only reason you caught me in the gut that night was because the Bouncer was holding me up."

Honeycat looked at Josh with a mix of amusement and intrigue as he rubbed the amulet around his neck.

"Yup, Honeycat, I don't know why I call you a motherfucker. I did your mom one time in a bathroom stall at a Bucharest whore house. She blew me too, you know."

Josh tried to laugh at his own oral assault on his captor. Unfortunately, the verbal attack on Honeycat was far less satisfying than Josh had hoped. His previous conversation with Noua had left him feeling as bad mentally as he felt physically. He rolled over on his side and looked toward the window in the back room at the trickle of sunlight hitting the floor.

"If only I could have that night back, Honeycat. I would have done things differently. You know what I mean? I would have banged Noua in my room and then found you outside and kicked you in the balls. Do you understand that, Dickhead? I would have kicked you in the nuts. You don't have the first clue what I'm saying.

"Who am I kidding? I wouldn't have done a thing different. Noua is hot. Far more beautiful than any woman I've ever been with. She has a helluva right hook, too. Did you know that, Honeycat? She's got a punch, but she is one stone-cold bitch."

Honeycat rolled a cigarette as Josh continued to ramble.

"That's what bothers me, Honeycat. You know what I mean? Of course, you don't. I'm not sure I do myself. Even knowing what I know now, I probably would have tried to leave with her.

"Can you believe that, Honeycat? Even knowing that I'd be kidnapped, I still probably would have tried to score with her. Man, that's what happens when a guy thinks with his dick."

Josh laid his head on the floor and tried to will himself to sleep.

Chapter 27

"It's my fault," repeated Griffith. "The whole goddamn thing is my fault."

"Do I want to hear this?" asked Thompson.

"No," replied Griffith. "No, not at all. But you're going to have to hear it at some point." He paused and looked down at the table. "I've been dreading this moment since it happened. As bad as I've felt because I fucked up that night, I've been dreading even more having to tell you about it. Jesus, Rick. If I could take it back, I would, but I can't."

"Tell me what happened, Griff," instructed Thompson. "Tell it all."

"This isn't going to be easy for me, Rick," said Griffith. "Ann, you're going to explode."

"Go on, Michael," Sue encouraged Griffith.

"The three of us had been out to dinner … me, Sue and Josh. After dinner, we headed back to the bar at the InterContinental to grab a few drinks. We had been there about an hour or so telling war stories."

"I get the picture. You were telling your war stories and Josh was listening," said Thompson. "Josh doesn't have any to tell. He's too damn young."

Griffith winced. "Right," he said. "You're right. I was doing most of the talking. So, like I said, we had been there about an hour when this young girl comes up to me and introduces herself."

"This girl starts getting real friendly with Michael," interjected Sue. "Real friendly."

"Excuse me," said Ann. "I don't even know who you are and why you're here."

"I met Sue on the flight over here," said Griffith. "We were spending a couple of days together before the real campaign work started."

"You were supposed to be watching out for Josh and you were shacking up?"

"Hey," said Sue.

"Don't be mad at her, Ann," said Griffith. "She's not at fault here. I am."

"Everybody calm down. Let's get back to the story. Go on, Griff," said Thompson.

"So anyhow," said Griffith. "This girl comes up to me and I think that she's some sort of power fucker, looking to grab me for a one night stand." He paused. "So I convince her that Josh is the real power player over here for the campaign, not me."

"What?" exclaimed Ann. "Why in the hell did you do that?"

"I wanted to get her interested in Josh, instead of me," said Griffith.

"Why?" asked Thompson.

"Well, first because I already had a date for the evening." Griffith looked right at Ann. "Please don't look at me like that, Ann. I feel shitty enough already."

"It's hard to look at you any other way right now, Michael," said Ann. "I'm pissed. But you said 'first.' Was there another reason?"

"Yeah, there was," replied Griffith. He paused and took a deep breath. "I also thought Josh needed to get laid."

"You've got to be kidding me!" exploded Ann. "Josh is missing because you thought he needed to get laid?"

"The kid had been working his ass off in D.C.," said Griffith. "I was trying to get him out of his shell. It was late. We'd been drinking. The woman was beautiful."

"And you thought a shot of pussy would do the trick?" asked Thompson.

"Yeah, I did. Goddamn, Rick, this girl attached herself to Josh like a fucking barnacle."

Thompson stood up and placed both of his hands behind his head, interlocking his fingers as he walked around. He took a deep breath and exhaled slowly. "Unbelievable," Thompson muttered. "Un-fucking believable."

"Look Rick, it's not like…"

"Shut up, Griff," Thompson held up his hand and cut Griffith off in mid-sentence. His abrupt interjection surprised even Ann. "Please, just shut the fuck up." All eyes focused on Thompson as he chose his words very carefully. "Here's the thing, Griff. You've been my best friend for a long time. Hell, I can barely remember a time in my life when you weren't around. I love you like you're my brother. I truly do."

"I know," said Griff.

"And that's the thing. People come up to me all the time and tell me they can't understand how we can be such close friends. When they say that they can't see us together, I tell them they don't know you as well as I do. I tell them the Michael Griffith they see on television is your public persona. I tell them they don't know the real Michael Griffith … the guy I know. The private Griffith is the guy who is like my own brother."

"Come on Rick … don't do this."

"The guy I know isn't the cowboy everyone sees on the talk shows." Thompson could feel the blood rising in his neck as his anger increased. He lightly bit his lower lip before he spoke again. "I say that to them all the time. But that's okay. I know that you like your reputation as the cowboy of D.C. politics. I mean, look at you … the shaved head … the beard … the cowboy boots and jeans. You live for your image."

"So where are you headed with this?" asked Griffith, suspecting he already knew the answer.

"You know where I'm headed, Griff. The kid idolizes you. He wants to be you. When he sees you living out the cowboy lifestyle, he's going to try and mirror what you do."

"So?"

"So?" Thompson's voice was quivering with rage. "Josh isn't a cowboy, Griff. He's not like you. He's a young kid with a great political future. If you wanted him to be like you, you could have taught him a hundred things. You could have taught him more Godfather Rules. But no, you had to …" Thompson tried to calm the fury from his voice.

"Go ahead and say it, Rick," said Griffith.

"You had to teach him to try and be a cowboy … just like you. You were the target and you got them to go after Josh. You may have gotten him killed."

Chapter 28

After Thompson's stinging indictment Griffith slowly turned and left the room. The truth of the charge was hard enough for Griffith to accept. He had known it was going to be a tough meeting. But to have such a harsh message delivered by his closest friend placed a burden on his soul that was too much for him to bear. After he left, Sue turned and gave everyone in the room a "please do something" look. When the response was a deafening silence, Sue turned and ran after Griffith.

"Don't you think you were a little tough on Griff?" Ann was the first to speak.

"No," replied Thompson, who was still pacing around the room, his anger still boiling. "You are just as pissed at him as I am. I just said exactly what you were thinking. Don't even go there."

"I don't mean to interrupt, but we've got other business right now," interjected Kline. "We're here to find your Chief of Staff. And by God, we're going to find him."

Thompson peered at the ceiling as if the cracks above his head were going to rain down on him some degree of personal composure. He took a deep breath. "You're right. I'll deal with Griff later. Josh is priority number one. What do we do next?"

"The local police chief is outside," interjected Morrison. "Do you want me to bring him in?"

"Yeah, and get us an interpreter," said Kline. "I know the language, but the Congressman and Mrs. Thompson may want to know what's being said."

"Gotcha. I'll see who they can dig up for us."

When the local police chief entered the room, Kline exchanged pleasantries with him in Romanian and introduced

Thompson. They waited to begin until Morrison returned to the room with an interpreter.

"This is Yorgi," said Morrison. "He was the only interpreter around the Embassy right now. Apparently, he's also the interpreter assigned to Mr. Griffith and Mr. Barkman. He was the one who told Mr. Griffith your Chief of Staff had been kidnapped."

Yorgi entered the room with the police chief. If the situation had not been so serious, Ann would have laughed out loud at the sight of the two of them. The police chief was an overweight, greasy-looking kind of fellow. His black police uniform looked about two sizes too small for his rotund body and his belly hung over his patent leather black belt. If he had to go for his gun he would have to fight against rolls of fat to pull it out.

Yorgi's appearance was quite the opposite of the chief. He was a smallish man, but he was not frail by any means. His jacket seemed to hang from his shoulders like a shawl on a scarecrow.

"Good afternoon, Meester and Meeses Thompson," said Yorgi, snapping Ann from her comical assessment of the pair. "I am Yorgi and I will interpret for you."

"Okay, Chief," said Kline in Romanian. "We need to know everything you know about the kidnapping of the American boy."

"I do not have much information, I am afraid," said the Chief. "We don't have any real strong leads."

"He doesn't know much," whispered Yorgi to the Thompsons.

"Great," whispered Thompson in response.

"Well, why don't we start by you telling me what you do know," said Kline. "I can ask you some questions after that."

"Here are the basic facts we have discovered. We know that the American boy left the bar around 1:00 a.m." The chief pulled a small piece of paper from a manila file folder and shoved it in front of Kline. "He charged his bar tab to his room about 1:10. Look at it. He had a lot to drink."

"He thinks Meester Yoshuua was drunk," said Yorgi.

"Anything else you know about before they left?" asked Kline.

"I spoke to the desk clerk at the hotel. She remembers seeing him leave with a beautiful Romanian woman dressed in a white leather skirt. They were quite enamored with each other. The clerk got the impression they were not going to sleep anytime soon."

"Mr. Yoshuua was ... uhhhh ... up very late with a preety woman," whispered Yorgi.

"The kidnappers grabbed the American about three blocks from the hotel. There was some sort of setup. No one would have seen them, but as they tried to throw him into the car, the woman started screaming. Two local men heard the screams and came running. The woman pulled a gun and shot and killed one of them."

"Meester Yousuua was grabbed close to the hotel," said Yorgi. "Some men saw it happen. The woman shot and keeled one of dem."

Thompson and Ann listened intently to Yorgi's interpretation of the facts. When he said the woman had shot someone both of their eyes grew wide.

"I am sorry, but that is all we know," said the Chief. "There have been no demands from the kidnappers."

"Okay," said Kline, continuing her Romanian conversation with the Chief. "That's not much to go on."

"I am very sorry," replied the Chief. "But our trail went dead at the site of the kidnapping."

"Dey do not know much," said Yorgi. "No one has claimed responsibility."

"Nothing?" asked Kline. "No descriptions of the other kidnappers?"

"Nothing concrete," replied the Chief. "Other than the

fact that it was an old black American automobile, we don't have too much else to go on."

"All dey know is dat Meester Yoshuua was tossed into an old black American car."

"Tell me about the car," instructed Kline.

"The second man, the one who wasn't shot at, gave us a general description. Black. Rusty. Old American style."

"Dey don't now much about de car," said Yorgi.

"Anything else," asked Kline.

"The man took a couple of pictures with his cell phone," the Chief replied. "But there is not much to them. You can see a wheel on one and part of the front quarter panel on another. But they are blurred and pretty bad."

"Dey have peectures of de car," said Yorgi. "But dey are very bad."

"Do you have them in the file with you?" asked Kline.

The Chief reached in the file folder and pulled out the pictures. They were blurred and obscured. "The man took the pictures while hiding underneath an automobile parked on the street. They don't show much."

Kline looked at the pictures and then gave them to Morrison. "Do these look like anything to you?"

"No," replied Morrison. "Just to be safe, I'll send a digital copy of them to headquarters to see if they can identify anything on them." Thompson stood up and walked over to where Morrison and Kline were sitting. He looked at the photos. Like the others who had looked at them, the photos had no particular significance to him. Thompson went back and sat next to Ann and Yorgi.

Kline thanked the Chief and asked that he make himself available for a future call if necessary. Once he was out of the room, Kline dismissed Yorgi, as well.

"That's not much to go on," said Ann.

"Yeah," said Thompson. "And that fat old bastard doesn't seem all that interested in helping us out."

"Look," said Kline. "Why don't the two of you head up to your room and get settled in. You've had a very rough 36 hours. Get some rest. We'll send these photos off and see if we come up with anything. In the meantime, I'll start contacting some of our covert sources on the ground here in the country to see if they have heard any chatter about Josh."

"We could use the rest," said Ann.

"And you'll keep us informed as soon as you know something?" asked Thompson.

"Absolutely," Kline replied.

As soon as Thompson and Ann exited the room and closed the door, Morrison turned and looked at Kline. "Sonofabitch," he said. "This kid is fucked."

Chapter 29

As Argo and The Fat Man pulled into the parking lot across from the Second Bank of New York, Leo Argo was beginning to understand some of the comments Congressman Richard Thompson had made about The Fat Man's anal-retentive nature. As planned, Argo had met The Fat Man outside the terminal at LaGuardia. From that point on, Argo wished he had let The Fat Man take a cab to their destination. Despite the fact that Argo was originally from New Jersey, The Fat Man had precise opinions on the route they should take from the airport to the bank. What really aggravated Argo was that somehow, The Fat Man's route actually turned out to be quicker.

Argo pulled into a parking space facing the street so he could survey the bank and its surroundings. The Second National Bank was housed in an old five-story brownstone building just outside of Soho. As they crossed the street Argo noticed the cornerstone on the building read 1814. An engraved stone over the door of the building read: "Jubal Shaw—Silversmith."

Argo nudged The Fat Man and pointed to the stone over the door. "Check it out. This is the place."

"Cool," said The Fat Man. "I told you I'd get you here."

After a detailed long-distance explanation via The Fat Man's conference room phone, Argo had been able to convince his boss at the FBI, that he had a lead in the investigation of "the stolen Mace" that was worth investigating. The fact that the lead was not about the theft of the Mace, which had been stolen only days earlier seemed to be a mere technicality which Argo could explain later. The Fat Man grabbed the next available flight to New York while Argo made the four-hour trek northward from D.C. in his own car. If the lead did not pan out Argo could be back in D.C. the same day.

"Right," replied Argo. "On my drive up, I called the lady who runs the bank."

"What did she say?" asked The Fat Man.

"Not much," replied the burly Cuban-American. "Specifically, she said she didn't know much about the history of the building and, other than the name on the outside of the building, didn't know anything about the Shaw family. But she was friendly and she's willing to show us around. She said they do have the original building plans for the bank."

"That's good," said The Fat Man. "I just hope the plans she has are readable."

"She said they're framed in the board room," said Argo. "I'm not expecting much. They are probably just a schematic showing the room layouts."

As Argo and The Fat Man made their way through the revolving front door of the bank, a tall and attractive, light-skinned African-American woman in a blue business suit made eye contact with the pair from a glass-encased office. She stood up and quickly made her way to the two standing in the lobby. Her sweet perfume complemented her attractive frame and pretty smile.

"Hi, my name is Leo Argo," said Argo, sticking out his hand as the woman approached.

"Cheri," replied the woman. "Cheri Pryor. We spoke on the phone."

The Fat Man, seeing Argo's instant attraction to the beautiful woman, cleared his throat to get Argo's attention.

"Excuse me," said Argo. "This is the gentleman I told you about on the phone. Cheri meet The Fa ..."

The Fat Man winced.

"Joe Bradley," said Argo. "Meet my friend Joe Bradley. He's an attorney from Kentucky who has been working with the Bureau on trying to find the silver rod I told you about. He'd like to look at the building plans you told me about."

"And you think there may be some clue about your silver rod in the building plans?" asked Pryor. "That's rich."

"Maybe," said The Fat Man. "The guy who commissioned this building to be built was a silversmith."

"Yeah," Pryor said. "Jubal Shaw. His name is over the door."

"There's a good possibility that Mr. Shaw may have known something about the 'silver rod' that disappeared back in the early 1800s."

"So what are you looking for, Mr. Bradley?"

"I have no earthly idea," replied The Fat Man. "But I'll know it when I see it."

"Where are the plans you told me about?" said Argo. "Framed on a wall somewhere, right?"

"Yeah," said Pryor. "They're in the conference room. It's right up there." She pointed to a room with one wall of floor-to-ceiling windows overlooking the lobby.

Argo and Pryor headed up the steps to the mezzanine with The Fat Man behind them pulling himself up by the brass banister as he huffed and puffed along. As they made their way up the steps, The Fat Man noticed the decorative plaster and metal work around the walls of the lobby. Ornate cherubs floated along the walls through crafted plaster vines and clouds. Gold leaf was tossed around the walls like Porter Paint.

"Is all of this original?" asked The Fat Man.

"The plaster work and stuff?" asked Pryor. "From what I know about the building, it is. I think it's been refurbished a time or two, but most of what you see is all part of the original building. It's on the National Register of Historic Places, you know." Pryor swung open the door to the conference room and turned on the light. "This room isn't original. We added it a couple of years back. Our board wanted a nice room to have meetings."

"I guess the whole idea of glass-enclosed conference rooms is relatively new," replied The Fat Man.

"There they are," said Pryor as she opened the curtains. The window lightened the room with natural light from the lobby windows and front door. On the walls were six different sets of framed building plans. "We wanted to keep the historic feel of the building. So we built this room to showcase the original plans and sketches. We like to show it off to big customers."

"They are in remarkably good shape," said The Fat Man as he got so close to the first set of diagrams that his nose nearly touched the glass covering the frame. "Great shape, in fact."

"Thanks," said Pryor. "I'll leave you gentlemen alone. Let me know if you need anything."

When Pryor had left the room, Argo wandered over to the window and nonchalantly looked down onto the lobby. "Seriously, Joey, what are you looking for?"

"I'm not really sure, Leo," The Fat Man replied. "Building plans from this era were not prepared with uniform precision. Standards were not exact. Architecture wasn't a strict science the way it is today. Every architect prepared them a little differently in order to suit his own needs. But when they designed buildings, they often made little hiding places for the building's owners that you'd never find without the plans. Jefferson did that with Monticello. He had little hiding places all over the house. Did you know that?"

"No," replied Argo. "I didn't know that."

"Sometimes," said The Fat Man, "the hiding places weren't even on the plans. There would be just some small clue or notation that only the owner would know what it meant. I am hoping these blueprints have that kind of a clue somewhere on them."

There was a long silence as The Fat Man looked over each set of plans with such painstaking detail he was leaving condensation on the frame's glass from observing them at such a close proximity. While The Fat Man studied, Argo continued to survey the lobby.

"Hey, Joey," said Argo. "What did this Mace thing look like?"

"I don't really know. There were no pictures of it, obviously," replied The Fat Man. "But according to the stuff I read, it resembled the one that was stolen."

"Was it about four or five feet tall?"

"Probably," replied The Fat Man. "It wasn't any taller than that, I suspect."

"A pole of some sort with a ball on top?"

"Yeah, it was a pole and it had a globe on top." The Fat Man squinted at another frame. "Why?"

"Well, you better come here and look at this," Argo said pointing at the sculpture in the interior arch over the front door of the bank.

The Fat Man turned and walked to the window overlooking the lobby. He focused his eyes where Argo was pointing. "Holy shit," was all he could mutter.

"I don't know about this," said Pryor as a custodian carried a ladder out to the front lobby of the bank. "I should really consult the bank's legal counsel first."

"Look," said Argo. "We could get the lawyers all wrapped up in this, but that could take time and cost us both a ton of money. All we want to do is get a close look at that sculpt over the door, chip off a piece of plaster and see if there is anything under it."

"And then what?" asked Pryor.

"Well," replied Argo, "if there's nothing under the plaster, then the FBI will hire the best plaster repairman in New York to fix it. In the end, everyone, including your lawyer, will be very happy."

"What if there is something under the plaster? What if this Mace thing that you're looking for is encased over my door?"

"If that sculpt is the real Mace then you need to know that it was stolen from the United States House of Representatives by a relative of Jubal Shaw around the time this building was being built. If that's the case, we'll have to remove it and take it back to Washington."

"Whoa, whoa, whoa," said Pryor. "You can't tear up my building."

"I am afraid that I can," replied Argo. "If that is the Mace up there, it belongs to the United States government."

"That's it," replied Pryor. "I'm calling the bank's lawyer."

"Hold on a minute, Ms. Pryor," said The Fat Man. "Before you make that call, I have a question for you. How much does a minute of advertising time cost on New York television?"

"What does that have to do with anything?" she replied.

"I am just curious. How much do prime time ads cost?"

"A bundle," Pryor replied. "We're a relatively small bank and we can't buy too much of it. We rely mostly on print advertising."

"That's what I figured," said The Fat Man. "Now if my instincts are correct and that is the Mace up there, every news station in town will be over here to do a story tomorrow about this bank. Hell, it will probably make the national news."

Pryor was nodding her head and suddenly started to smile.

"In fact," he continued, "if I were you—and your shareholders—I'd be praying the Mace is up there. We knock it out. The FBI pays for the repairs and your bank get news exposure that you couldn't even think of buying."

"You're pretty persuasive, Mr. Bradley."

"I'm sure the FBI public affairs office would even help out," added Argo. "But of course, if this gets tied up in lawyers, the bank looks like it's hoarding a national treasure."

"We'd never do that," smiled Pryor. She looked at the custodian. "Mr. Kenady, set the ladder up for these gentlemen. Let's see what they find."

The Fat Man and the custodian held the ladder steady while Argo made his way up the side of the wall. He pulled a small pocket knife from his pocket and chipped away at a tiny section of plaster that was already cracked. He cleared another chip or two with his knife, leaned forward and blew away the dust.

"What is it? What do you see?"

"Silver, my friend ... I see silver."

Chapter 30

Richard and Ann Thompson, fresh from a nap and hot shower, were sitting in the restaurant at the U.S. Embassy, each sipping on a cup of coffee, when Jane Kline and Mark Morrison entered the room.

"Do you mind if we join you?" asked Kline.

"Naw," said Thompson. "Have a seat."

"You certainly look better than you did a couple of hours ago," said Kline.

"Thanks," said Ann. "The shower was a great suggestion. I feel like a new woman." She paused. "Same problems, but a new perspective."

"Anything new?" asked Thompson.

"Not much," said Morrison. "We sent the pictures to D.C. As we suspected, they didn't tell us much. One picture was a tire. They were able to make out some writing as a Romanian brand, but nothing else. The other photo was an air vent."

"What do you mean an air vent?" asked Ann.

"A lot of older American cars apparently had air vents on the sides of the quarter panels," said Morrison. "They were mostly for show. I don't think they did much to keep the engines cool."

"You said apparently," interjected Thompson. "I assume that you are not old enough to remember that design?"

"He's a pup, Congressman," said Kline. "I sure remember them, though. My dad had one like that … a big old boat with air vents. I learned to drive in that car."

Thompson sat back in his chair and contemplated Kline's words. The conversation continued, but he was not listening.

"I'm headed over to the InterContinental next to interview the witnesses," said Kline. "Maybe our friend the Chief missed something. Agent Morrison will be around here if you need something."

"Say that again," instructed Thompson.

"I'm headed over to the InterContinental," said Kline.

"No, before that," said Thompson. "Say what you said about the car."

"My old man owned a car with air vents," said Kline.

"Yeah," said Thompson as he leaned his chair back on its two hind legs. "What kind of car was it?"

"Why?" asked Ann.

"I've got a hunch," said Thompson. "What kind of car did you say your dad drove?"

"A Buick Electra," Kline replied "Why?"

Thompson put his hands in front of his face and spoke slowly and deliberately. "I have a hunch that I know this car."

"What do you mean, Richard?" asked Ann. "How do you know that car?"

"It's Nixon's car," replied Thompson.

"I'm sorry, Agent Kline," said Ann. "I apologize. My husband is a Nixon freak. He knows everything about the man. What in the hell does Nixon have to do with this?"

"When President Nixon visited Romania in 1972, he gave Nicolae Ceausescu a black Buick Electra. The same kind Jane learned to drive in."

"Keep going," instructed Kline.

"So Nixon gave Ceausescu this cool car in an attempt to try and turn him against the Russians. Ceausescu loved the car and took excellent care of it. He kept it at his home up in the mountains and used to drive it around town himself. When Ceausescu was killed, his houses were looted by locals and even by some of his own troops. The car disappeared. I was over here right after that, working the post-revolt election with Michael Griffith."

"And you think this car is the same one?" asked Ann.

"Who knows, but we used to joke all the time about that car," said Thompson. "How many old black American cars can there be in this country?"

"That's pretty fucking tenuous, Congressman," said Morrison.

Kline shot Morrison a piercing look. "In any event," she said. "We'll check it out."

Chapter 31

"It's absolutely unbelievable, Rick," said The Fat Man into his cell phone. He was standing outside the Second National Bank and the traffic of New York generated such a loud white noise he nearly had to yell into the phone.

"That's great," replied Thompson from his bedroom at the embassy in Romania. "So it was hidden right there in plain sight … right above the doorway."

The Fat Man walked around the corner of the building in an effort to deaden the sounds of the busy city street. When movement didn't work he jammed the index finger from his free hand into his open ear canal. "Yeah, I was looking at the plans of the building trying to spot any clues or secret hiding places. Then Leo spotted it on the wall."

"Sounds like you've had an exciting couple of days," replied Thompson. "You know I really appreciate what you've done there. You've gone above and beyond what I've asked."

Personal recognition from Thompson caused The Fat Man to grin a big toothy smile. "Thanks, Rick. That really means a lot to me." He leaned against the wall of the bank building, still smiling.

"Well, you deserve it, man," said Thompson. "You might even get a commendation from Congress for this."

"Do you think so?"

"Hell, you should. In fact, I'll see to it. You found something that's been missing since 1814."

There was a pause. The Fat Man knew that Thompson's use of the word "missing" had brought Thompson back to the sad reality of Josh's situation. On Thompson's end of the call he had just closed his eyes in a painful recognition of his own words. "Speaking of missing, how's the search for Josh going?"

"Not well, my friend," replied Thompson. "Not well at all."

"I'm sorry to hear that. You sound horrible."

"We may have gotten a break today. I think that we've been able to identify the car the kidnappers used to nab Josh."

"That's something."

"The CIA doesn't think it's much to go on. In fact, they think I'm nuts for suggesting it."

"Too bad. How's Griff?"

"I'm pretty pissed at Griff right now. He's the reason Josh got nabbed."

"No way. How?"

"I don't want to talk about it."

"Okay, so I'll drop it. If you need me, I'll be in New York for a day or so."

"You want to see them take it off the wall?"

"Yeah. That, and the Yankees are in town. I've got tickets on the first base side tonight. Then, I'm headed back to Northern Kentucky in the morning."

Chapter 32

"Where are you calling from?"

"Do not worry. I am using a secure phone."

"Did you meet with the Americans?"

"Yes. There are two agents there. They are probably CIA. The Congressman for whom the boy worked was also there. He and his wife are unimpressive, very common."

"So what did you learn?"

"If the CIA knows anything they did not indicate it at our meeting."

"Too bad."

"Those bugs we placed in the salt shakers in the cafeteria worked. We were able to pick up a conversation the agents had with the Congressman and his wife."

"And …"

"It is just as you had suspected. The rebels in the Transylvanian Alps have the American boy. Their leader still drives the car he stole from Nicolae at the end. Should we send our people to the mountains and rescue the boy?"

"No. Tell the CIA officer that you know how to find the car and the rebels. Let them go and get the boy themselves."

"But there could be bloodshed."

"We can only hope. If the CIA kills the idiots in the mountains we are rid of our Romanian problems. If the CIA agents and the boy die, we blame the U.S. for interfering. Either way, we gain the upper hand."

Chapter 33

Thompson and Ann had been sitting quietly in the visiting dignitary bedroom at the American Embassy for over an hour. Although both had a deep desire to talk about the events of the day, neither seemed to have the energy or emotional constitution to rehash what had transpired earlier. In fact, the couple had barely spoken since they left the conference room. Dinner conversation had not progressed beyond small talk about the quality of Romanian wine.

When they returned to their private room, Thompson immediately went to bed and sipped on a Manhattan made from a bottle of Makers' Mark he slipped through customs. As he drank, he pretended to review the campaign briefing book prepared for him about the upcoming Romanian election.

How did it come to this? Thompson thought to himself. *How did everything in my life get this far out of control? A couple of days ago, I was riding high at Fancy Farm. I was the rising star of Kentucky politics. People were talking me up for Governor or Senator. Tonight I may be responsible for the death of a young man I really care about. There is no in between. I've gone from one extreme to another.*

All right God, if this is some sort of test, I failed. Okay, I admit it.

Ann had seen her husband in this kind of funk before. They both understood his studying act was just a ruse. When Thompson put his noise-canceling headset on, it was a signal that he just wanted to be alone with his thoughts. Ann was a political spouse, she knew her role in these uncomfortable situations when her husband wanted to be alone and to be with her all at the same time. The headset brought him solitude. Ann's presence brought him the comfort of knowing that if he broke down, she was only steps away.

As Warren Zevon blasted a song of international intrigue into his waiting eardrums, Thompson tried to gather all of the day's events into a place in his brain where he could get a better perspective on his place in the world.

What the fuck am I thinking about? Twenty-two million people and I'm trying to find one black Buick Electra. This is nuts. We'll never find that car and we'll never find Josh.

Josh—I wonder where he is right now. Is he alive? What am I thinking? Of course he's alive. That's the one thing I have to believe right now. I can't give up on that hope.

Still, how the hell are we going to find him?

And what about Griff? I may have alienated my best friend ... not that he didn't deserve getting ripped. He does. He fucked up. Still, he does seem to feel as bad about all of this as anyone. I may have gone a little over the top today. Blasting Griff won't help us find Josh.

And Ann—God look at her. She's beautiful, sitting there in that black silk robe. Despite all of this, it's hard not to sit here and admire how alluring she looks right now. And she knows what's going on in my head right now. She's wearing that robe for me. She knows that I enjoy tension sex as much as campaign sex. Hell, she may know me better than myself.

"Hey, babe," Thompson took off his headset and broke the silence in the room. "What are you thinking about?"

"You," replied Ann, as she put her book aside. She stood up and readjusted the robe before joining Thompson on the bed. "You. Josh. Griff. The whole ball of wax. My head is so filled with thoughts right now that I don't even know where to start."

"Me, too," replied Thompson. "Me, too. Finding Josh is number one. If we can do that, I can deal with everything else later."

"We'll find him," replied Ann, not sure if she believed herself, but knowing that her husband needed to hear her say it out loud.

"Yeah," said Thompson. "We'll find him."

"And then what?"

"Then we get the hell out of Romania," said Thompson.

"You know what I'm talking about," replied Ann. "Griff. What are you going to do about Griff?"

"I don't know, Ann," Thompson said. "I want to let him up on this one, but I don't know if I can. He was in charge. I can't get it out of my head that he's ultimately responsible. I just don't know what to do."

Ann thought briefly that it was time for sex. She knew her husband well. The best thing to get him to disengage from any situation was sex. It would not take much. Her nipples were sticking out from her black silk robe. She had noticed him looking at them as they spoke.

Any thoughts of a Romanian quickie were soon extinguished by a knock at the door.

"Who is it?" shouted Thompson, as he looked at his watch.

"It's me … Agent Kline. I need to talk to you."

Thompson got up out of bed, while Ann did her best to cover up her body with the otherwise revealing robe. Thompson opened the door and gestured Kline into the room.

"Sorry for the intrusion, Congressman … Mrs. Thompson," said Kline. "But I have some information on Josh."

"Josh?" asked Ann. "You've found him?"

"No, I misspoke," said Kline. "We've not actually found Josh, but we do have some information on the car. We've gotten a tip on its whereabouts."

"Where?" asked Thompson with excitement in his voice. "Where is the car?"

"You were right, Congressman. It was Nixon's black Buick Electra. Apparently, it was stolen by an old Securitate officer who lives in the foothills of the Carpathian Mountains. We made a call to Washington and we have a file on the old man. The guy's name is General Alexandro. He was one of Ceausescu's top aides and closest confidants.

"I remember the name," said Thompson.

"Back when you were over here the revolutionaries would have liked to have killed Alexandro along with Ceausescu, but he escaped."

"And he got away in a black Buick Electra?" asked Thompson.

"According to a source we've developed, apparently so. The old man keeps to himself, but when he heads into the closest town, which is Brasov, he's in a black American car. It's too coincidental. It's got to be the same car."

"I have heard of Brasov," said Thompson.

"It's up in the Carpathian Mountains," replied Kline. "It's rough country. There was a lot of rebel activity around there. There are lots of gypsies up there too."

"What now?" asked Ann. "Do we call the police chief?"

"No," said Kline. "Now this is a matter for Agent Morrison and me to handle. The only people we can trust with this information are the people in this room. Anyone else is a potential leak. Involving governments and police will only endanger Josh's life."

"All right," said Ann. "We won't tell anyone."

"Good," said Kline "Agent Morrison and I will head up to Brasov in the morning."

"Just the two of you?" asked Ann. "We can't wait to get some more agents to help you?"

"I'll take that as not being an insult," smiled Kline. "Our information indicates that it's a small group of rebels. Agent Morrison will be all that I need to extricate Josh."

"I'm going with you," Thompson immediately interjected.

"No, you are not," replied Kline and Ann, simultaneously.

"Jinx," added Ann. "And Richard, what the hell are you thinking?"

"Ann, this is something I have to do," said Thompson. "You know that. If Josh is up there, I have to be with them."

"I know you feel strongly about this, Richard. But I don't like it at all. I am really against this."

"This is not a negotiation, babe," replied Thompson. "You know I love you, but if that kid is up in Brasov, I'm going. This isn't up for discussion."

"Nice try, Congressman," said Kline. "You're right. It isn't up for discussion. This is my call. I can't have you going with us."

"See, I told you the woman was in charge," muttered Ann.

"Sorry, Agent Kline, but this is not your call," said Thompson, ignoring his wife's comment. "According to the Chairman of the Select Committee on Intelligence, all I have to do is place a call to him and I get whatever I want on this trip."

Thompson peered at Kline. The determination in his eyes was unmistakable. "That's right—I spoke with the Chairman before we left." He looked down at his watch. "It's going to be late afternoon in Iowa right now. The Chairman is not going to like me bothering him at home during the district work period with a CIA problem. Clowns in Action—that's what he calls you guys. Then he will call the Director, who's enjoying the fact that Congress has left town. And the Director calls you and chews your ass out and I'm on the trip anyway. You're a lifer. You know how this works. My politics will trump your ground game." He paused for effect. "Let's just skip the bullshit, shall we, Agent Kline? What time are we leaving?"

Kline stared back at the steely resolve in Thompson's eyes. The silence seemed like an eternity. "Meet Morrison and me out front at 5:30 a.m. sharp. Don't be late. I hate people being late. I won't take it from my partner and I won't wait for you." Kline turned and left the room, firmly shutting the door behind her.

"When did you have time to speak to the Chairman of the Select Committee?"

"I didn't."

Chapter 34

Dream sequences for Josh varied between idyllic scenes from his boyhood and nightmarish visions of death and dismemberment, sometimes all in the same dream. The cold, drafty floor provided little comfort, and dreams that started peacefully usually ended just as he felt when he awakened—cold and alone.

"Wake up, boy," Noua said as she used her booted foot to rustle Josh from a light sleep.

Josh jumped at the feel of Noua's hiking boot against his side. "What?" he shouted in an edgy response.

Noua laughed at his nervous reply. She knew he was expecting her to kick him in the side again. "Oh, Mr. America's Brain, you don't seem so clever right now. Wake up. I have some food for you. Eat."

"Thank you."

"Don't thank me," replied Noua. "I do not want your appreciation. I am not doing this for your personal enjoyment. You will need your nourishment for the trip."

Josh looked around. There was a bowl of borscht and some bread lying on the floor next to him. He quickly devoured the bread. The soup was very hot and tasted like, well, it tasted like hot boiled red beets. Josh hated beets. But then again, he had not eaten this much in days. He sure as hell was not going to argue with the chef about the menu selection at this point.

"What do you mean, trip?" asked Josh as he drank from the bowl without a spoon.

"We are leaving the house for business in the city."

"What business? What city?"

"You talk too much," replied Noua. "Shut up and eat."

After Josh had finished eating, Bouncer came in, picked

him up and carried him outside, Josh's bound feet dragging the ground behind him. The sun had not yet risen, and Josh could see his breath form an outline against the clear Romanian night sky. He shivered slightly from the cool damp air. But the cold did not matter. It was the first time he had seen the outside of the house since the night he had been kidnapped. The air smelled fresh.

Outside the house there were several other men. Honeycat stood next to an older man with long dirty grey hair. He seemed to be giving orders to everyone, including Noua. When he yelled at her, Josh recognized the voice as the man who had been inflicting the abuse on Noua in the room next to the one where he was being held. Another man with a scruffy black beard, whom Josh recognized as the driver from the kidnapping, stood by the old man. A man in a suit stood next to him.

Bouncer navigated Josh to a domestic Romanian vehicle, parked next to the black American car which had brought him to the mountains. Bouncer placed Josh in the back seat of the car, but when he pulled out a blindfold, Josh protested.

"No, please," said Josh. "Not the blindfold. I haven't seen the sky for days. I have no idea where I am." When he realized that the language barrier had kept Bouncer from understanding his request, he pled his case to Noua. "Noua, please don't. A blindfold has no meaning for me. I don't know where I am and have no idea where we are going. Please let me go without the blindfold."

Noua laughed and motioned to Bouncer to place the blindfold around Josh's head, covering his eyes. The last thing he saw was Honeycat getting into the car on the passenger side. Josh listened as Noua engaged the other men standing by the house in a brief conversation. Then Josh heard the car doors slam shut, the engine started and the car began to move.

After they had driven for about five minutes, Noua said something to Honeycat, who reached in the backseat and removed the blindfold from Josh's head.

"Let him see the sky," Noua said to Honeycat in Romanian. "It is the least we can do for our American guest. Let him enjoy tonight. For in two days, I will personally deliver him to the gates of hell."

Chapter 35

In order to make sure Kline and Morrison did not leave without him, Thompson headed to the front lobby of the American Embassy about a half an hour before the designated departure time. He suspected Kline meant what she said about leaving him behind if he was late. She knew he would have little to complain to the Director about if he missed the departure time. 5:30 a.m. sharp meant 5:30 a.m. sharp.

Despite Thompson's protests to the contrary, Ann went to the lobby with him to see him off on his dangerous expedition.

Normally impeccable in her appearance, Ann looked as distraught as she felt. The dark semicircles under her eyes indicated she had not slept at all the night before. The sexy black robe had been replaced by tight jeans and a rumpled t-shirt. Her hair was straying in several directions at once, daring a hair brush to venture in.

During the night, Ann had become almost frantic at the thought of Thompson going into the mountains with the two CIA agents in search of Josh. The strain of her own thoughts was showing on her pretty face.

Thompson made love with Ann shortly after the late night visit from Kline. It began as a gentle act of love making, with the pair gently touching and caressing each other in erotic recognition of their mutual feelings and desires—sexually and silently recognizing the potential deadly consequences of Thompson's decision to go to Brasov. As the pair progressed, the act itself transformed to a sweaty and noisy raucous act that went beyond making love, where Ann had to dig her finger nails into her husband's back in order to keep her low orgasmic moan from turning into a scream. For both, the act itself had been as much of a stress reliever as a consummation of their love for each other.

Thompson had fallen asleep shortly after they made love. For Ann, however, the late-night sex session had only acted to energize her own mind to further thoughts of the dangers of Thompson's pending voyage into the mountains. Ann was dealing with more than fear about her husband's safety. She was also worried for her children. The unthinkable thought of them growing up fatherless was embedded in her mind. Her fear was coupled with a creeping guilt she felt about placing her husband's personal safety and own desires over that of Josh's. The conflict of emotions in Ann's soul was extreme. Sleep was impossible.

Ann was a recovering alcoholic who had struggled with her sobriety since Thompson's election to Congress. The stress of her thoughts had not helped last night. She wanted a drink and it was Romania. She could not just pick up the phone and call her sponsor. After tossing and turning in bed for about an hour, Ann slipped out of bed, dressed and left in search of a cigarette. She quit cigarettes when she quit drinking, but she still had to have a smoke or two when her stress level would have compelled lesser disciplined persons to drink.

Ann bummed a harsh European brand smoke from the night watchman at the front desk. As she sat on the front steps of the Embassy and took the smoke deep into her lungs, she felt the first wave of nicotine rock her body. A second and third cigarette had followed with Ann trying to gather her conflicting thoughts about Thompson, Josh and Griff.

After she had stamped out her last cigarette on the sidewalk in front of the Embassy, Ann slipped back into the room and sat quietly in a chair, watching her husband sleep until the harsh buzzing of the alarm clock at 4:00 a.m. had made her jump.

Thompson looked over at Ann sitting in the chair. "You been there all night?"

"Pretty much so," she replied. "There's no chance of talking you out of this, is there?"

"Not gonna happen."

Ann sat still in the chair while Thompson showered. When he came out of the bathroom, he tried to make small talk. "What does one wear to a rescue?"

"Not funny, Richard," was all that Ann could muster. She had a bad feeling about the trip and wanted to talk him out of going. But in her heart she knew that any talk to the contrary would be futile. She also knew that Richard going was probably the right thing to do—but that did not make it any easier. "I'm sorry, hon. I didn't mean to snap. I just didn't sleep much last night and I'm worried about this trip."

"It will be fine," Thompson said. "I'll be back late tonight with Josh in tow. Then, we can have some real hotel sex in this place."

"Don't make jokes, Richard. Not now. I'm serious."

"I know you are. It's going to be all right."

"Be careful and I love you." She had paused. "If something happens to you, I swear I will kill you."

Now Ann stood quietly aside as Kline, Morrison and Thompson looked at a map for the route from Bucharest to the town of Brasov. "We've got a GPS and a lot of other gear," Kline explained to Thompson. "But sometimes in these remote places, the map is the only way to tell where you're going." Thompson nodded his understanding. "I always like to visualize the route before some voice tells me where to turn."

As Kline was folding the map, Morrison walked over to where Ann was standing. He had not been able to break the ice with the Congressman's wife on the flight over to Romania. As Thompson helped Kline plot their journey, he thought he would give it another try.

"Don't worry, Mrs. Thompson. I'll keep an eye on him," said Morrison. "Couple of hours up, find the kid, and we're back in time for a late dinner."

"Don't patronize me, agent," said Ann. "I know what's at stake here and I'm worried about it."

"I'll keep him out of trouble," replied Morrison. "Trust me, I don't want a dead Congressman on my resume."

"Did you have to use that word?"

"Sorry," said Morrison, realizing that even joking about Thompson's death was not endearing him to Ann. "Hey, I'm already taking care of the Congressman. I've got us a couple of thermos jugs of coffee for the ride."

"I'm good to go," said Thompson as he put on a green canvas rain jacket over his blue jeans and long sleeve sweat shirt. His hair stuck out from underneath a khaki colored ball cap.

"Bring him back in one piece," Ann warned both of Thompson's traveling companions.

"We will," said Morrison as he jumped into the front seat. Kline got into the car on the driver's side.

Thompson walked over to Ann. He hugged her and, while kissing her on the cheek, he whispered in her ear. "I love you. Think about where we should take Josh for dinner tonight."

Ann was so filled with emotion that she was unable to voice her reply. She mouthed "I love you" as Thompson pulled back. He turned and got into the back seat of the SUV.

"One piece," Ann mumbled, as she watched the red tail lights disappear around the corner.

Chapter 36

Benny Vesper had worked for several presidents, so he knew of the many distractions that one encounters in roaming the halls of the White House. Staffers engrossed with their own self-importance walk around the West Wing at the pace of Olympic speed walkers and they tend to talk in either extremely loud or extremely soft voices in order to accentuate their own superiority to others. The office for the Chief of Staff was so close to the Oval Office that the ceaseless flow of people and problems could easily consume the entire day. So when Vesper went to work for President Mocker, he made sure that he secured a second secret office hidden in the Old Executive Office Building where he could escape for actual work.

The OEOB was built in 1888 and Mark Twain called it the ugliest building in America. President Dwight David Eisenhower agreed and he once commissioned a study to determine the cost of tearing it down. However, since much of the interior of the OEOB is built with fireproof cast iron, Ike found the project cost prohibitive. In an ultimate twist of irony, today the building bears Ike's name.

The office of the Vice President is in the OEOB and several presidents have maintained hideaway offices there. When President Mocker declined such a hideaway office, Vesper grabbed the space for himself. The office was on the northeast end of the second floor, and it gave the Chief of Staff a view of the television cameras regularly stationed on the north lawn.

Every morning, Vesper would start his day extra early by spending an hour or so in his OEOB office. Though it was the size of a regular business office, by comparison to the Oval Office, it was a silent cubby hole. From there he could focus on an issue or two before hurling himself into the political quagmire that is the West Wing. Inasmuch as only he had a key to the office, he did not bother at keeping it tidy. The desk was piled high with papers and files. Bankers boxes, filled mostly with personal files, lined the walls.

Benny Vesper was shocked when President Mocker burst into his office unannounced. "Did you see the news this morning?" He paused and looked around. "God, this place is a mess. No wonder you won't tell anyone else where you go. How the hell do you work in here?"

"Good morning to you, too, Mr. President," responded Vesper as he promptly stood up.

"Yeah, yeah, yeah," responded Mocker to Vesper's ceremonial reply. "Sit down."

"Sorry, sir. You're still the leader of the free world."

"Did you see the news this morning?"

"I never watch the news in the morning, sir. You know that."

"I know. You've told me before that you spend the early part of the morning preparing me for the morning security briefing."

"That's right, sir. And the Press Office tells me what I need to tell you about the overnight news clips."

"Well," said Mocker, "I did see the news this morning and I want an immediate full report about the story I saw."

"Wow. You're sure fired up."

"The Mace, man. They found the Mace in New York."

"That's impossible sir. The Mace is in Romania. I put it in the belly of the plane myself."

"Not that Mace. They found the original Mace … the one that was stolen from the House when the British invaded Washington during the War of 1812."

"So, there are two stolen Maces, and one's been found."

"Yeah. The reporter said the FBI is investigating."

"I'm afraid I'm not following you, Jack."

"Get the Director on the phone. I want him over here ASAP. I have an idea."

Chapter 37

Ann was sitting at the restaurant in the basement of the American Embassy, mindlessly prodding her fork through runny scrambled eggs, when she heard a voice. "Mind if I join you?" It was Sue, the woman who had accompanied Griff on the night Josh had been kidnapped. Ann looked up with a blank face, shrugged her shoulders and pointed her fork at the empty chair across from where she was sitting.

"They told me I'd find you here," said Sue. "Michael had to go to a morning campaign meeting for President Krasterich. I thought that I'd come over and try a second introduction. We really didn't get off to a good start yesterday."

"Nothing about this trip has been good," replied Ann. "And that includes introductions. Sorry about yesterday. I'm a little stressed out."

"I can certainly understand," replied Sue. "Josh is a good kid. I've only known him for a couple of days, but I think the world of him."

"He's easy to love," said Ann. "The blue eyes … the blond hair…" Her voice trailed off as tears welled up in her eyes and left her unable to complete her description of Josh. Memories of the first time he entered the campaign office dashed through her mind. She pictured the cute grin he gave when she first asked him his age. Ann cut her thoughts short. She did not want to lose all control in front of someone she had just met.

"Hey, look, I'm sorry," said Sue. "I didn't come over to get you all emotional."

"It's all right," said Ann, taking a gulp of coffee and a deep breath. "It's a pretty emotional morning. In any event, yeah, Josh is a very special kid to Richard and me."

"I know," said Sue. "Michael has told me how special

he is to you two. That's what I wanted you to know. He's a special kid to Michael also."

Ann was too tired and emotionally drained to let her anger with Michael Griffith overtake the conversation. "Griff loves Josh as much as we do. I know that. Richard knows that, too."

"You don't even know how much," said Sue. "Michael is literally despondent over the whole thing. I know that you're mad at Michael and blame him for what has happened, but you can't even imagine what he's going through right now."

"I know in my heart that I have to let Griff up," said Ann. "I know that he has to be going out of his mind."

"And it's been made worse for Michael because he feels he can't talk to his best friend about it," said Sue. "Last night, he just walked around the embassy grounds by himself for hours."

"I can't do anything about that right now," said Ann.

"Look, Ann," said Sue, "we've just met, and I know that you don't really like me to begin with. But Michael has only known me for a few days. He desperately needs someone to talk to. He needs someone he trusts. I'd like to get Michael and your husband together later today."

Ann wanted desperately to tell Sue—or anyone for that matter—that Richard could not talk to Michael because he was out looking for Josh. She wanted to shout out that her husband was on a trip to the Carpathian Mountains from which he might not return. She wanted to scream a string of curse words at the top of her lungs. Griff needed to talk—well, goddamnit, she needed to talk. But she was a Congressional spouse. She needed to remain calm and not say a word. Her thoughts and emotions had to remain bottled up inside her for only her to see when she looked in the mirror.

"I'm sorry," said Ann, as she pushed herself back from the table. "That's impossible." She got up and, fighting back tears, turned before slowly walking out of the restaurant. "Congressional spouses don't cry in public," she mumbled as she walked.

Chapter 38

The weekday morning flights out of LaGuardia are generally filled with business men and women heading to and fro on missions of varied corporate importance. Men in dark suits, French-cuffed shirts and power ties mingle in the lounges with women with identical hair styles and equally conservative suits and dresses. As they sip their soy-lattés they text each other on their smart phones about the latest stories they all read in the *Wall Street Journal*.

The Fat Man waited in the midst of these corporate icons for his morning flight home to CVG. In contrast to the Brooks Brothers sea of pinstripes around him, The Fat Man was wearing a Yankees pin-striped jersey he had picked up at the ball game the night before. It had Mickey Mantle's number eight on the back and his long speckled gray hair stuck out from underneath a navy blue New York Yankees ball cap. To a casual observer he would have looked like a bad Michael Moore impersonator waiting for his one-way flight to hell.

The Fat Man was finishing a phone call with his wife when two uniformed officers approached him.

"Excuse me," said one of the officers. "Are you Joe Bradley?"

"Who's asking?" replied The Fat Man, looking at the officers' badges.

"Officers Parsons and Hoffman, New York police," the female police officer replied while showing her badge and ID card to The Fat Man. "Are you Mr. Bradley?"

"Yes, I am. Although you seem to know that already. You walked right up to me."

"We had a description. You weren't that hard to pick out of the crowd."

"Thanks. You're a real confidence builder. What can I do for you, officers?"

"We've been given instructions to escort you to the international gate in Terminal 3."

"Really? And just who gave you those instructions?"

"FBI Agent Leo Argo. He said he'd explain when you got there."

"This is absolutely insane," The Fat Man said to Leo Argo as they walked across the tarmac at LaGuardia.

"Welcome to my world," replied Argo. "You wanted to be a superhero. Welcome to crime fighting. Why do you think I'm single? No woman would ever put up with this kind of shit."

"And you think my wife will?" replied The Fat Man.

"The bottom line is that I'm headed to Romania and I need you to go with me."

"My wife is not going to like this one damn bit."

"Tell her it's at the request of the President of the United States," came a voice from inside the airplane.

Chapter 39

Ann was lying on the bed in her room with a damp cloth over her eyes. The coolness of the cloth seemed to ease the pain of her psyche like ice on a swollen muscle. She was craving another cigarette, but she did not have the emotional energy to get out of bed and find another person to give her one.

She was just about to fall asleep, finally, when there was a knock at the door. Assuming that it was the Embassy's room cleaning service, she shouted at the door: "I'm sorry. Not right now. I'm trying to get some rest. Just leave some towels in front of the door. I'll get them later."

"It's me, Ann," said Griffith from the hallway. "I need to talk to you."

Ann pressed the cloth firmly against her forehead. "Fuck me," she mumbled to herself. "Leave me alone, Michael. I can't talk right now."

"Come on, Annie," Griffith pleaded. "We've got to have this conversation sooner or later. Please let me in."

"I can't do this now," said Ann.

"Don't do this to me, Ann," replied Griffith, as he leaned his head against the door. "I really need to talk to you."

Ann exhaled slowly and used the cold cloth to wipe her face. She looked in the mirror and tried to adjust her hair. "You look horrible," she mumbled pointing at her own reflection. She walked to the door and opened it, silently gesturing Griffith's admittance.

"Thank you," said Griffith as he walked into the room. Once inside, Griffith paused and looked at Ann. He had known Ann before Thompson, and he had actually introduced the couple when they all had worked on Capitol Hill. "Jesus, Annie. Sue was right. You look like hell."

"If that's what you came to tell me, Michael," Ann replied, "you're too late. They do have mirrors over here. I know how I look."

"Sue said she came over here this morning to talk to you," said Griffith. "She said you were all shook up over Josh."

"I'm fine," Ann said looking out the window. She felt like crying again, but she was not sure if her body could take it.

"Yeah," said Griffith. "I can tell. Where's Richard? Is he around?"

With that one simple question Ann lost it completely. She began crying uncontrollable. The string of curse words she had repressed earlier in the morning at breakfast with Sue suddenly flowed from her mouth with a reckless abandon and ease. "Fuck, shit, hell, damn…"

"Annie. What is it? What's wrong?"

Ann turned and faced Griffith, her left hand hoisting her hair out of her reddened face. Tears were flowing down her cheeks. "I've got to tell someone this, Michael. You're the only person I can trust over here. What I am about to tell you has to stay in this room."

"Of course, you can trust me," said Griffith. "What the hell is going on? And where is Richard?"

"Sit down, Michael," said Ann. "You're about to find out what a living hell my life has become."

Griffith sat and listened as Ann rambled in an unformed rant about the whereabouts of his best friend. She told him about the black Buick. She told him about the conversation with Kline. She told him how they had made love the night before. She told him she felt guilty for being so mad. She told him how she really needed a smoke. Finally, she told him she was deathly afraid she would never see the father of her children alive again.

When she was finished, Griffith was almost as shaken as Ann. He fumbled in his pockets for his pack of cigarettes.

Finding them, he pulled two out and silently flipped one to Ann. He pulled a single match from a pack he had tucked in the cigarettes and tried to light it. His hands were shaking so badly he could not get the match to light. One strike. Two strikes. When a third and a fourth strike produced no flame, Griffith threw the matches against the wall and shouted out loud: "Motherfucker!"

In desperation, Griffith picked up an ashtray from the table and threw it hard against the wall. It smashed into several large pieces and, seemingly, a thousand smaller slivers. Ann jumped as it hit the wall and Griffith cut loose with a litany of four-letter words. When he stopped, he put his head in his hands and began taking large, deep breaths. "I'm sorry, Annie."

"Just an ash tray," replied Ann.

"Not just the ash tray," said Griffith. "I am sorry about everything."

"I know you are, Griff," said Ann.

Griffith bent over and picked up the matches. Hands still shaking, he pulled out another match and lit it on the first try. He put the cigarette in his mouth and lit it. As he drew in, he offered the lit match to Ann who had already placed her cigarette in her mouth. "Two on a match," he said deadpan. After the cigarette was lit, he kissed her on the forehead. Then he proceeded to the table where Thompson had left his bottle of Makers' Mark. He opened the bottle and drank straight from the neck. "If anything happens to those two," Griffith said as his voice trailed off with no particular end to the sentence in his mind.

Chapter 40

The ride to the village of Brasov in the Carpathian Mountains was long and arduous for the trio of Americans in the Romanian SUV. The narrow and ill-kept Romanian roads were made far more treacherous by the wild drivers who took each bumpy curve at top speed.

Forget the rebels, Thompson thought to himself as they drove, *I may die in a car wreck.*

The trio had stopped a couple of miles away from where they thought the kidnapper's house was located in order to change drivers. Kline wanted Morrison to drive the car past the house so she could adequately survey the surroundings. Morrison drove the car past the house and around a bend in the road. When he was sure the hillside sufficiently hid the car from view of the house, Morrison pulled over. "So what's the plan, boss?" he asked Kline.

"The house sits back off the road up against the hillside. There isn't much brush for about ten or fifteen yards," replied Kline.

"Yeah," said Morrison. "This ain't gonna be easy, is it?"

"No," she said. "Here's what I want you to do. You and the Congressman get out and circle back to the cabin. I'm going to give you ten minutes to get into position."

"What are you going to do?" asked Morrison. "How are you going to approach the house?"

Kline took a breath. "I am going to drive the car up to the front of the house and knock on the door."

"That's a bit ballsy," interjected Thompson.

"Trust me," replied Morrison. "She's got bigger balls than either you or me."

"It isn't ballsy. The front door is our only way in," said Kline. "The surrounding terrain sucks. Full frontal assault is our only option."

"You're in charge," said Morrison.

"I am going to go knock on the door and act like I'm an American who is lost in the countryside," said Kline. "You've been over here, too, Congressman. That's believable. Isn't it?"

"Oh, hell yeah," replied Thompson. "It's easy to get lost. They know that with the election and all, there are a lot of Americans over here getting lost."

"I'll survey the situation and keep them occupied," said Kline. "Mark. After I'm in, you need to wait a couple of minutes and then make your way to the house. Check out and see if there are any alternate ways in or out. There are none facing the road, but there must be at least one or two in that little house somewhere. If you think you can make your way in, do it. That way we can hit 'em from two sides. Remember, getting the kid out alive is the top priority."

"What do I do?" asked Thompson.

"Not a goddamn thing," replied Kline. "Do you understand me? You don't do a goddamn thing. Wait in the brush. We'll extricate Josh. He may come out first. You get him to cover. We'll take care of the rest. Kline looked Thompson square in the eyes and handed him her cell phone before she continued. "If we do not come back out, you get the hell out of here and contact the embassy to let them know what's happened. The number is programmed into the contacts list on this phone. Ask for Stephenson. She will know what to do. And Congressman…"

"Yeah?"

"It is extremely important to keep your cool. This may get ugly."

Chapter 41

As Kline waited ten minutes to allow Morrison to get himself into position, she put her game face on.

This is what I train for, Kline thought to herself. *I don't design the mission, I just execute it. I don't question the morality. I don't look for a reason. Those decisions are made for me. I do what I do because I'm the best at it in the Company. I have saved more lives than I have taken.*

Kline turned the car around and headed back to Alexandro's home. She parked her vehicle behind the old rusty Buick Electra and turned off the engine. She took a deep breath, grabbed the door handle and exited the car. She put a stupid smile on her face as she approached.

The mountain air outside the cabin was thin and damp. The cold wind cut through the mountains and left a cold, wet film on her face. She knocked on the door.

General Alexandro could hardly believe his good fortune when he opened the front door. A pretty woman stood at his doorstep, looking forsaken and lost. By her clothes and general appearance she did not appear to be Romanian. She clearly was not a gypsy.

"Good afternoon," she said in English, trying to make sure she appeared completely unversed in the Romanian language. "I am an American and um… um … lost."

"Lost?" said Alexandro in broken English. He didn't speak the language often anymore, but he knew enough English to communicate effectively with most Americans. In particular, he understood the woman's assertion that she was lost. He returned her smile. Maybe she was the insurance policy he needed in case the efforts with Noua and the boy failed to work according to the plan. "I am sorry to hear that. Please. Please. Come in."

Kline stepped inside and quickly surveyed the premises. Three men sat around a table staring at her. There was at least one side room. The configuration of the house was such that there might be another one. Josh was probably in one of the side rooms. Kline assumed there was at least one guard in the room with him. Morrison would figure that out as he entered the house from one of these two side rooms.

"So," said Alexandro. "You are lost?"

"Yes," Kline replied. "I am afraid so."

"And how did you come to find your way so far out of the city?"

"That is a long story," replied Kline. "I am an American official sent to Romania to observe the election for your government. I am supposed to be in headed to Suceava and somehow I must have taken a wrong turn. I am very lost. I do not speak Romanian and have been looking for someone who speaks English to get me back on my way. I am so glad that you speak English."

"Well, how fortunate for you," said Alexandro. "I do speak some English. Come. Sit with my friends and me. I am honored to have an American election official in my home." Alexandro turned to his colleagues and, unaware that Kline spoke fluent Romanian, spoke freely to them in his native language. "This lady is an American official who is here to observe the election. How lucky for us that she is lost. I will act as if I am giving her direction, but you need to get ready to get a hold on her. If Noua is unsuccessful in her mission, we will have this pretty lady as a backup."

Kline, understanding every word, immediately drew the obvious conclusion that the men intended to kidnap her. Her heartbeat increased.

"Certainly. Certainly," Alexandro said in broken-English as he returned his attention to Kline. "Please sit. I will make you some coffee and then explain how to get back to the city. We will draw up a map for you to get back to Brasov. Once you are there you can get further directions to Suceava."

Thompson and Morrison made their way through the brush, up over a hill and down towards Alexandro's small home. The thick brush gave them cover, but made the going slow. About a hundred yards or so from the house, Thompson tripped and fell to the ground so hard he knocked the wind out of himself.

Morrison chuckled lowly as he looked at Thompson on the ground. "What's wrong, Congressman?" asked Morrison. "The going a little tougher than you expected?"

"It's definitely not what I read in the job description," replied Thompson on his hands and knees. Morrison reached for his arm, but Thompson declined by yanking it away. *I'll do this myself,* he thought. He slowly stood up, brushed himself off and tried to catch his breath.

"Try to keep up," said Morrison as he continued to move. "Kline should be on the move any minute now."

"You go as quickly as you need to. I'll keep up."

"When we get into position behind the house, I need you to stay out of sight."

"Don't worry about that," replied Thompson. "I know I'm out of my league."

"Good. Well, we may have to cut your friend loose and send him out quickly," replied Morrison. "If we do, you get him into the woods with you as quickly as possible. Duck for cover until we give the all-clear."

"Check."

The SUV was pulling up in front of the house and Kline was approaching the door. Morrison and Thompson kept moving.

"See that back window," said Morrison as they approached the back of the house.

"Yeah," whispered Thompson.

"Kline's gone in the front. I'm going in that window."

Morrison pulled a gun and a couple of ammo clips from

a back pack he had been carrying. He pulled a second gun out of the backpack and stuck it in a shoulder holster.

"What about me?" Thompson asked.

"What do you mean?" asked Morrison. "What about you?"

"I mean, do you have a weapon for me?" said Thompson.

"No way."

"I really don't want to stay out here by myself without a gun. If everything goes as planned, Josh is going to be headed out my way. What if someone follows him?"

Morrison looked at Thompson. "No one will follow him. You may have forced your way onto the mission, but I'm not giving you a piece."

"Really," said Thompson. "Think seriously about this. Do you want me to stay out here by myself without a weapon?"

Morrison pulled the gun he had just put in the shoulder holster and looked at it. "Have you ever shot a gun before?"

"I'm a Congressman. I get invited to police shooting ranges all the time."

"And you're a good shot?"

"No," said Thompson. "I'm a lousy shot. But I'm not going to shoot someone unless they are right on top of me. And if they're right on top of me then everything has gone to hell. If that's the case, I better have a fucking gun in my hand. At that point, that gun may be my only way out."

Morrison looked up at the sky and shook his head in disbelief. Morrison took the 9mm Sig Sauer he had been holding in his hand and handed it to Thompson. "I really shouldn't do this."

"I won't tell anyone. I promise," said Thompson, as he accepted the gun by looking down the backside of its barrel.

"Don't make me regret this. I'm in deep shit with everyone right now as it is."

Morrison took his remaining gun and pointed it at the ground as he approached the house taking quick steps in a crouched-down posture. Thompson watched from the brush as Morrison made his way to the back of the house. In a quick motion, he raised up, looked in the window, and then ducked back down. Morrison pulled a small pocket knife from his pants pocket and cut the screen from the frame of the window. He reached in and jimmied the window open.

Morrison looked back at Thompson as he lifted himself upward and attempted to lift his muscular body into a position that would allow him to lower himself through the window. As he lifted his body to its most prone position, a portion of the window frame, worn from years of wet weather and dry rot, gave way. Morrison fell into the house, landing on the floor with a thud loud enough for Thompson to hear from the brush.

"Sonofabitch," Morrison grumbled as he hit the floor. He looked down at his ankle which was turned sideways with a serious compound fracture. *Sonofabitch.* Morrison looked to the door and steadied his weapon for the onslaught that he knew was inevitable.

Alexandro grabbed a worn porcelain coffee cup from the cabinet and placed it on the wooden counter top. He took the tin pot off the old stove and poured a steaming hot cup of dark java. He placed the hot cup of coffee in front of his guest and then freshened up the cups of his colleagues. Kline looked at the broken veins in the cup and wondered when it had last been washed. She sipped some bitter coffee.

"So," said Alexandro as he stood behind a man in a white shirt—Abel Bogdan . "You are from America and have come here to help us in our election."

"Yes," replied Kline.

"That must be very exciting," Alexandro commented as he walked from behind the man and started around toward the kitchen cabinet. "Have you been to Romania before?"

"No," Kline lied. "This is my first time."

"And what do you do back in America?" asked Alexandro.

"I am an attorney. I work for a large law firm in Washington," replied Kline. "I do a lot of lobbying of the United States Congress."

"You do?" said Alexandro. "That sounds quite exciting. Why did you decide to come to Romania for our elections?"

Kline was just about to answer when there was a loud crack followed by a thud from behind the closed door to the other room. Alexandro immediately opened a kitchen drawer and pulled a Russian revolver. He lowered it at Kline who sat motionless with her coffee cup in her hands.

"What is it?" asked Kline. "What's wrong?"

"I am not sure," replied Alexandro as he gave the weapon to Bogdan. "Keep an eye on her," he said to the man in Romanian as he pulled another revolver from the same drawer. "Stay still," Alexandro instructed Kline in a whisper as he moved to the door. "Did someone come here with you?"

"No," said Kline. "I don't know what you are talking about."

"If you are lying, I will kill you."

Thompson did not have to be a covert agent or an employee of "the Company" to know that when Morrison fell into the room, their mission and their lives were in danger. He crouched down behind a large rock and closed his eyes in contemplation.

This is bad. This is real fucking bad, Thompson thought, as his breathing quickly went shallow. *Breathe deep. Slow down. Breathe deep.*

Hell, someone may have already slit Josh's throat, Thompson thought to himself. *I've got to move and move quickly.* He rose up from behind the rock and looked at Alexandro's house. He decided against following Morrison. Instead, sprinting at a diagonal to his right, Thompson made his way to the side of the structure. On that side he found another window about a third of the way back from the front of the house. Based on its position, Thompson assumed the window would give him a view of the front door and, hopefully, Kline.

As Thompson caught his breath beside the window at the side of the house, one thought kept making its way through his mind. This is crazy. *This is absolutely fucking crazy.*

Thompson placed his back against the outside wall of the building. The window was just past his left shoulder. He slowly looked to the corner of the window and saw a man at a table holding a gun on Kline. There were two other men at the table, but they were unarmed. A fourth man was standing at a door to another room, talking to Kline and looking like he was about to enter the adjacent room. He too, had a gun in his hand.

"Don't interfere," Thompson mumbled as he leaned his back against the house, pointing his gun at the ground. *These guys are the pros. Let them do their jobs. They're pros. They'll get out of this.*

Alexandro opened the door and cautiously looked into the adjacent room. Kline sat still in her chair and looked past Alexandro. She thought about how she would get her gun from her shoulder holster underneath her down jacket. As Kline anticipated how the scene might play out, she could see into the next room. From what she could tell, there was no one else in the room. So, if Morrison was not in that room, there must be a third room. Morrison would therefore have to be in that third room. *More importantly,* Kline thought as she looked around, *Josh is not in there.*

Alexandro surveyed the room slowly and then entered a step or two further into the room. After a few seconds, his shoulders seemed to relax, and he walked around the room in a natural way. Apparently satisfied, he came back out into the main room and closed the door behind him.

Alexandro paused for a moment, and then his eyes moved to another part of the back wall of the house. He took four steps to another doorway that was around a corner and out of the line of sight. He looked back at Kline. “If there is someone in there, I will kill you,” he whispered. Kline nodded her head negatively, trying to look scared.

Alexandro paused again, just long enough to look down at the gun in his right hand. He grabbed the door knob with his left hand and quickly swung the door open, lowering his gun as he stepped into the doorway.

Morrison, anticipating the entry, immediately opened fire. His bullets hit General Alexandro with deadly accuracy. Alexandro, however, simultaneously returned fire at the man lying on his floor. In an instant, Alexandro was dead and Morrison was gravely wounded.

Kline had no time to move as Bogdan jumped up and pointed the gun at her head. He barked instructions for one of the other men to peek around the corner. The man, the one Josh had referred to as Bouncer, looked into the room. “The General is on the floor,” Bouncer said. “He’s been hit. He’s not moving.”

“General,” shouted Bogdan. “General, can you hear me?”

When there was no response from the other room, Bogdan moved to Kline and placed the gun at her temple. “Out,” he said to Kline in broken English as he began to roughly frisk her. “Tell him to come out.”

Kline’s situation had suddenly gone from bad to worse. Any move for her weapon would result in a bullet in her head and he was sure to find Kline’s weapon at any moment.

When Thompson heard the gun fire he jumped. Once he had regained his composure, he stood up and looked through the window into the kitchen. One of the men at the table had stood up and moved to Kline's side. He was holding a gun to her head. His back was to the window.

Oh, shit, thought Thompson. *Gunshots mean that someone has fired on Morrison. He's not barging into the room, so he's been hit. Fuck. Morrison is down. It's up to me.* For a few seconds Thompson stood there perfectly still and out of view of the window. He closed his eyes for a moment and raised his chin in defiance of his own civil mores. *God forgive me, but please... please give me the strength to do this.* Thompson stepped back and squared his shoulders to the window. He sighted his gun at the head of the man who was hovering over Kline and pulled the trigger.

When Thompson's bullet smashed through the window and shattered the head of the man holding the gun, Kline reached into her jacket and pulled her own weapon. One of the two remaining men went for the dead man's gun, which was now lying on the floor. Kline lowered the angle of her weapon and shot him. He stumbled across the room and then crumpled slowly to the floor just in front of the stove. Kline swung around to face the remaining man. "Don't move a muscle, Comrade," she said in perfect Romanian.

The man sat down in the chair and lowered his head. Hearing her speak in his native language, Bouncer knew he was screwed.

Chapter 42

"Josh. Josh Barkman," Jane Kline shouted. "Josh, are you in there?"

There was no response to Kline's call.

As Thompson entered the house through the front door, Kline looked at the man sitting at the table. "Thanks," she said to Thompson. Thompson, in turn, was frozen—looking at the body on the floor—at the body of the man he had just killed. "Nice shot."

Thompson did not move and he continued to stare as a pool of dark blood began to form around the dead man's head.

"The first kill is always the toughest," said Kline. "Welcome to the Company. But I still need your full attention." When Thompson still did not move, she shouted at him. "Congressman!"

Thompson looked at Kline with a blank, pale look on his face. "Snap out of it, Congressman. I still need your help here."

"Okay, okay," he replied, as Kline turned her attention to the remaining man sitting at the table.

"Where is he, Comrade?" she shouted at him in Romanian. "Where is the boy?"

Bouncer shrugged his shoulders.

"Keep your gun on him," Kline instructed Thompson. "I'm going to clear the house. If he moves, shoot him, but not to kill. We may need him."

Kline entered the adjacent room with her weapon in firing position, her finger on the trigger. Spinning hard to her right she made sure no one was in her blind spot. In a motion just as quick, she turned hard to her left. She could see Alexandro lying motionless in another spreading pool of blood. His gun was on the floor by his side.

"Shadow. Shadow. Can you hear me?

"Yeah," came the weak response. "This room is clear." Morrison's voice gurgled as his lungs filled up with blood. "It's all right. The room is clear."

Kline looked into the room and saw Morrison lying on the floor, blood spreading around him as well. "Shit, I'll be right back." She holstered her weapon and went back into the kitchen area. "Keep the gun on this fucker," she said to Thompson as she looked around. Kline pushed the body of the man she had shot out of the way and spied a roll of duct tape on a cabinet. She grabbed it and tossed it to Bouncer. "Now, tape your legs to the chair," she instructed in Romanian.

After he had taped his ankles to the chair, she moved over to his side and taped the man's wrists to the arms of the chair. "He isn't going anywhere," she told Thompson. "Now go in and see if you can help out Morrison."

As Kline paced around in the main room pondering her next move, Thompson went to the storage room and knelt on the floor next to Morrison. He straightened out Morrison's body, pulling his legs out from underneath him. He took off his jacket, rolled it up and placed it underneath the back of Morrison's neck. Morrison looked up at Thompson with knowledge of his dire situation showing in his eyes. His left leg was twitching and there was a slight rattle in his chest as his lungs continued to fill.

"Sonofabitch," he grunted from the pain.

"Don't worry," said Thompson. "You're going to be all right."

Morrison smiled back and in a faint voice replied: "Nice try, Congressman." He winced again. "Was that you that made the kill in there?"

"Yeah," Thompson replied.

"I thought I told you to stay put."

"Sorry," replied Thompson. "I wanted to get in on the action."

"Aw, sonofabitch," said Morrison. "And I missed it. It was my gun, so I get half a notch. Right?"

"You know it," Thompson replied as he continued to kneel by Morrison's side. "I'll be right back," he said as and walked back out into the main room where Kline was taping Bouncer's fingers—all except each pinkie—to the arms of the chair. "You better come look at this," said Thompson. "Morrison is in bad shape."

Kline left the room, walked over to Morrison and knelt down low. "What's up, Shadow?"

"You know what's up, boss," replied Morrison. "I'm dying a slow death here."

"We'll get you help," interjected Thompson. "I've got the cell phone. We can get a chopper out here, can't we?"

"No," said Morrison. He looked at Kline. "No choppers. No help."

"You sure?" she asked.

"I'm not leaving here alive," he whispered. "You and I both know that. We can't have this mission leave this crap-hole of a house. Get it over with."

Kline looked at Thompson and pulled her gun from her holster.

"What the hell are you doing?" asked Thompson.

"I'm ending it," said Kline.

"You're going to kill him? But, we can get help."

"In your world, Congressman, people get help," Morrison whispered. "In our world, people die. It's over."

"He's already dead. He's got no chance," added Kline. "I'm making a foregone conclusion a reality. I'm going to put him out of his misery."

"You can't do that," replied Thompson.

"Why?" replied Kline. "Because you're here? This is what we do, Congressman. We kill people. That's our dirty little secret. We kill people. And you approve of it every time you vote us a new appropriation bill."

"This is fucked up."

"Listen to his lungs," said Kline. "He's dying. Even if we could call for a chopper, it's a twenty minute flight up here. He doesn't have twenty minutes. He's never going to make it." Thompson just stood there. "Get out of my way, Congressman Thompson. This is part of my job."

Kline walked across the room and lowered the gun at Morrison's head. "I'm sorry, Shadow," she said.

"*In coelo quies est*," Morrison replied in Latin.

Kline looked at Thompson, who still had not turned around following their conversation. Kline looked directly at her partner and pulled the trigger sending a single bullet through Morrison's head. The loud bang made Thompson leap. The man taped to the chair twitched against the tape restraining him to his chair.

Kline walked back into the kitchen where Bouncer was taped to the chair and pushed the gun against his temple. "Where is the boy?" she asked in Romanian.

"Kill me," Bouncer replied. "Kill me and you'll never know. Let me go and I will tell you."

"Ah, we're negotiating now," Kline replied.

"Yes, we're negotiating."

Kline looked around at Thompson. "He wants to negotiate. The sonofabitch kidnapped your staffer and his buddy shot my partner." She looked back at Bouncer. "And the sonofabitch wants to negotiate."

Kline lowered the gun and placed it on the table. Bouncer smiled.

"Okay, so we'll negotiate," said Kline in Romanian. Switching to English she spoke to Thompson, "Go find me a knife and some shears."

"What for?" replied Thompson.

"Negotiation."

"Negotiation?" asked Thompson. "I don't get it."

"We're going to negotiate… my style."

"What are you going to do?"

"Well, he's going to tell me where Josh is located and I'm going to let him keep his fingers," replied Kline.

"What?"

"He tells me everything I want to know," said Kline, "or I'm going to start cutting off his fingers."

"Torture?" asked Thompson. "You're going to torture him?"

"You call it torture," replied Kline. "I call it negotiation. I'm going to negotiate with him. I want information. He wants his fingers."

"I can't agree to this," said Thompson.

"What do you mean, you can't agree to this? You don't have a choice, Congressman. In fact, you don't even have a vote. This isn't the U.S. where there are laws and rules. This is Romania—there are no rules here."

"But…"

"We do this or Josh dies," said Kline in a matter-of-fact, but harsh tone. "Live with that because that's what we live with everyday. Sometimes we do things we don't want to do. Sometimes we do things that are not moral or pretty, but we save American lives. That's what you pay me to do."

"I don't know," said Thompson, shaking his head.

"Look, you can leave if you want," said Kline. "But I have been trained to find out where they have taken Josh. I know how to get the information and every minute we waste is another minute when Josh may die. Let me do my job and he might live." Kline looked squarely at Thompson, "With you or without you. This is going forward." His affirmative nod indicating that he would help was barely noticeable. "Good—now go find me some scissors, shears, a knife…anything sharp."

Thompson went to the kitchen cabinets and began looking through the drawers and cabinets. Kline turned her attention to Bouncer.

"Well, well, Comrade," said Kline in Romanian. "Let's start negotiating. Here's the rules. You give me something and I give you something. Understand?"

"Sure," said the man. "I tell you a clue about where the American boy is and you untape my leg."

"Something like that," replied Kline.

Thompson returned and put an assortment of knives, shears and scissors on the old wooden table. Kline looked over the tools, holding each one in her hand as she closely examined it. "Can't we just water board him or something?" asked Thompson.

"Don't be cliché," she replied. "Water boarding takes days, maybe weeks, to build up fear and fatigue. It's really not all that effective. If you want information quickly, cut off a finger or two."

"Jesus," said Thompson with revulsion and disgust in his voice.

"The biggest guy in the world will give up his own mom if you cut off both pinkies," said Kline as she picked up some shears. "Now, go behind him and hold his shoulders down."

"Won't the tape hold him down?" asked Thompson.

"Yeah," replied Kline. "It's just for effect."

Thompson walked behind the man and placed his hands on his shoulders. Kline switched back to Romanian.

"Okay, Comrade," said Kline. "Here's our first negotiation. You tell me who took the boy out of here and I'll give you one of your cigarettes."

"Noua," said Bouncer after only a moment of hesitation. "She's the General's daughter. She left here with the boy and another man early this morning."

Kline grabbed a pack of cigarettes from the table popped one into her mouth and lit it up with a wood match off the table. She took a couple of puffs to get it going and placed it in Bouncer's mouth. He took a couple of puffs before Kline removed it and placed it on a plate on the table.

"Now, see how easy that was?" Kline said in Romanian. Bouncer smiled in return.

"So, who are your friends?" Kline continued.

"The one in the other room is General Gheroghe Alexandro. You have killed a great man. He is the leader of the Communist Party in Romania. The one in the tie, he is

Abel Bogdan, a Member of the Romanian Parliament. The other one is a local supporter of the party. He is probably of no concern to you, but was a friend of mine." He paused and pondered his point of negotiation. "Now give me a shot of vodka. It's up in the cabinet. My throat is dry."

Kline nodded to Thompson to get the vodka and pour a shot. Thompson walked to the cabinet and found the vodka and a glass. His hand shook as he poured some of the clear liquid into the glass. Despite Thompson's urge to drink it himself, he went back and raised the glass to Bouncer's lips. Bouncer drank until it was gone.

"Good," said Kline. "Let's go to our next negotiation point. You tell me everything that you know about the boy and I'll let you keep your little finger."

Bouncer laughed. "You are a funny woman. This is how you want to negotiate?"

"You're right, you're right. I should not take your entire finger. Let's start with the top of your little finger…just above the first knuckle. Give me everything you know about the boy and I will let you keep the top part of your little finger."

"Let the boy die," Bouncer snarled.

"One more chance," said Kline. "The top of your little finger for the boy?"

Bouncer spit on Kline's pant leg in defiance. Kline smiled.

"Last chance, Comrade."

"I do not fear you, woman."

Kline looked at Thompson and spoke in English. "That's the problem here. Old Romanian males have been taught to disregard women. This dumb fucker doesn't think a woman can follow through on this. Hold his shoulders."

As Thompson pressed down on Bouncer's shoulders, Kline placed the shears on the man's first knuckle.

"Last chance…"

"Fuck you!"

Kline started to press the shears against the Bouncer's

skin and then stopped. Bouncer smiled at her hesitation. His smile indicated he thought Kline would not follow through on her threat. Then, in a swift movement of sudden violence, Kline snapped the shears closed. The smug look on Bouncer's face was replaced with pain. He let out a blood curdling scream. Thompson felt a chill go down his spine.

"You cut off my finger," he screamed. "You are crazy. You are crazy."

"No, I'm negotiating," Kline shouted directly into the man's ear. "I'm negotiating, and I'll let you keep the rest of this finger if you tell me where the boy is."

Bouncer screamed and wriggled back and forth, trying to escape his restraints.

"Hold him steady," Kline said as she took the shears and cut off Bouncer's finger at the second and then quickly the third knuckle. "The General is dead and you're giving up your fingers for his memory. Touching, but I really don't care. I'll keep doing this until you have no fingers and then I'll start on your toes."

Kline grabbed for Bouncer's other hand. He struggled to keep her from gaining control over it. "Motherfucker," Kline mumbled as she grabbed a knife from the table. She raised her arm and slammed the knife through Bouncer's hand and into the wood arm rest on the chair. Blood splattered from the vicious impact. Some hit Thompson in the face. "There. That will keep your hand steady."

Thompson's eyes grew wide and his stomach queasy. Kline picked up the shears and grabbed Bouncer's other pinkie. "Go ahead; lose them all for the memory of a fucking dead man."

"No, wait," screamed the man, looking at the blood gushing from the knife wound on one hand and his lost finger on the other. "I will tell you. I will tell you everything."

"Okay," said Kline. "Now we're negotiating."

"Please stop the bleeding on my finger."

"Tell me where the boy is."

"But my finger is bleeding."

Kline picked the shears back up and snapped the tip of the little finger off of Bouncer's left hand. He screamed in agony. "Noua took him. Noua took him."

"Noua," screamed Kline. "You already told me that. Who is Noua?"

"Noua is the General's daughter," he whimpered. "She took him."

"Is Noua the woman who kidnapped the boy?" asked Kline.

"Yes, yes. Noua did so at her father's command."

Kline looked at Thompson. He was pale, visibly shaking and sweating profusely.

"Where?" asked Kline. "Where did Noua take the boy?"

"I don't know," he cried.

Kline placed the shears on Bouncer's second knuckle and began to apply pressure. "No, no, no," he screamed. "Enough. I will tell you everything."

"Good," said Kline. "You're a shrewd negotiator." Changing languages, she told Thompson: "Let go of his shoulders, he's ready to talk."

"Noua took the boy to the city. They are going to attend the rally in Bucharest for President Krasterich."

"Why?" asked Kline. "Tell me why they are going to the city."

"Please do not cut off any more of my fingers," replied Bouncer.

"Then tell me why Noua took the boy to Bucharest."

"She's going to kill him at the rally," said Bouncer. "She's going to kill him in front of the Americans on the stage and then when everyone is looking at the boy, she is going to assassinate the President."

Kline relaxed her voice. As Bouncer continued to moan in pain, Kline explained to Thompson that the woman who had kidnapped Josh was taking him to the rally in Bucharest to kill him and President Krasterich.

"Please stop my bleeding," begged Bouncer. "I told you what you wanted. Please stop the bleeding."

Kline pulled her revolver, turned and shot Bouncer between the eyes. He fell back with such force that he flipped the chair onto the floor. "That will stop your bleeding."

"What the fuck?" shouted Thompson. "What did you do that for? He gave us what we wanted. Why did you kill him?"

"He knew what I looked like," replied Kline.

Thompson ran to the sink and threw up...once...twice...and then a third time. As Thompson wiped his mouth, Kline grabbed all the guns. "Take these," she said to Thompson, "and go get in the car."

When Thompson walked outside the cool damp air hit the cold sweat which was now covering his entire body. The sensation did not help his uncontrollable shaking.

Inside, Kline had gathered up some old newspaper and towels. She threw them on top of the stove and started the burners. When they were lit, she kicked over the table and chairs and threw the lit rags under them. The dry wood caught fire quickly. She grabbed more towels and set fire to them before placing them against a wood wall of the house. She opened all the windows to feed the fire and met Thompson outside.

"I don't think I want to know what you just did," said Thompson as he sniffed smoke in the air.

"There can't be any evidence. In this country there won't be any autopsy. No one will ever look at burnt corpses for bullet holes or missing fingers. Let's get out of here."

As they started to get into the car Thompson stopped and leaned over to throw up again. The small wooden structure was quickly being engulfed in flames. Thompson wiped his mouth again and he stared at the swift progress of the fire.

"Get in," said Kline.

Thompson stood still, looking at the flames rising in front of him.

"Get in, Congressman. We've got to haul ass back to Bucharest."

Chapter 43

Thompson leaned his head against the door of the car and closed his eyes. He wished he had retrieved his jacket from underneath Morris' head before they left the house. The rough bumps of the narrow mountain road caused his head to bounce against the car door window. If he had his jacket maybe he could fall asleep.

With sleep, maybe he could forget the horrors of the day. Maybe he could forget his sense of impending doom for his young friend, Josh. Maybe he could sleep and it would all go away.

When he did open his eyes Thompson stared blankly at the beautiful countryside. The streams, fed from the majestic snow capped mountains, were a blur. He looked at them, but he had no focus.

With his eyes either opened or closed all he could envision was a flaming house that contained the burning corpses of several men, one of whom he had killed and another whom he had helped to torture.

Somewhere between Bucharest and the mountains was Josh. He did not know what to do, so Thompson closed his eyes and prayed. *Lord, I know that I do not do this often enough, but I need you right now. Forgive me. God please forgive me for what I did back there. I need your guidance and strength to help find Josh. His eyes started to tear up. He's just a young man, Lord. Please let me find him alive. If someone must die, let it be me. For what I did back in the mountains, take me, but let Josh live.*

As Kline drove the car over the bumpy road she recognized that Thompson's quiet brooding was hiding some serious thoughts. She thought she would break the ice. "It got pretty crazy back there."

Thompson remained silent.

"Look, Congressman," said Kline with true empathy in her voice. "I don't expect you to understand what happened back there."

"I'm trying," said Thompson. "I'm trying."

"Don't," replied Kline. "Trying to understand is going to give you a reality you don't want to know about."

"Maybe I do. Maybe I need to."

"No, you don't," replied Kline. "No one really wants to know what we do. You vote, but you don't know the implications of those votes. You don't want to know."

"Not if it's all like what just happened," said Thompson.

"It isn't always like that," replied Kline. "Covert doesn't always mean blood and guts."

"But it did this time."

"Hell, Congressman, it does a lot of times," said Kline. "But that's part of the game I'm in."

"Game? This is all a game to you?" asked Thompson.

"Yeah," replied Kline. "It's a game. We know the rules and so do they. Do you think that Alexandro never killed anyone? I did the research. He was a real rat bastard. He is probably responsible for the deaths of more men and women than anyone who was at the Securitate. We did the world a favor today."

"When I was in high school," said Thompson, still staring out the window, "there was this kid that everyone else in the school picked on. Even the teachers treated him like dirt. I stood up for him one day…actually got into an argument with a teacher who was making fun of him in front of the whole class."

"What happened?"

"I got suspended," said Thompson. "My parents were pissed. So I showed up at the next school board meeting to appeal my suspension. I made my case and won. That was the day I knew that I wanted to be a lawyer. The next year, the class elected me to be President. They said they wanted someone with the balls to stand up to the school board and principal."

"And, from all of that, you learned that you wanted to be a Congressman," injected Kline.

"No," he replied. "From that I learned that I always wanted to be on the side of the good guys. I wanted to help people who couldn't stand up for themselves. I did what I was supposed to do. I went to school, got involved in politics and ran for office as a way to help. Today wasn't what I signed up for. Today was way beyond the pale."

"Congressman," said Kline, "you're far too experienced to sound that naïve."

"I'm not," replied Thompson. "Really I'm not. When I was younger, I spent a lot of time helping on foreign campaigns. I spent my vacation time in a lot of dumps giving seminars on grassroots organization. I saw some serious shit back then."

"Yeah?" asked Kline. "Like what?"

"This one time," said Thompson. "Griff and I were working a campaign in the Caribbean."

"Caribbean?" said Kline. "Sounds like tough duty."

"It really was. In fact, it was much tougher than you might expect. I'm working every day at the headquarters for the free market party. They were the opposition to the ruling party. I showed up at the office one morning and the place is surrounded by police. I go inside and one of my candidates was lying on the floor, dead." Thompson paused. "He had his testicles cut off and had bled to death on the floor."

"Sounds pretty gruesome."

"Damn gruesome," replied Thompson. "I started questioning why I was doing what I was doing. I remember thinking that I did what I did to beat the bad guys. It never dawned on me that I might be the bad guy someday. Today I'm just not sure whose side I'm on."

"Sometimes," said Kline, "it's hard to discern the good guys from the bad guys. In Europe, the farther east you go, the more blurry the line becomes. People don't always wear white hats or black hats. Sometimes they wear gray ones."

Thompson looked out the window and contemplated Kline's words. "When we were over here in the 90s, we had the white hats on."

"Do you think so?" said Kline, reflecting on the mission she had in Romania years prior. The hit she executed was ordered precisely because the fall of Communism in Romania had led to a robust drug trade in the country. A market economy had meant free trade, both legal and illegal. Still, she wasn't going to bring that up with Thompson on this ride.

"Yeah," said Thompson. "Do you know how many twenty-year-olds there are over here named Reagan?"

"A bundle," replied Kline. "The parents of those kids loved Reagan and the freedom he brought to them. But how many of them today even know the legacy of their namesake? Not many, I bet. Do you know why they have such low unemployment numbers here?"

"No," replied Thompson. "Why?"

"It's because all of those little twenty-year-old 'Angels of Democracy' are leaving Romania in record numbers. They don't want what you gave them. You gave them free enterprise and their leaders use it to launder drug cartel money through legal casinos."

Despite Kline's reassurances to the contrary, Thompson felt that his moral compass had lost true north for the first time in his life.

"So what happens now?" asked Thompson. "Will there be a file somewhere that tells about what happened?"

"No, you're clear," replied Kline. "Covert doesn't put stuff in writing."

"I didn't mean that," said Thompson. "I'm not worried about covering my own ass."

"I know what you meant and I'm going one step further and telling you not to worry about anyone knowing what happened back there."

"So how do we find Josh?" asked Thompson. "They've probably got more than a hundred thousand people coming to the rally. Foreign rallies are huge social events. There will be people coming in from all over the country."

"I don't know yet, but we've got two things in our favor. They don't know that Alexandro is dead and we know they're coming."

Chapter 44

"So, where did you go to law school, Mr. Bradley?"

"University of Kentucky," replied The Fat Man to the question from Presidential Chief of Staff, Benny Vesper. The plane flight had been relatively quiet thus far. Other than acknowledging a very basic introduction by Leo Argo at the airport, Vesper had not spoken more than a few words since the flight had begun. The words about law school seemed like a welcome break to the uneasy silence.

"How nice," he smugly replied. "I'm sure that prepared you well for a career practicing law in the Commonwealth."

"I understand that Mr. Bradley finished first in his class at UK," added Argo, as if to try and add credibility to The Fat Man in Vesper's eyes.

"How about you, Mr. Vesper?" interjected The Fat Man. "Didn't I read somewhere that you were a lawyer?"

"Yes, I am, Mr. Bradley," replied Vesper. "I went to Yale."

I'm sure that prepared you well for your career as an asshole, Argo thought to himself.

"Really," replied The Fat Man. "I was offered a full trip there, but decided to stay home."

Nice play, fat boy, thought Argo.

"Really?" replied Vesper. "Well, I never really wanted a day-to-day law practice. Yale suited me well for what I've done."

"And you've sure done a lot," said The Fat Man, hoping a little bit of suck up would endear him to the Chief of Staff. "You've been at the side of several presidents."

"Yes, I have," replied Vesper smiling at The Fat Man's acknowledgment. "It's been a fun career."

"I can only imagine," said The Fat Man. "Any one of them a favorite over the other?"

"Mocker," replied Vesper with a smile. "The current President is always my favorite President."

"Good call," replied the Fat Man. Feeling that he had established some credibility with Vesper, The Fat Man changed directions. "So do you mind if I ask you a question, Mr. Vesper?"

"Sure. Ask away. I may not answer you. But feel free to ask."

"My question is real basic," said The Fat Man. "I'm curious. Why are you here?"

"Where?"

"Here … on this plane … right here, right now. You're Chief of Staff to the President of the United States. Don't you have more important things to do than head to the Presidential elections in Romania with some ancient American historical relic?"

"I'm sorry, Mr. Bradley, but my role in Romania is strictly classified," replied Vesper. "I warned you that I might not answer your question."

"All righty then," replied The Fat Man. "I'll change directions. What about me? What the hell am I doing here?"

"Ask Agent Argo," replied Vesper. "I didn't particularly want you on this flight."

"I requested clearance for you, Joe," replied Argo.

"You, Leo?"

"Yeah, I can't tell you much, but we're headed over to Romania on an assignment related to your friend Josh Barkman."

"You think you know who has Josh?"

"I can't tell you that, but our mission involves the mace," replied Argo.

"Our mace," replied The Fat Man. "The one we found?"

"Yeah," said Argo. "Anyway, you know more about the mace than anyone alive. We may need you."

"Well, if it will help find Josh, I'm all in," replied The Fat Man. "But, I have to warn you, I don't have my passport with me. When we started out we were only going to be in New York for a day or so. I don't have much in my bags."

"We'll have special diplomatic papers waiting for you at the airport," said Argo.

"And clothes?"

"You'll have full access to someone at the American Embassy in Romania," Vesper interjected. "They'll help you get some clothes."

"Yeah," said Argo. "The government is paying for everything. Go out and get some nice clothes. If you want to, get something tailor-made."

"What?" replied The Fat Man, looking down at his belly. "The gypsy tent makers aren't already busy enough?"

Chapter 45

Michael Griffith stared out the window at the setting of the evening sun. It was just touching the rooftops on the opposite side of the square from Thompson's room at the embassy.

After Ann had explained Thompson's mission into the Carpathian Mountains, Griffith had gone down to the restaurant at the embassy to retrieve a second bottle of bourbon. It was not Maker's Mark, but at this point his taste buds were not being picky. When he returned to Thompson's room, he poured himself yet another tall glass without ice. Unlike his normal routine, he found himself unable to savor the taste.

The view out the window was more than simply a focal point for Griffith to become lost in his thoughts. He stared at everything in his field of vision and nothing, all at the same time. Michael Griffith was lost ... period. The liquor and view were just outlets to numb his consciousness.

Griffith was not just bothered by Thompson's stinging indictment regarding his role in the fate of Josh Barkman. He had known that was coming as he headed into the meeting. In fact, he had felt that pain coming as soon as he had learned that Josh had gone missing. Josh was gone and Griffith felt to blame. Nothing Thompson could have said would have made him feel any more responsible for Josh's fate. Of course, Thompson had done nothing of the sort—instead, he had piled on the guilt.

The sting Griffith was feeling stemmed, in part, from the self-realization which had followed Thompson's condemnation of Griffith's own character. Griffith spent the last 24 hours realizing he had indeed built a cowboy image for himself in the world of politics. The image worked for his clients and the media, but he was starting to wonder if it worked for him.

Now, with Josh missing and Griffith feeling to blame, he was forced to examine his cowboy image in light of its impact on himself and politics. Suddenly, and for maybe the first time, he realized the image he had created for himself was not the guy he was or, more important, had wanted to become.

"Look at that scene," Griffith mumbled to himself. He took a gulp of bourbon while gazing out the window, looking at a young couple playing with their kids.

The scene particularly disturbed Griffith because over the last 24 hours, Griffith had come to realize that when he came to Romania back in 1990, he had believed. His belief back then was not like the wide-eyed Pollyanna belief of Thompson, who felt that democracy brought streets paved with gold. But Griffith did believe that bringing free elections to people meant freedom. He believed the casting of one simple vote could allow the individual to feel empowered. He worked elections in his youth because he believed he could teach people how to win elections with an electorate who felt empowered.

Griffith came to the painful realization he was in Romania this time, not for some basic core belief, as in years gone past, but for money. He had no idea who Krasterich was or whether his presidency was good for the couple in the park. He only knew that Krasterich had the money necessary to pay his fee.

"Am I here because I believe," he mumbled as he took another drink of bourbon, "or am I here because I can convince Krasterich that I believe?"

Griffith paused as he contemplated his answer. "Fuck, I was afraid that was the answer." He took another drink and continued to stare, so wrapped up in his own self-reflective pity he had not heard Ann let Sue into the suite.

Ann nodded to the window. "He's been there over an

hour, just staring out," she whispered. "Staring out and drinking bourbon."

"Yorgi's frantic," replied Sue softly. "He's been looking all over the place for Michael. The President's rally is tomorrow and Krasterich wants to practice his speech in front of his campaign consultant. Unfortunately, no one seems to know where the consultant is right now."

"Lots of luck getting him out of here," said Ann. "He's been drinking pretty heavily."

When Sue walked up along side of him, Griffith barely acknowledged her presence. Both avoided eye contact and stared out the window.

Sue finally broke the silence. "What ya thinkin' 'bout?"

"Dinner the other night," replied Griff.

"Really?"

"Yeah, it was good," replied Griffith.

"Really?" Sue repeated.

"In fact, it was great."

"You've been here for an hour drinking and looking out the window and thinking about dinner?" asked Sue.

"Yeah. I was thinking how nice it would be to take the Congressman to that same place tonight for dinner. When we were here in 1990, the food was so damn bad. I've been thinking how much fun it would be to take him out for a good meal. It would be symbolic of the change we made here when we were kids."

Sue gently grabbed Griffith's hand and quietly stared out the window with him. "So, where is the Congressman?" she finally asked.

"I can't tell you."

"Do you want to take a walk around that park?"

"No, I can't go out there with those people in the park. I've let them down."

Sue looked over at Ann for guidance as to what that comment meant. Ann simply shook her head at Griffith's ramble. She turned her attention back to Griffith.

"President Krasterich would like to see you today," said Sue.

"Fuck him," replied Griffith.

"All right," Sue responded. "So, what do you want to do?"

"I want to stand by this window until my friend walks through that door."

Chapter 46

The drive back from Alexandro's now charred house had been surreal for Thompson. As they drove, he looked out the car windows as the mountains changed colors with the dramatic contrasts of a child's paint-by-numbers picture. But Thompson's personal situation had become more than a youngster's attempt to stay within the lines. Thompson had gone way outside the lines and the internal moral struggle he was experiencing was as dramatic as the changes in colors on the mountains.

Thompson had witnessed more than he had ever dreamed in his worst nightmare. More significantly, he had participated. He had killed a man.

Although he was aware that he and Kline had spoken during the drive, Thompson could not recall the exact substance of their conversation.

As the view out of his window changed from mountains to countryside, to suburban, to urban, Thompson's viewpoint had switched as well. When he saw the skyline of Bucharest in the distance, he felt compelled to utter words.

"So what do I tell folks when we get back?" asked Thompson, hoping that he had not already asked the question previously during the drive.

"About what?" replied Kline.

"What do you mean, about what? Jesus Christ. Don't do this to me."

"Nothing happened today, Congressman," said Kline. "We went to the mountains. We found the house. And by the time we got there, everyone was already gone. We found some evidence they are going to show up at the Krasterich rally, but we saw no one."

Thompson looked out the window for about a mile or so. "What about Morrison? When we left this morning, Morrison was with us. We've come back without him."

"Mark Morrison got called back to America. We dropped him off at the airport on the way in."

"God, I don't know how you do this and sleep at night," said Thompson.

"We say the same thing at the CIA every time you vote on the Hill," replied Kline.

"Yeah, but..."

"Knock it off, Congressman. You wanted in on the mission. You threatened to call the Chairman of the Joint Committee. Now, you are living with the consequences of your actions. We keep everything that happened today to ourselves. We don't tell a soul. You can't even tell your wife."

"But I've got to tell Ann."

"Not a fucking soul, Congressman. You aren't getting this. Alexandro was the head of the Communist Party in Romania. I know there isn't supposed to be any Communist Party here, but there is ... well was ... a party out there. They had even set up a relationship with an existing Member of the Parliament. We killed them both. Hell, we killed everyone in the party except some crazy broad who is running around somewhere in the city with Josh.

"If there was a Communist Party then they had direct access to the Kremlin," she continued. "Do you want the Kremlin to find out that some piddly-ass Congressman from Kentucky and some CIA agent eliminated their entire presence here?"

"I never thought about that."

"Well, you better fucking think about it. We're talking international incident here."

Chapter 47

As unpleasant as the memories were, Josh knew exactly where he was when the car came to a halt. He, Noua and Honeycat were about a block away from the place where he had been thrown into the trunk of a car. A strange *déjà vu* shook his body, as he relived those memories in the actual location of where they had been seared into the core of his soul.

Noua stopped the car just outside the city to allow Honeycat to drive the car for the remainder of the trip into Bucharest. Now they were in town, Noua was talking constantly to Honeycat in Romanian. Josh hoped it was just mindless chatter about traffic and directions, but he understood that, more likely than not, their conversation had a lot to do with his fate.

"What is our plan for tomorrow?" asked Honeycat in Romanian.

"I will go to the rally with the American boy," replied Noua. "I will get him within eyesight of the main stage. An American singer with Romanian heritage will be singing songs."

"An American singer?" asked Honeycat.

"Yes," replied Noua. "Do you really think that the idiot Krasterich would be able to draw 100,000 people on his own? The people are coming to hear the singer. They do not care about Krasterich. They only know there is a singer and free food."

"True," replied Honeycat.

"When he finishes his last song, I will be near the front of the stage with the boy. I will get the attention of the President and the Americans. When I have their attention, I will put a bullet in the boy's head."

"But, they will see you," said Honeycat. "You will surely be killed."

"Martyred," replied Noua, "not killed. After I kill the boy, I will put the gun to my own head. I shall be martyred in the name of the Communist party and all we represent. I will die, but my name will live forever."

"And what is my role?" asked Honeycat.

"You will be in eyesight of us at all times," Noua said. "When I shoot the boy and myself you take aim on the President and kill him. All eyes will be on me. If you are on the side of the stage by the President it will be easy. You should be able to escape unharmed."

"Why? Why should you die and I live?"

"When the act is done," Noua said, "return to the mountains. Tell my father what has happened. Tell him to be proud of the sacrifice made by his daughter and that what I have done was done in his name. This selfless act will rally our party. From the blood that pours from my dead body the Communist Party will rise again in our country."

As they spoke, Honeycat had circled the car around one particular block several times. It was far enough away from the InterContinental Hotel that the new buildings of the rebuilt city had morphed into the dilapidated row houses and deteriorated apartment buildings more commonly seen across Eastern Europe. The buildings looked acceptable and quaint from afar, but as you looked at them more closely you knew they bore the internal scars of years of misuse and neglect.

Honeycat was parallel parking the car on a side street when Noua finally spoke to Josh in English. "Well, Mr. America's Brain, we're here," she said. "Do you recognize this place?"

"Yes, I do," replied Josh.

"Good," said Noua. "You tried to take advantage of me at my apartment, remember? Well, I really do have an apartment here. We are going there for the night."

"All right," Josh replied.

"Just remember, when we get out of this car, don't try anything out of the ordinary. I will have my gun aimed at you at all times. If you try to escape, I will kill you." Noua Alexandro made her point clear by letting Josh see the gun. "I have killed men before, and I have no problem with putting a bullet into your head if you try to escape."

"Understood," replied Josh as he surveyed the surroundings, looking for an opportunity to escape. "You'll get no problems out of me."

Chapter 48

When Ann heard a key in the door to her room, she jumped up from her chair and looked to the door in distressed anticipation of who would be holding the key on the other side. When the door swung open, revealing the deflated frame of her husband, Ann made a sound that varied somewhere between a squeal and a gasp. She ran across the room and literally jumped into Thompson's arms, wrapping her legs around him in a protective cocoon of spousal fortification.

Ann hung tight to Thompson's body for what seemed like a loving eternity. Suddenly, she realized there were others in the room and loosed the buttressed grip she had on her husband. She kissed him before turning to the others in the room. "Sorry," she said.

"You're allowed, Annie," Griffith replied. "Feel free to act like we're not here."

"Hey, Griff," said Thompson. "You been here long?"

"All freakin' day, pal," Griffith's words slurred slightly from all the alcohol he had consumed.

Thompson went over to Griffith, who met his advance with a warm embrace. "I'm sorry," Thompson whispered in his ear. "I was wrong to be so hard on you yesterday."

"No," Griffith whispered back in Thompson's ear. "You may be more right than you've ever been in your life. We'll work it out later."

"Where's Josh?" asked Ann, waiting for the two friends to separate their clinch.

"We found the place where he was being kept," said Kline. "Unfortunately, the bad guys were gone by the time we got there."

"Yeah," inserted Thompson. "We must have just missed them."

Ann looked around the room. She saw Kline, but suddenly realized that Morrison was missing. "Where's your partner? Where's Mark?"

"Called home," said Thompson, jumping on top of Kline's reply. "Mark had a new assignment and he had to rush home. We dropped him off at the airport on the way in." After speaking, Thompson looked at Kline in order to confirm the pact that they had agreed to during the car drive home.

Ann looked at Thompson. She saw the quick exchange of glances between her husband and Kline. Instinctively, she knew that he was lying. She would question his statement, but not now ... not in front of everyone else. There would come a time. Ann was a political spouse—she would know when.

"We've got a lead on Josh," said Kline. "We know that the kidnappers are going to bring him tomorrow to the Krasterich rally."

"The rally?" said Sue. "There's going to be a ton of people there."

"That's okay," said Griffith. "We've narrowed it down from twenty-two million people to a couple of hundred thousand. I'm good with that. It's a start."

"So, what's our plan?" asked Ann.

"Right now, the plan for you and the Congressman is to get some sleep," replied Kline. "We've had a pretty exhausting day and I'll need both of you fresh tomorrow. Me, I've got some homework to do. I want to map out a strategy. Then I want to see everybody here in the conference room at 0700 sharp."

Chapter 49

Once they parked the car, Honeycat cut the tape from Josh's ankles before escorting him up the rickety wooden stairs of the worn building to Noua's small flat. The decaying residence had an efficiency kitchen that attached to the living room and one bedroom with two single cots against the wall. The living room had a couple of pieces of old furniture covered in old sheets. There was one bathroom.

Josh expected to be bound again as soon as they entered the room but, after a conversation between Noua and Honeycat, Noua informed Josh she was going to allow him to shower and shave before they tied him up for the night. Josh couldn't help but notice that somehow Noua's attitude towards him had changed in the drive from the mountains to the city.

Having not bathed since he had been kidnapped, even the thought of a shower sent a shiver of anticipation down Josh's back. Inasmuch as there was no hot water coming from the shower head, the actual shower itself sent real shivers through Josh's entire body. Despite the cold water, he took a long time scrubbing the dirt and grime from his frame.

As Josh stepped from the shower, he was startled to find Honeycat sitting in a chair in the doorway carefully watching him as he moved around the bathroom. Josh pointed to the narrow window in the room. "What's wrong, Honeycat," Josh had said, "afraid I'm going to sneak out that window?"

Honeycat, having no idea what Josh had said, simply smiled. Josh did not let Honeycat's presence deter the enjoyment of his few minutes of unbound freedom. With Honeycat looking on at Josh's naked body, Josh had shaved with soap and a disposable razor as if he was the only person in the room. When Josh had finished, Honeycat tossed him some new underwear and a t-shirt.

"You've got to be kidding me, Honeycat," Josh said. "This is yours, right? This stuff is about two sizes too big for me."

"It is clean," Noua shouted from the other room. "Put it on."

Josh looked at the underwear he had been wearing since his whole ordeal had began and contemplated the disgusting thought of putting it back on. Unable to bear that thought, he tossed the old underwear and undershirt in the wastebasket.

When Josh emerged from the bathroom, clad in the oversized underwear, the door to the bedroom was closed and Noua was nowhere to be seen. Honeycat motioned Josh to lie on the floor and bound his ankles in plastic ties. He then placed a pair of handcuffs around the ties and connected the other end of the handcuffs to the metal apparatus of an old beat up recliner chair.

If Josh was going to escape, he would have to take the recliner with him. Honeycat went to the couch and turned on a small television set that showed a picture in some shade of yellow/green. Honeycat placed the gun on a table and stared at the television.

Maybe it was the fact that Josh had been living captive in little more than a mountain shack for days, or it could have been the physical exhaustion. Whatever it was, after being bound, Josh fell fast asleep. He was sleeping as deeply as he had in days when he was awakened. The deep level of his sleep was aroused by what he initially thought was nothing more than an erotic wet dream.

When Josh looked up, Noua was sitting next to him naked. The light from the moon outside the window was shining on her near perfect body. Her nipples were so erect that the light cast shadows of them across her breasts. The fly on Josh's boxers had been opened. The feeling he thought he was having in a dream turned out to be Noua's oiled hand slowly masturbating him.

With a start, Josh tried to sit up but the ankle restraints bound to the chair kept him from doing so. As Josh struggled to sit up Noua shoved him back down to the floor before continuing her slow deliberate assault on his manhood. “Be still,” she whispered, “or you’ll wake my friend in the next room.”

Once he had grown to full hardness in her hand, Noua climbed on top of Josh and lowered her body to his, fusing their two bodies into one sexual unit. “Back in my father’s home, I heard what you said. They couldn’t understand you, but I was in the next room. I heard what you said. Do you really think I’m beautiful?”

“Yes,” was all that Josh could say as Noua began to slowly rise and fall on top of him in a deliberate ballet of sexual pleasure. As much as he tried to resist, Josh stopped his struggle and began enjoying Noua’s movements.

Josh and Noua simultaneously exploded in personal gratification. With sweat dripping down her subtle breasts, she looked down at Josh.

“I don’t understand,” he whispered.

“I didn’t expect that you would,” she replied. “This is all about something more important than you could ever understand.”

“But…”

“Tomorrow you will understand,” Noua said as she gathered up her clothes and went to the bathroom to shower.

When Noua emerged from the bathroom, she went to the bedroom. Honeycat was awake. “I heard what happened out there,” he said. “Why did you do it? Why did you fuck the American?”

“Because, now, tomorrow he will trust me,” Noua replied. “Americans are like that when they have sex with a woman. They are weak to a woman’s ways. He will not try to escape.”

“What should I tell your father about your actions tonight?”

“Tell him the boy and I became one. When I killed him, I also had to kill myself.”

Chapter 50

Thompson struggled to sleep as thoughts of the hell that had defined his day ran through his head. The *chargé d'affair* had brought him some sleeping pills which, despite Ann's protest to the contrary, he washed down with bourbon. Despite the combination of chemicals and booze, Thompson stared at the walls and ceiling.

It wasn't for lack of trying to sleep. Each time Thompson tried to close his eyes, he would repeat the day's sequence of events over and over in his head. The drive up and back ... Morrison's final words gurgled to him as blood filled his lungs ... Kline's methodical torture ... it all rattled around in Thompson's brain, blocking sleep. When he had been able to close his eyes, he seemed to count gun shots and missing fingers like sheep jumping over a fence.

Exhaustion finally had its way with him and sleep crept into Thompson's head.

Even in his dreams, Thompson continued to relive the events of the day in a slow motion sequence of unstoppable frames. During each step towards Alexandro's house, he tried to stop his own progress. His body yelled at his nocturnal likeness to stop, but in this dream he had no control over his own actions.

Thompson watched as if from outside of his own body as Morrison fell through the window. His own approach to the house continued despite inner demons screaming for him to stop. When he got to the window of Alexandro's house, Thompson felt a gun in his hand. He looked inside the rundown home. The men he had seen earlier in the day were there, flames rising from their bodies.

Again and again in slow motion, Thompson lifted the gun and squared his shoulders, taking aim at the man standing in the center of the room. It took all of his strength to pull the trigger. But instead of firing, blood dripped out the end of the barrel.

The man whom Thompson was trying to kill in his dream turned and looked at Thompson. Instead of being one of the Romanian rebels who had been killed, it was Josh. He looked at Thompson, smiled and pointed a gun at Thompson's face.

At the sound of the explosion of the gun, Thompson yelled out loud "NO" as he awoke in a cold sweat.

Chapter 51

"Wheels down, gentlemen," said the pilot over the intercom as the plane carrying The Fat Man, Argo and Vesper touched down for a fuel stop at Charles De Galle Airport in Paris. "We'll have about a four-hour layover as we fuel up and get clearance from France into Romania. While we are on the ground, you will have access to the private aviation terminal, but you will not be allowed to clear security."

The pilot paused for a moment and then added: "Mr. Vesper, as soon as we're at the terminal, we'll set up a secure line for you to the White House."

Vesper leaned forward in his leather chair and spoke to his traveling companions. "It's early, but I've arranged for some staff from the embassy in Paris to drop by and bring you some sundries and food. Mr. Bradley, they've found some larger-sized clothes that should hold you over until you are able to do some shopping in Bucharest. You'll be able to change out of the Yankees uniform."

"Thank you," replied The Fat Man. "I hope they're not European cut."

Vesper smiled, a big expression of emotion for a man who rarely laughed. "We'll make sure we get you taken care of."

"Take your luggage into the terminal," added Argo. "I've been here before. The private aviation terminal has showers for travelers to use. I don't know about you, but a nice hot shower sounds pretty good right now."

"And I don't mean to be rude, but once the secure line is set up, I'll need to be alone," Vesper said. "Even the pilot will have to get off the plane."

"I understand," said The Fat Man. "Tell President Mocker I said 'howdy.'"

"I'm sure he'll be impressed," replied Argo.

"You don't know that," replied The Fat Man. "I sent him fifty bucks in the last election. I'm sure he remembers that."

"Gentlemen, we're at the terminal," came the announcement from the pilot. "Feel free to move about."

"You're all set, Mr. Vesper," said the pilot. "The White House operator is locating the President right now."

"Thanks, Colonel," replied Vesper.

"Let me get out of here and secure the door," replied the young pilot as he put his military jacket on. "When you're done, hit the cancel button. That'll terminate the secure line."

"Got it."

"I'll be in the terminal getting a shave and a shower, if you need me."

Vesper put the headset over his ears and adjusted the mouthpiece to hang just in front of him. After a minute or so, Vesper heard President Mocker's voice over the line: "Benny, ya there?"

"Yes, Mr. President," replied Vesper. "I'm here. We're in Paris for a couple of hours while we get final clearance into Romania."

"How was the flight?" asked Mocker.

"Good," replied Vesper. "We had some weather as we hit the European mainland. It got a little bumpy. But it was no big deal."

"So how are your traveling companions?" Mocker said, asking the first question for which he was really interested in getting an answer.

"The director was right about Argo," said Vesper. "He's a good agent. He's definitely a 'by-the-book' kind of guy. But I think he'll understand his role when we get to Bucharest."

"How is the civilian? What's his name, Bradley?"

"Smart guy," Vesper replied. "He's a big-fish litigator at some small-pond law firm in Kentucky. He was Congressman Thompson's law partner before Thompson got elected."

"Is Bradley politically astute?"

"Well, he gave you a contribution in your first campaign."

"Okay, he's smart," said the President. "But will he understand what we're doing over there?"

"He'll question it," said Vesper. "That's for certain. Still, he seems like one of those patriotic types who'll do whatever his President asks of him."

"Good. Tell him that his President appreciates his service to the country."

"Have you spoken to the Kremlin yet?" Vesper asked.

"Yeah," said Mocker. "I spoke to them last night. They were more than glad to agree to the new deal. They didn't trust their rebel contacts up in the mountains. They were more than willing to cut them loose."

"Dumb bastards," said Vesper. "They're sitting in the mountains right now thinking the Russians are on their side." Vesper smiled at the thought and paused. "Do I have a contact in Bucharest yet?"

"Yes."

"Who is it?"

"I don't know," said Mocker. "They wouldn't tell me a name. When you land, go straight to the Presidential Palace. Krasterich is having a rally out on the lawn today. Go straight to the east gate. Apparently, it's right next to the Palace. Someone will approach you once you're at the gate."

"Got it."

"And, Benny…"

"Yes, Mr. President."

"This deal is important. If you pull this off, things stabilize. My second term is a sure thing."

"I understand, Mr. President."

Argo stood at the sink in the men's locker room. With nothing but a towel around his waist, he lathered up his face before dipping his razor into the hot water. Steam was pouring out of the shower as The Fat Man let hot water pour down on his head.

"Hey, Leo," asked The Fat Man, "is the locker room still empty except for you and me?"

"Yeah," said Argo. "I can't expect they get much traffic in here at this hour of the morning."

"You're probably right," The Fat Man replied. "Since we're in here alone, tell me what you know about Vesper."

"He's worked for several administrations and has a pretty good reputation around D.C.," Argo replied.

"Hey, Leo. Are you gay?"

"What? No."

"I didn't think so."

"Why the hell did you ask me that?"

"Because you're doing a real bad job at jackin' me off right now," The Fat Man said. "You get me on a plane to Romania and you're giving me a public affairs prepared response when I ask you about Vesper. I mean, I give you the historical discovery of the century and you're going to…"

"Calm down, Joe," replied Argo. "All right, all right, I'll give you the skinny on Vesper."

"And don't use the word skinny with a fat man."

Argo smiled at The Fat Man's rant as he ran the razor blade over his face. "Vesper is a big deal with the President. They all seem to want him somewhere in their administrations. Some people seem to think that an incoming president wants Vesper for his institutional knowledge. Others think that he knows so much about the presidents themselves they're afraid of him. They'd rather have Vesper with them than against them."

"What do you think, Leo?"

"He's smart," said Argo. "There's no denying that."

"But..."

"But, personally, I don't trust him. Hell, no one at the Bureau trusts him. We do what he says because he's acting with the authority of the President. Between you and me, I think he believes he's better than the President. He likes to give people the impression that he actually gives orders to the President instead of the other way around."

"So, what are we doing on a plane to Romania with Benny Vesper and the mace?"

"Truthfully, Joe," replied Argo, "I have no earthly idea."

"Okay. Then who do you think is giving the orders?"

"If I knew the answer to that one, Joe, I'd be working at the White House."

Chapter 52

Jane Kline had a very busy ten hours. After leaving the embassy and the tearful reunion between Thompson and his wife, she contacted the Company to inform them the employment of Mark Morrison had been terminated. As always, there were no questions asked or reports demanded. Shadow Six was now, just as his code name had implied, no more than an electronic file that needed to be washed from the Company's computer mainframe.

After the transmittal of Morrison's fate, Kline spent the remainder of the evening reviewing schematics and photographs of the grounds around Krasterich's Presidential Palace where the rally was going to take place. She knew that if someone wanted to kill the President they would have to be close to the stage. Therefore, as soon as she left Thompson's room, she requested that the security personnel in charge of the rally divide the grounds into quadrants with fences and sawhorse barricades. Supporters headed to each section would have to go through separate gates. The east gate was going to be the only gate where anyone who wanted to be close to the main stage and the President could go to gain entrance.

The mission had been slightly complicated by the fact that Kline did not share her knowledge of the attempted assassination plot with Romanian officials. She noted that when she spoke with the portly Chief of Police, he was skittish. His force was already taking numerous precautions to assure Krasterich's safety. She knew if she conveyed the actual threat, the rally might be cancelled. So Kline had convinced the Chief it was standard operating procedure for whenever a United States official attended a foreign event. If the President wanted

Congressman Thompson and the other American observers to attend the speech, this would have to be the setup. Fearing that no Americans being on stage with Krasterich would be blamed on him, the Chief complied with Kline's demands.

Once the Chief agreed to her plans, Kline began reviewing a map of the area to determine where to place people. The area would be small enough that, from any of several locations, Josh could be spotted and extricated long before the President's arrival on stage.

Once her plan was devised, she got a couple of hours of sleep before getting dressed, downing a couple of hits of speed and heading downstairs for a meeting with the people who had gathered in Thompson's room the night before.

Kline was pouring coffee into a cup emblazoned with the seal of the United States Department of State, with the words "Romania Desk" underneath, when Richard and Ann Thompson walked into the embassy's conference room.

"You look tired, Congressman," said Kline. She offered the cup of coffee she was pouring to Ann as if she had been intending the first cup for her all along.

"I didn't sleep very well last night," Thompson responded.

"He kept yelling out in his sleep," interjected Ann.

"Well, here then," Kline said, pouring more coffee. "You get cup number two. You'll need to be sharp today if we're going to pull this off. I'll need your full attention."

"I'll be ready," Thompson replied.

"I'll get you some speed if you need it," said Kline. "Greenies are a food group for us in covert."

"I said I'll be ready, goddamnit," snapped Thompson. Ann looked at her husband somewhat surprised. He was normally the picture of cool and calm. She was shocked at his quick-tempered response.

"All right," Kline replied. "The staff put some fruit and bread together for us. Grab some grub and we'll get going as soon as Mr. Griffith arrives."

Ann filled her plate with fruit and noticed that her husband was not eating. "Do you want some of my kiwi?" she asked.

"If I wanted some fruit, don't you think I would have gotten it myself?" said Thompson.

"Well, excuse me," Ann replied.

Griffith walked into the room with Sue and Yorgi. "Morning, gang," said Griffith as they entered the room.

"What's he doing here?" asked Thompson, pointing to Yorgi.

"Sorry," said Ann, gesturing to her husband. "He didn't sleep well last night."

"Don't apologize for me," said Thompson. "I want to know why he is here."

Ann shrugged her shoulders at Yorgi.

"No offense take, Mees Ann," said Yorgi.

"Yorgi knows what Josh looks like," Griff said. "At this point, we need everyone in the country who knows what our boy looks like."

Ann frowned her disapproval at Thompson, who in turn purposefully disregarded her glance.

Kline began to go over the plan for the day. "Congressman, you and your wife will be on the stage as soon as the gates open."

"Why on stage? Shouldn't we be in the crowd?"

"No," Kline replied. "I want you and Ann on stage early. You'll have seats in the front row with the other observers and Romanian dignitaries. While you're sitting through a whole bunch of speeches you don't understand, you'll have the perfect vantage point to view anyone trying to get close to the stage. You'll have the widest field of vision. Keep scanning the crowd. Josh will be out there somewhere."

"Got it," said Ann.

"Where do you want me?" asked Griffith.

"We need to make this look normal," said Kline. "So I want you in the television production truck. Tell your production team that you want lots of close up shots of happy Romanian voters. Keep having one camera pan the crowd close to the stage. You keep your eyes on the monitor for that camera."

"Check," said Griffith.

"Sue and Yorgi," said Kline, "I want you working the crowd with me. One of you take the gate, and one of you mingle through the crowd."

"I weel take the gate," said Yorgi.

"All right then," said Kline. "Sue, you're in the crowd. Everyone grab an earpiece and a transmitter." They each picked up an earpiece and fiddled around with the device to become comfortable with it. "'May Day' is what I want to hear when you spot Josh. Give me your location and then stay out of sight. I'll take it from there."

"You're not going to shoot, are you?" asked Thompson.

Kline stared back at Thompson. "No, Congressman, I'm not going to shoot in a crowd. I will approach them from behind and stun her. I've got a stun device that will knock her out. She'll collapse and I'll grab her. Whoever is closest to Josh, grab him and get him backstage immediately."

"How the hell we going to do this?" asked Thompson. "This isn't Fancy Farm. There's going to be 100,000 people there today."

Kline ignored the comment. "I'm headed over early to review the grounds. I need everyone else in place when the gates open at noon. I'll see everyone there."

As the others began to exit the room, Kline grabbed Thompson's attention. "Congressman, can I have a private moment with you?"

"What do you want?" Thompson asked in a sour tone.

As the door to the conference room closed and the two were alone, Kline came at Thompson in such an intimidating manner that it caused him to step back as she approached. "Get it together, Congressman. You've got to shake what happened yesterday."

"I'm sorry, but I can't do that."

"Yesterday wasn't Gitmo, Congressman Thompson. It wasn't some exercise where you get to hold Congressional hearings about what was proper procedure. There are no second judgments in the field. We did what we had to do to save an American life. You think that it's all about morality. It isn't. It's about survival."

Thompson glared back at her.

"You balked yesterday when I said this was a game. Well, it is and in a couple of hours it's game time. Winning and losing this game is about life and death. Josh is going to be somewhere in that crowd. I need you to be fully focused if we're going to find him. I lost my partner yesterday, and if you're not on your game today, we're liable to lose someone else. This is not the day to freak out. Save that for tomorrow."

"I can't," said Thompson.

"You're so full of shit," replied Kline.

"Excuse me?" replied a shocked Thompson.

"You heard me," replied Kline. "You told me that you think of this kid like a son."

"I do," replied Thompson.

"I don't believe that," said Kline.

"You've got no idea how I feel."

"Let me ask you something, Congressman," said Kline. "Where are your kids right now?"

"Back in the states with their aunt," Thompson said. "You know that."

"Well, what if they were here? What if they had been in the next room yesterday? Would you have thought twice about killing Alexandro if it had been one of your and Mrs. Thompson's real kids who had been kidnapped?"

Thompson froze at the question and looked right through Kline.

"You keep telling me that everyone thinks of Josh as family," said Kline. "Start treating him like it. You'd kill to save your own kids. If you think that Josh is family, start getting it in your head that what you did yesterday may have saved his life."

Thompson bit his lip and looked to the side, avoiding her gaze.

"And get it together. If we lose someone today, it could be Josh or someone who was around the table this morning, including your wife."

Kline moved to the door and, as she reached for the doorknob, she turned back to Thompson and added: "So snap the fuck out of it. You've got a couple of hours to get it together."

Chapter 53

Thompson asked Griff and Sue to take care of Ann for a couple of hours before they left for the Presidential Palace. Kline was blunt and abrasive, but she was right. He needed to change his mood. He needed to get his game face on. Changing his attitude was not going to happen with others in the room. It was only going to happen with solitude.

So Richard Thompson sat alone in his room. His ear buds were in his ears, but the iPod was silent. For once in his life, Thompson did not know what kind of music would change his dismal mind-set.

Lou Holtz was right, Thompson thought as he stared at the ceiling. *Happiness is no more than having a poor memory. Yesterday happened. I can't change it and I'll never be able to shake it. The only thing I can do is justify it...learn to live with it.*

Kline hit it right on the head. I tell everyone that I consider Josh my oldest son, but I'm putting my own morals ahead of what I should value most—his life. I killed a bad guy to save a good guy. Kline's alive today because I had the guts to pull the trigger. Josh may be alive or dead tomorrow based on what I have the guts to do today. That's the only judgment call I need to make about myself. Fuck any judgment others may make. I'm keeping people I value alive and I'm willing to live with any consequences.

I am a liar if I tell myself that my principles are more important than the lives of my families.

There's still one quarter left in the game. And this is a game where people die. It's going to be them, not us. Good guys aren't supposed to die. That's my value. That's my new moral compass.

Thompson twirled the dial on his iPod looking for music.

This city has changed since 1990, but the country side we saw yesterday is still the same. That broken down little house where it all happened was still third world. We did some good over here, but it never got out to the countryside.

I blasted Griff the other day about being a cowboy, but it's still the wild, wild, west up in the mountains. There is no law in the mountains. The only law in this situation is what I say it is. I'm the law. These bastards better live by what I say. I'm the law.

I was probably wrong about Griff. I told him he needed to back off the cowboy image. We need a cowboy right now. We need someone who will ride in with guns blazing to establish justice.

Thompson sat up in bed and sent a text to Griff. "WHERE R U?"

"OUTSIDE. NEEDED A SMOKE."

"COME TO MY ROOM—ALONE."

"WHAT'S UP?"

"I NEED UR BOOTS."

Thompson leaned back in the bed and dialed up an old Billy Joel song, softly singing along as it played:

From a town known as Wheeling, West Virginia,
Came a boy with a six-gun in his hand,
And his daring life of crime,
Made him a legend in his time,
East and west of the Rio Grande.

Chapter 54

It was about 11:00 a.m. as Richard Thompson gazed out through the wrought iron fence waiting for the motorcade that would take him, Ann, Yorgi, Griff, and Sue to their destination. He was focused, ready and wearing Griff's snake skin boots. As he walked along the fence the scene on the streets of Bucharest was so unusual it made an instant impression upon him.

The streets around the embassy were abuzz with energy as tens of thousands of Romanians slowly made their way through Bucharest anticipating the big political rally at the Presidential Palace in support of President Krasterich. The excitement had been building since early in the morning as families made their way in from the countryside, sometimes piling more people into cars, vans, and buses than the vehicles themselves were ever meant to hold. Even the Roma—the Gypsies of Romania—leaned out of windows in cramped vehicles waving flag poles hoisting the red, yellow, and blue Romanian flag.

When Thompson and Griffith had been in Romania previously, the nationalism displayed by the people had often been ugly. Groups had fought and killed those who had differing views about what Romania should become. Today, they waved flags in support of elections to make that decision.

Thompson noticed the clothing on those milling outside of the American Embassy made it easy to pick out those who were from the cities and those who were from the country. The city people dressed casually in jeans and khakis, wearing t-shirts with Romanian slogans supporting one party or another. Krasterich t-shirts were being given away for free on street corners and, as the day progressed, more and more city dwellers were wearing simple white t-shirts bearing his name and campaign slogan in fire-engine-red letters.

On the other hand, the country folk came to the city dressed in their finest clothes. Most of the men were wearing old suit pants, sweat stained white dress shirts and ties. The women wore drab colored but tasteful dresses. They had saved their weekly bath for this historic event.

What the four Americans did not know at the time about the Bucharest traffic was that, the closer one got to the Palace, the more congested the traffic became. All morning, volunteer police in yellow vests tried to clear intersections and direct traffic, but to no avail. Romanians had begun simply double- and triple-parking their cars and walking to the grounds. The only vehicles actually moving were motorcycles and scooters that weaved in and out of cars, which largely remained stationary on the road.

As they waited for the car to meet them at the back exit to the embassy, Ann pulled her husband aside. "What's with the boots?"

"It's a big day. I needed a little something to get me focused."

"And you went with Griff's boots?"

"Yup."

"You're weird."

"You married me."

"So, I guess this means you're not going to tell me what's been bothering you?"

"No," Thompson replied. "Not now."

"Then when?"

"Someday." He paused, knowing that the look on Ann's face indicated his response was woefully insufficient. "I'm sorry. There are so many voices in my head right now I'm struggling to make them all get in line and only speak one at a time. Once they're all through talking, I'll have it figured out. The day I understand all of this, I promise you'll be the first one to know. Today we have a job to do and we need to do it with pinpoint accuracy. Josh is depending on us."

Jane Kline left the American Embassy immediately following the meeting with the others so that she could survey the grounds where the rally was going to be held. She, along with the other Americans, had been given special credentials which allowed full access to the grounds.

Outside the gates to the Palace, the city was bustling. Inside the grounds, it was quiet. As Kline walked around, the only sign of an oncoming political rally was the swirling smell of smoke coming from the food vendors cooking various kinds of skewered meat just outside the fenced-in grounds.

As the plans had indicated, the stage was on a hill that was sloping down away from the stage. Kline walked to the fence line and started walking backwards, all the time looking at the front row of seats where the President would be sitting. After moving about twenty yards backwards, she stopped. "Good," Kline mumbled. "This is the spot. Noua is going to have to be right here or closer to get a shot off. She'll realize immediately that the closer to the fence line she gets, the better shot she'll have at Krasterich. Bitch, I'll see you coming from a mile away."

Leo Argo, The Fat Man, and Benny Vesper sat in a car on the streets of Bucharest, wondering how long it would take for the traffic to clear up. The *chargé d'affair* from the American Embassy had gone to the airport to greet the trio, provide special papers for their entry and personally drive them to the Presidential Palace. She had been told, by her direct superior in the United States, to keep Vesper's visit top secret. She thought it was best to handle the arrival personally. Even the American Ambassador to Romania did not know of the trip.

Now, however, the Charge was not so happy about her decision to personally handle the drive from the airport. The other two men in her car had been pleasant enough when she had met them, but Benny Vesper, the Chief of Staff to the President of the United States, had been rather rude to her. With no more than a handshake and a mumbled greeting, he had thrown a large case in the trunk of the car.

Vesper now was clearly agitated, the car was stuck in traffic, surrounded by masses of people from the countryside who had been pouring into the city all day, clogging the streets of Bucharest. The honking of the car horns from all directions only seemed to increase Vesper's ire.

"How far away are we?" asked Vesper.

"Just about a mile," replied the Charge.

"Come on, boys," Vesper said to Argo and The Fat Man. "Grab the case. We're walking the rest of the way."

Noua watched as Honeycat cut the tape from Josh's ankles. She held her gun in her right hand and a shoulder strap purse in the other. As Honeycat finished his work, Josh kept eye contact with his female kidnapper. Noua's amulet was still around her neck, but, despite his blue-eyed glare, she did not rub it.

The night before had been confusing for Josh. He had barely slept since Noua had fucked him. He realized that was exactly what Noua had done to him. After all the abuse she had dished out to him over the past several days, he still became sexually aroused when she woke him up. He should have resisted, but he let her fuck him. What really pissed him off was that he had enjoyed it. When he was finally free of the restraints, he stood up and began to put on his clothes.

"All right boy," Noua said. "We're going to walk to the rally for the President now."

"Why?" asked Josh.

"I have to meet members of the Romanian Communist Party who will be there in the crowd," she replied. "I have to show them that we have taken one of the Americans captive as a political prisoner."

"And, after that, what happens to me?"

"After I meet with them and they see you, we will let you go."

"That's it?" asked Josh. "They see me and then you let me go?"

"We are trying to gain control of our party. How do you think my party will react to my father's faction if they see we are willing to capture Americans for our cause?" Noua smiled a knowing smile at Josh. "You are America's Brain. You figure it out. We will be heroes."

"Okay," said Josh.

"But don't forget one thing, lover," said Noua. "I have a gun. And if you try to run before you meet my comrades, I will kill you. I need you to help establish my family's place in the party. After that, I will have no further use for you and I will let you go. I am sure that you can find Mr. Griffith somewhere in the crowd."

She looked at Honeycat and in Romanian said: "He's all mine. Follow us from about a block behind. Today, my family's name will be forever etched in the annals of the party's history. Tell my father that I died a proud death."

Chapter 55

On the way to the Presidential Palace, Benny Vesper weaved in and out of the people in front of him like a race horse rushing to the finish line, switching the black case from hand-to-hand like a jockey's whip. Argo was keeping up fine, but The Fat Man was huffing and puffing heavily as they reached the grounds of the Presidential Palace.

"Wait here," said Vesper. "I have some business to do at the gate."

The Fat Man was bent over—one hand on his side, the other on his knee. "Not a problem," he replied. "I'll just wait here."

"Are you all right?" asked Argo. "You're breathing heavier than an obscene phone caller."

"I'll be fine," said The Fat Man. "Just let me get my breath."

As The Fat Man tried desperately to catch his breath, he turned and placed his hand on the fence. His exhaustion caused him to look aimlessly through the chain links at the people entering the grounds. As he gained his breath, be began to pay more attention to what was happening inside the fence. He looked beyond the crowd at the main stage. "Hey, Leo," he said. "Look, there's Rick and Ann."

"No shit," replied Argo. "Where?"

"Up on stage," said The Fat Man. "Right in the front row. I wonder what he's doing up there?"

"I don't know," said Argo. "But that's good news for Josh. They must have found him. The Congressman probably wouldn't be up on stage if Josh hadn't been found already."

"Good," said The Fat Man. "That's really reassuring. We'll have to grab them tonight after the rally and see how they found him." The Fat Man turned and propped his back up against the fence. Still breathing a bit heavy, he spotted something out of the corner of his eye that caught his attention.

"Hey, Leo," said The Fat Man as he slowly moved toward the gate, with Argo following him. "Did you see that kid who just headed through the gate ahead of us?"

"No," said Argo. "Where?"

"Up there. The kid with the blond curls sticking out from under that ball cap. Is that Josh?"

"I don't know," said Argo. "I don't know him as well as you do."

"He's about Josh's size," said The Fat Man as he slowly started to follow the man with the curls. "I'm almost sure that's him." As The Fat Man and Argo approached the gate themselves, they noticed Vesper was talking to a smallish Romanian man in a hound's-tooth suit.

"Hey, Josh," The Fat Man yelled as they walked past Vesper and the man. "Josh, Josh Barkman."

Josh didn't turn, but The Fat Man looked at Argo. "I'm sure that's him, Leo. I know that's Josh." As The Fat Man said that, Argo noticed that the small man who was speaking to Vesper abruptly pushed the Chief of Staff aside and spoke into a small microphone being cupped in his hand: "May Day. May Day. Entering the east gate. Etts Meester Yousuaa."

"What the hell?" said Vesper as he bounced against the fence and stumbled slightly. He righted himself, grabbed the case and watched in stunned silence as the man with whom he had been speaking walked away from him without any explanation.

At Yorgi's announcement, Kline began moving quickly towards the east gate. "We got a sighting," said Kline. "Get a camera on him, Griff. See if you can get a positive identification." She fumbled with the taser in her vest pocket as she moved through the crowd.

Hearing the chatter on the transmitter, Thompson stood up and looked toward the east gate. "Mayday. East Gate," he whispered to Ann.

"Camera three, let's pan in on people entering through the east gate," said Griffith, looking at a monitor. He saw a couple, one of whom had blond curls sticking out from under a ball cap. "Pan in on that couple in the lower right of the screen. The one with the cap." He paused as he stared at the monitor. "May Day. It's him. It's Josh."

Seeing Yorgi moving quickly past him, Argo realized that something was happening. He reached to grab The Fat Man's shoulder in an effort to try and stop him from yelling again. Before he could do so, the Fat Man yelled in a loud voice, "Hey Josh!"

Josh turned and looked toward The Fat Man. "Joe?" said Josh. "What the hell are you doing here?" Noua turned as Josh stopped at the call of his name and she immediately grabbed for the gun inside her purse. "Aw, fuck," Josh mumbled. "This is it."

As Noua was in the process of pulling the gun from her purse, Yorgi jumped in front of Noua, acting as if he was drunk. "Hey, pretty lady," he said to Noua in Romanian. "Here's to President Krasterich."

"Get out of my way, you drunk," Noua replied as she tried to walk herself and Josh around Yorgi.

"Join me in a toast to our president," Yorgi said, reaching into his suit coat as if he were pulling out a bottle of alcohol from which to drink. Instead of a flask, Yorgi pulled a small revolver with a silencer on the end. He placed it at Noua's chest and pulled the trigger. The bullet made a dull sound as it pierced her heart. She slumped and fell forward into Yorgi's arms.

"Yorgi, no!" shouted Josh. Then, watching her fall, Josh gently called her name.

Griffith, who was watching the whole scene on his monitor, drew back in horror. "Holy shit," he gasped.

Argo watched as the small caliber bullet pierced Noua's chest. Instinctively, he pushed The Fat Man to the ground, knocked Josh out of the way and tackled Yorgi. As Yorgi struggled against the force of Argo's tackle and Noua's dead body, Argo twisted Yorgi's wrist twice and grabbed the gun from his hand.

Behind the scuffle, Honeycat could see that something was happening twenty or thirty yards ahead of him. He started to walk faster in an attempt to narrow the distance between Noua and him. When he saw someone apparently tackle Noua, he broke into a sprint, pulled his revolver and began forcefully throwing people aside as he ran.

Kline had had a bead on Noua and Josh when she saw Yorgi jump in front of the couple. "What the hell?" she muttered as she watched Noua slump forward. Then she watched as the FBI agent who had brought Congressman Thompson and his wife to the plane in Quantico tackle both Yorgi and Noua. She saw Argo grab the gun and a large Romanian man approach all of them from behind with a drawn weapon. "Behind you!" Kline shouted as Honeycat approached the pile of people on the ground.

Argo, eyes focused, glanced quickly at Kline when he heard her warning and then turned. He saw Honeycat running toward him with a drawn weapon. He knew he had no jurisdiction in a foreign country, but his split second decision meant life or death. Argo gritted his teeth, went to one knee and leveled Yorgi's weapon at the man.

Benny Vesper had been watching all this happen from a distance, when he noticed the man he had been talking to, appeared to tackle a woman. Then Argo had barreled into both of them. As the scuffle had intensified, he moved closer to it. He was nearly trotting as he stepped in front of Honeycat.

Honeycat grabbed Vesper by his shoulders half a second before Argo shot. The bullet hit Vesper on the left side of his chest. Vesper's eyes were wide, and looking squarely at Argo, as his mortally wounded body lurched backwards into Honeycat's arms.

By the time Vesper's body had hit the ground, Kline had pulled her weapon. Honeycat was struggling to disentangle himself from Vesper's body which gave Kline just enough time to fire. Honeycat knew his fate. He looked defiantly at Kline as she pulled the trigger. Honeycat fell like a sack of rotten Romanian beets.

Within a matter of seconds Noua Alexandro, Honeycat and Benny Vesper all lay dead within 30 yards of the east gate to the grounds of the Romanian Presidential Palace.

Pandemonium followed. People began screaming and running in every direction. Sue had arrived and froze at the sight of the dead bodies on the ground. "Grab Josh," Kline instructed Sue. "Get him backstage pronto."

Sue continued to look at the dead bodies.

"Now!" shouted Kline.

Sue grabbed the hand of Josh, who looked scared and confused. "Come with me," she said.

"But…" Josh resisted.

She grabbed Josh by both sides of his face and looked squarely into his eyes. "It's me. Sue. This is no time to question what is happening. Come with me. All right?"

"All right," Josh said as he looked over his shoulder at the blood stain growing on Noua's shirt.

Once Sue had Josh under control, Kline quickly turned her attention to the mild-mannered interpreter from the American Embassy. "Yorgi? What the hell?"

"FSB" said Yorgi in perfect English with only the slightest hint of an accent. "We don't like to be called the KGB anymore—uh, certain negative connotations.

"Well, I'll be damned," replied Kline.

Yorgi flashed Romanian credentials to police who were arriving with guns pulled. "These people were trying to kill the President. Let's get their bodies into the Palace. Quickly! You," said Yorgi pointing at The Fat Man who was slowly getting up off the ground. "Are you with him?" He gestured toward Argo.

"Yeah," said Argo. "He's with me."

"Good. Go grab that case over by the dead American and follow us."

The Fat Man looked at Argo, who nodded his approval. The Fat Man went back up the hill, grabbed the case and followed the others to the door of the Palace.

Chapter 56

When Yorgi, Argo, The Fat Man, and Kline had gotten the bodies in the side door of the Palace, Kline immediately called for Griffith. "Griff, are you on the air?"

"Yeah, I'm here," he replied. "What the fuck is going on down there? It's fuzzy on the film, but it looked like somebody got shot."

"They did," replied Kline. "But we cleared the area pretty quickly. Security has shut down the east gate."

"Damn. What about Josh? Is Josh okay?"

"Yeah," replied Kline. "He's with Sue. Get someone out onstage to assure the crowd that everything is under control. There are 100,000 people mingling around out there. Get someone onstage quick. This happened in a small section near the front of the stage. If word starts spreading that someone was shot, we'll have a riot on our hands. Get someone from the president's staff out there. Have them tell the crowd that someone fell and hurt themselves, but they're all right."

"Kline...where are you?" came Thompson's voice through the ear piece.

Yorgi had kicked open the door to an office on the first floor of the Palace and, along with Argo, he started pulling dead bodies into the room. Kline stood in the corridor outside the office and looked above the door. "Congressman, I'm in room 107. Get here as soon as possible. We have a major problem."

"But I heard you say that Josh is all right," Thompson replied.

"He is. He is," Kline repeated. "Josh is with Sue. But I've got a major cluster-fuck on my hands down here and I need your assistance in a big way. Let's not talk about it on the line. Just get here quickly."

"Got it," replied Thompson. "There's a lot of security between you and me. It'll take us a few minutes."

"Sue," asked Kline. "Are you out there?"

"Yeah."

"Get to room 110 as quickly as possible. I'll get it open for you. Get Josh there and wait for my instructions. Don't let anyone into the room unless it's one of us."

When everyone was accounted for, Kline turned her attention to Yorgi: "So you're our number-one interpreter in Romania and you're working for the Russians?"

"Yeah," replied Yorgi. "Do you think that when the republics split off, we quit our covert?"

"Hell no," replied Kline, "We figured the FSB is as deep as the KGB ever was. We know you're out there, but our research shows that you don't have any strongholds in Romania."

"We don't," said Yorgi. "That's why I'm here. We've been working on building a new base of support here."

"You're building a new base of support from our embassy in Romania?" said Kline sarcastically.

"Brilliant, isn't it?" said Yorgi. "Using your embassy and doing it with the support of your government?"

"Before the shooting, I saw you talking to Vesper," interjected Argo. "Is that why he was here? Were you the contact he was supposed to meet with?"

"Yes," said Yorgi. "I was to meet Mr. Vesper at the gate. He was early. I didn't expect to see him for at least another hour or so."

"Well," said The Fat Man, "when we landed, he wanted to come straight here. He didn't want to stop at the embassy because he thought he might be late."

"He sure as hell was early," said Kline.

"Yeah," Yorgi replied. "Just early enough to be killed by one of your people with my gun."

Chapter 57

Thompson knocked on the door to Room 107. "It's me. Thompson," he said in a loud whisper.

Kline opened the door and looked up and down the hallway, before allowing Thompson and Ann to enter. "Come on in," she said.

When Thompson entered the room, his forward progress into the remainder of the office was impeded by three dead bodies. "Holy shit," he said as he surveyed the corpses on the floor. With his gaze drawn to the bodies, he did not even notice Leo Argo standing against the wall. "Dear Lord, is that Benny Vesper?"

"Yeah," replied Kline.

"Oh, my God," said Ann as she entered the room behind her husband. She stood motionless looking at the three corpses.

"What happened?" asked Thompson.

"It's complicated," said Kline. "I'll explain it all later. First, go find Josh. He's in Room 110 with Sue. Check him out and make sure he's okay. As soon as you're convinced he's in good shape, get back in here. Believe it or not, I need you right now more than Josh does."

Ann continued to stare at the dead bodies on the floor. Thompson had to literally drag her out of the room by her arm. When they were outside the room, Ann looked at her husband. "Dear God, Richard," she said. "What the hell is happening here?"

"I have absolutely no idea," he replied.

"Wait!" said Ann.

"What?"

"There was a third person in the room back there," she said. "He was against the wall. I swear I think it was Leo."

"It can't be," Thompson replied. "He has no authority over here."

"But …"

"But, nothing," said Thompson. "I need you to focus right now. Let's find Josh and make sure he's okay." Thompson walked the corridor until he found an office on the opposite side of the hall labeled Room 110. He knocked gently on the door.

"Who's there?" asked Sue.

"It's me. Congressman Thompson."

Sue unlocked the door and let Thompson and Ann into the room. Josh was sitting at a desk with his head in his hands. When he looked up, the blankness in his blue eyes revealed his shock. Ann literally ran across the room and embraced Josh in a strong hug. She began to cry as she pushed his head back to look at his still bruised eye. "Josh? Are you all right? What did they do to you?"

"I'm fine," Josh replied. "It probably looks worse than it feels."

"We've been so worried," Ann said.

"I was afraid I'd never see you again," said Thompson, as he placed his hands on Josh's shoulders. Ann stepped aside and Thompson leaned into Josh until their foreheads were touching. The pair held that simple position for a long time. Ann put her hand over her mouth to fight back her own emotions.

For the first time since being captured, Josh's eyes began to fill with tears. "I'm sorry, Boss. I didn't listen to Griff. He told me not to leave the hotel alone, but …"

"Don't worry, son," replied Thompson. "It's over. It's all over. You're safe now."

Not knowing which emotion to grapple with first, Josh looked with sad eyes at Thompson. "Yorgi killed her," Josh said. "He killed Noua."

"Yeah," replied Thompson. "I know."

"Honey, she was going to kill you," said Ann, placing a hand on Josh's arm.

"No, she was going to let me go," replied Josh. "She told me so."

"I'll explain this all to you someday, Josh," Thompson whispered, his forehead again resting on that of his young staffer. "But trust me on this one, son. You were her decoy to assassinate the President. She was going to kill you and then President Krasterich."

"No. No," was all Josh could muster, suddenly confused with the notion that the shot which took Noua's life might have saved his.

Ann grabbed Josh's hand, as much to comfort herself as to comfort Josh. "Listen to him, Josh. This was real."

There was another knock at the door and Sue let Griffith into the room. Griffith entered and saw the scene with Josh and Thompson. When Griffith saw she was there he walked over and embraced her.

Thompson did not actually see who had entered the room, but apparently he could sense Griff's presence. "Come over here, Griff. I've got someone who wants to say hello."

Thompson leaned back and opened his left arm to allow Griffith to join the reunion hug. "I'm sorry," said Griffith in a hushed voice. "Josh, I am so damn sorry."

"What for?" asked Josh, sounding genuinely surprised.

"For letting all of this happen to you."

"You didn't let anything happen," replied Josh. "I did this to myself. I left the hotel when I knew I shouldn't."

"I told you the kid has a future in politics," said Thompson. "Next time, though, let's learn about accountability in a little less dangerous setting."

Throughout the emotional reunion, no one had noticed The Fat Man was also in the room standing quietly against the back wall. Once all of the emotional greetings had been played out, The Fat Man cleared his voice. Ann was the first to look up. She was literally speechless. When she tugged at Thompson's arm, he looked at the spot in the corner of the room to which she was pointing.

"Joe … what the hell are you doing here?"

Kline was alone in the other room with Yorgi, Argo and the dead bodies. She turned to Yorgi with an air of professional curiosity. "So, comrade, what's going on here?"

"Do you think I am going to reveal that to you?" Yorgi asked. "You are the enemy."

"You damn well better tell me," said Kline.

"I don't think so," replied Yorgi. "You won't kill me. The repercussions of killing an FSB agent would be too severe. You know that very well."

"Listen, Yorgi, or whatever your name is, you better come clean. We're both in really deep shit right now. What happened here today could potentially cause a war between our two countries. That body just to the right of you is the White House Chief of Staff and that's a Russian intelligence service bullet in his chest."

Yorgi paused to think about Kline's words. "You are persuasive, but why should I trust you?"

"You can trust me because I'm as deep into this as you are right now," Kline replied. "The President's Chief of Staff was killed on a mission in Romania while an FBI agent and I were at his side. Personally, if we don't find a way to make this work out, I don't think I'm going back to the States. I'm going deep rogue to never be seen or heard from again. We're partners in our own dilemma."

"True," said Yorgi.

"And when Argo gets back to the U.S., he'll claim that you killed the old fucker on the floor. Ballistics will prove it's your weapon. Once that is the point of contention, you'll spend the rest of your life in some Siberian work yard. You're right, I will not kill you, but your superiors just might."

"You are convincing," Yorgi said as he stepped over the body of Noua and walked to the window. He paused, considered his options and then spoke. "All right. Let us figure out how to handle this."

"Great," said Kline. "Let's start at the beginning. Why are you in Romania?"

"It is true that we do not have an official presence in Romania. We lost it after you brought elections and democracy to the country. But over the years we have been building support in the Parliament and disguising it under the name of many different parties."

"That is just as we have suspected," said Kline. "Keep going ..."

"The parties are all independent of each other, but they have a common leader. It is a man by the name of Abel Bogdan from the north. He has been accumulating support from all of the varying interests. He is one of ours and he is close to gaining enough support to control the Parliament."

Internally Kline winced at the mention of Abel Bogdan, the man whom Thompson had killed in the home of General Alexandro. Externally she showed no sign of any emotion whatsoever.

Yorgi continued. "On the other hand, the President is a puppet of your government. He shamelessly wraps himself in the American flag. Krasterich coddles to your embassy and he bows to their every demand. When he speaks of capitalism, he does so as if it is the great salvation of Eastern Europe. The man thinks he is Ronald Reagan with a Romanian accent."

"All right," said Kline. "We own the President and you own some legislators. Why is all of that important?"

"Because this could be the next confrontation," said Yorgi. "Here ... Romania ... this could be the start. Both countries want influence, but neither is ready for the consequences of full control."

"Consequences?" asked Kline.

"The consequences of ultimate control are huge," replied Yorgi. "Eastern Europe lies in the balance. Secretly, the hard-liners do not want to start the next Cold War here and now. We own some legislators, but not quite enough to control the Parliament. The President is with you. There has to be a balance. So, we had cut a deal with your president to split power in Romania."

"You cut a deal with President Mocker?" interjected Argo.

"Of course, I didn't do it personally," replied Yorgi. "There is an old hard-line group at the Kremlin. They cut the deal. On your end, the U.S. was going to help us win the several remaining seats we need to control the Parliament. In the plan, you were going to supply us with a symbol from your country that we could burn in effigy and rally support. It would be something that would play to the lowest common denominator of anti-American sentiment."

"The Mace," replied Argo.

"Yes," said Yorgi. "The Mace."

"You Americans play on anger in the voters all the time," said Yorgi. "There is resentment of America in the north. To burn a symbol of your power would harness their rage."

"And in the end you get a Romanian stalemate," said Kline. "What are we supposed to get?"

"We know that a balance of power in this country comes with a price. Our end is oil. When we gain control of the Parliament, then we start selling oil to the U.S. at a very lucrative price."

"How much?" asked Argo.

"Let's just say that we would sell you enough oil to lower U.S. gas prices just before your next election."

"Damn," said Argo, unable to hide his disgust for the timing of Mocker's deal.

"So what happened?" asked Kline.

"The rebels we had enlisted went rogue on us," Yorgi said. "They had their own plans."

"They did the kidnapping on their own," said Argo

"Yes," said Yorgi. "The kidnapping of the American was not part of the plan. It caused us great distress and nearly ended the deal."

"So the death of two Romanians will not distress you or your bosses," said Argo.

"Not in the least," Yorgi replied.

"There are more than two," said Kline.

"Still not a problem," said Yorgi.

"What if one of the dead men was Abel Bogdan?" asked Kline.

Yorgi's eyes focused on Kline. "Well …"

Kline cut Yorgi off. "And I can prove that Bogdan was part of the kidnapping."

Yorgi thought for a minute. "We care about control. We can determine our puppet leader later. Unfortunately, with all of this I do not see how you can control your end of the bargain."

"Don't worry about our end of the deal," Kline replied. She turned to Argo and continued. "Apparently, we've got to make sure that Yorgi's candidates win a seat in the election."

"And, in case you've forgotten, we need to come up with a story to cover this," Argo said, pointing to the floor.

"We do not need a story for the dead woman and her colleague," said Yorgi. "As I said, they had become liabilities to us. I was on orders to kill these two and her colleagues in the mountains."

"And Vesper?" asked Kline.

"That is up to you," said Yorgi. "He was here to deliver the Mace. Your President sent him. We would have preferred someone of lesser stature than Mr. Vesper. I take no responsibility for him. The story for his death rests on your shoulders."

"So," said Argo, "we need a cover for Vesper's death, and we need to throw an election in the mountains."

"What about the rebels who are still up there?" asked Yorgi. "How do we deal with them?"

"I can assure you that we won't have to worry about them," replied Kline.

Just then Thompson, The Fat Man, and Griffith walked into the room. The Fat Man and Griffith immediately began to stare at the bodies on the floor. Thompson, on the other hand, looked over at Argo. "My wife was right. It was you, Leo."

"It's me, Congressman," Argo responded, shrugging his shoulders. "How's Josh?"

"Physically he seems to be all right," said Thompson. "He's got a shiner around his eye and a few bruises on his ribs. We'll get the doctor at the embassy to check him out later, but he'll survive."

"And mentally?" asked Argo.

"That's going to take a bit longer," said Thompson. "He's pretty shook up right now." He pointed to the dead body of Noua on the floor. "I think she really got in his head."

"I knew she was going to kill him," said Yorgi. "Her father would have expected her to do nothing less. I wanted to get to her before she killed your friend."

"Yorgi, what the hell happened to your accent?" asked Griffith.

"Sorry to disappoint you, Mr. Griffith. I'm really not a silly little eastern European man acting as your interpreter. I'm Russian security."

"I'll be damned," replied Griffith.

"Griff," said Kline, "you said that you have the shooting of Vesper on tape?"

"Like I told you on the wave," Griffith said. "It's a little fuzzy, but I got it on tape."

"Did anyone else see it?"

"No, I had it channeled to my private monitor."

"Good."

"And, Congressman, you're a big Nixon fan, right?

"Sure," Thompson responded. "Why?"

"Dust off your bag of campaign dirty tricks. We've got an election to throw."

Chapter 58

It was very late in the evening as Michael Griffith sat alone in the production truck parked just outside the grounds at the Presidential Palace. About the size of a small moving van, the truck was much smaller than most production trucks Griffith was used to working with in the States. However, it had a solid wall of monitors and editing equipment which was more than sufficient for producing quick thirty-second television and radio spots. The lights from the eight television monitors were enough to light the entire van.

The truck sat in a lonely parking space by a now-quiet loading dock on the back side of the palace far away from the street traffic of the night. The speeches ended long ago, and the crowds had been dispersed for hours. Griffith sat in solitude and sipped a cup of bad coffee as he ran a tape backwards and forwards over and over again. The low hum of the equipment was white noise obscuring the other sounds of the night. When there was a knock at the door of the truck, Griffith jumped in his seat.

"I'm busy," Griffith shouted. "I told you I'll have it tomorrow morning."

"It's me," said the voice outside. "It's Jane Kline. Let me in."

Griffith got up from his chair and moved to the door of the production truck. He opened the door and let Kline in. "Sorry," he said. "I thought it was someone from the President's campaign. They want an ad made from the footage of his speech tonight to go up on the air tomorrow. They've been bugging the shit out of me."

"Too bad," replied Kline. "I've got dibbs on you right now. What do you have on the shooting?"

"Check it out," Griffith instructed, pointing to the main

monitor. He hit the button and played a twenty second clip on the screen. He ran it backwards in fast motion and played it again. "I converted it to black and white to make it look authentic."

Kline peered at the screen with the intensity of an art connoisseur looking at an original work of art in the Louvre. "Play it back again," she instructed. Griffith adjusted a couple of knobs and played the clip a third and fourth time. "This is perfect," Kline said. "Good job. Make me a copy and destroy the original. I've got to get this to the embassy. They've got a secure line. I'll transmit it from there."

"Where's the Congressman?" asked Griffith.

"Observing," replied Kline.

"Observing?" asked Griffith.

"Absolutely," said Kline. "That's what he was sent here to do."

Griffith chuckled. "I assume he is heading up to observe the casting of votes in the provinces up north?"

"Yeah," said Kline. "Apparently, they anticipate having some problems up there with their voting machines. They needed someone to observe them up close."

"And they're going up there in the middle of the night?"

"It seems they felt an arrival while it was still dark outside was key for their observations," replied Kline.

"Good call," said Griffith as he fiddled with the production board to copy the video footage to a DVD. "He took an interpreter with him, I suppose?"

"He's using our number one guy at the embassy."

"Great." Griffith paused. "I know we're not supposed to talk about this, but don't you find this whole thing kind of odd."

"What?"

"Well, an American Congressman is tossing an election in Romania while being escorted around by an FSB guy and an FBI agent."

"Don't question the mission," said Kline. "That's the first thing they teach us at the Agency. I don't know what we got as our end of the bargain, but it has got to be better than the alternative."

"What's the alternative?" asked Griffith.

"The truth," replied Kline. She reached in her backpack and handed an envelope to Griffith. He opened it up and saw that it contained pictures of Krasterich's opponent, buck-ass naked and in many compromising positions with several naked women at once.

Griffith looked at the pictures. "What the hell are these?"

"Yorgi asked me to give these to you. He said that you might be able to use them."

"Now the Russians are working to defeat their own candidate," said Griffith "Weirdest damn election I've ever seen."

"Me, too," Kline laughed. "Hey, since we're being honest here, I've got a question for you."

"Shoot," said Griffith.

"Why the hell was Congressman Thompson wearing your boots when he headed out tonight?"

Chapter 59

Zig zagging around ancient potholes, the Romanian-made SUV carrying Thompson, The Fat Man, Leo Argo, and Yorgi moved briskly down the mountain road. Gravel constantly bounced against the under chassis of the car so loudly it sounded like an army of tiny soldiers trying to break through the bottom of the car with mini sledge hammers. As the car rounded a sharp bend, Argo looked out his rear passenger window. The full moon was bright enough to allow him to notice there was no guard rail on the outside of the turn protecting them from the severe drop-off on the other side.

"Jesus, Yorgi, slow down," said Argo. "I thought the drivers in D.C. were wild. You're scaring the living shit out of me." He looked over at The Fat Man, who had a white knuckle grip on the back door arm rest. "You ought to see this damn drop-off over here."

"No thanks, Leo," replied The Fat Man, staring straight ahead. "I'm doing just fine with my eyes focused on the horizon and practicing my deep breathing."

"Knock it off, you two," said Thompson from the front passenger seat. "We're on a tight schedule. We've got to get to the Union Liberty Party headquarters before sunup."

"That presumes that we actually make it off the mountain," said Argo.

"You sound a little nervous, Leo," laughed Thompson. "I expected Joey to be a little uneasy about the ride, but not you. You're really blowing the FBI tough-guy image for me."

"Shit," shouted The Fat Man, as the car hit a deep pothole that bounced the car's inhabitants like pinballs in an arcade game.

"Calm down, Joey," said Thompson. "It's just a pot hole.

We have them all over back home in Kentucky."

"Which is where I'd like to be buried when I die," The Fat Man replied in a whisper just loud enough for Thompson to hear. "Someone please write that down. When they find us, years from now, I'd like that to be my final wish."

"Awww, and miss seeing the Romanian countryside by night," said Argo, his eyes nearly as wide as The Fat Man's.

The Fat Man sat rigidly in his seat, with a death grip on the arm rest, contemplating the purpose of their trip. After a minute or two of hearing nothing but gravel hitting the undercarriage of the car, The Fat Man finally got up the nerve to ask the question that had been on his mind ever since they left the embassy. "Okay, Rick," he said. "Please explain this to me again. Use small words that even I can understand. Why are we throwing the election for Romanian Parliament?"

"We're not really throwing the election, Joey," responded Thompson. "Throwing the election implies that we are going to rig the voting machines. We're not going to do that. People will cast their votes for whomever they want."

"So, then how would you classify what we are doing?" asked The Fat Man.

Thompson thought for a second. "We're simply supplementing the campaign literature they consider before casting their vote."

Yorgi, understanding the Congressman's difficulty with his friend, jumped in. "The most influential party in the north is the People's Rights Party," he said, as he turned the wheel hard to avoid a pot hole. "There are so many parties in the north. The PRP does not have any candidates on the ballot. They simply endorse others who are running."

"That is important to me because..." asked The Fat Man.

"On election day, the PRP gives out sample ballots at the polls. The ballots have check marks next to the candidates they support. Those candidates always win."

"I'm still not following you," said The Fat Man.

"We're going to supplement the PRP's supply of sample

ballots," said Thompson. "Yorgi is having some new sample ballots delivered. The ones they give out on Tuesday will have a new candidate marked on them as an endorsed candidate."

"How are you going to convince the PRP to accept a new candidate?" asked The Fat Man. "The election is only a day away."

"We're not," said Thompson.

"Then how are we going to get the ballots into the hands of the poll workers?" asked The Fat Man.

Thompson did not say anything in response. After a few seconds, The Fat Man glanced up at the front seat and noticed Thompson giving him a look with arched eyebrows and a knowing grin. Then he understood the unspoken answer.

"You're planning for us to break into the PRP's headquarters to plant the ballots, aren't you?" said The Fat Man.

Thompson just turned to the back seat and grinned wider in response.

"When did you come up with this one?" asked Argo

"I didn't come up with anything," said Thompson. "It was done in Mississippi in a Congressional election back in the '80s. Someone broke into an office of a voters' rights group and switched the sample ballots. On election day they handed out marked sample ballots for the wrong candidate. By the time they figured it out, it was late in the day and the election was over. They never caught who did it."

"So we're breaking the law," said The Fat Man.

"No," replied Thompson.

"I don't like this," muttered The Fat Man. "I don't like this whole thing. It's getting worse with each minute."

"Listen, Joe, it was illegal in Mississippi, but not here," said Thompson. "Romania has no election fraud laws."

"I bet breaking and entering is still illegal."

Kline had told Thompson just enough of the full story to convince him that throwing the Romanian election was in the interest of America's national security. "The ends justify the means, Joe," said Thompson. "The ends justify the means."

Ann and Sue sat with Josh at a table in a secluded corner of the embassy restaurant. He had just joined them and was still not talking much about what had happened. Despite his silence, it was apparent to Sue and Ann he had a lot going on in his head.

"How were your mom and dad?" asked Ann, trying to break the awkward silence.

"I spoke to them," said Josh. "I didn't tell them anything. The CIA folks debriefed me and told me I couldn't tell them. It's best they don't know. They couldn't deal with it anyway."

"We are parents, honey," said Ann. "That's how we are. We can't deal with our kids in pain."

There was another pause. "I should have gone with them," Josh said.

"No way," said Ann. "There was no way I was going to let you go back into the mountains."

"So I get to stay here with the girls."

"Josh, I am not letting you out of my sight until we get back to the States," said Ann.

"I'm fine."

"I can tell that you are not fine," interjected Sue. "The bruises have not gone away. And I suspect that those bruises are pretty deep."

Josh paused and stared off into the distance, somewhere far beyond the space defined by the walls of the room. "The drive back to the city was something," he said. "They took my blindfold off and I got to look out the window as we drove.

"Sue, you like the city. So do I. Bucharest is a great town. But I'll tell you something—it is not like the country. There is extreme poverty out there in the countryside. You know I didn't see a single school while we drove. Most of the houses were rat holes and the people were hardened poor.

Capitalism and democracy may have changed the cities, but it's still the same old oppression out in the country. It's just a new oppressor."

Neither Sue nor Ann knew quite what to say. "I don't know if I can go back to the Hill," said Josh.

"Richard will give you some time off, I'm sure," said Ann.

"That's not it," said Josh. "I don't need time off."

"Then what is it?" asked Sue.

"It's something more," said Josh. "It's like there's something more out there for me. I don't need some time off. I need some time here."

"You're still having a tough time," said Ann. "Things seem a little fuzzy right now."

"Ann, I love you and the Congressman," Josh replied, "but nothing in my life has ever been more clear."

Chapter 60

The television anchorwoman sat at her desk adjusting her expression. When the light came on, her blank look broke into a large, toothy smile.

"Before the break, we told you about other stories making news today besides President Mocker's upcoming press conference. On the international political front, we've been following the elections today in Romania. In an exclusive you'll only see here on this channel, we have a story on the open elections in the former communist country of Romania today. We'll go live now to our international political reporter, Stuart Edwards, with continuing coverage. Stu, what do you have for us?"

"Thanks, Caroline," responded Edwards, speaking into a microphone with the Presidential Palace in the background. "What has been described to us as a minor internal party skirmish which occurred on the grounds of the Presidential Palace three days ago has not damped the enthusiasm of voters today in Romania. It's been a brisk day of voting here in the capitol city of Bucharest. Polling places in the city have been experiencing moderate to heavy lines, but no problems or protests have been reported.

"Of note is the huge turnout being reported in the northern provinces of Baia Mare and Satu Mare, which will not have a major impact on the presidential election, but may impact the makeup of Romania's Parliament.

"I am joined now by Michael Griffith, one of America's premiere political consultants, over here in Romania to consult in the campaign of President Krasterich and one of our frequent guests here on our political broadcasts. Welcome to the broadcast, Griff."

"Thanks, Stu," replied Griffith. "It's great to be here."

"Good turnout in the cities today … what does this say for your candidate, President Krasterich?"

"Well, it's definitely good for President Krasterich and his reelection effort. Krasterich has worked hard to restore jobs in the factories and create wealth for Romanians. His strength is definitely in the urban areas."

"So you think that Krasterich wins?"

"Definitely."

"No comment about your impact on the reelection campaign?" asked Edwards.

"Naw," replied Griffith. "Krasterich had a pretty good campaign organization and he'd done a good job. I think he could have won with you running his campaign, Stu."

"Okay, well what do you make of the big turnout in the north?"

"There does seem to be a rather large turnout up near the Ukraine and Hungarian borders. That's a rugged area up there. Turnout can be driven by local issues. You can never really tell what drives the vote up or down."

"Early results indicate that a few unknowns may gain seats in the Parliament. What do you know about them?"

"Never heard of them before, Stu," Griffith replied.

In the studio the anchor was waiting for the red light to come back to the camera in front of her. "That was our very own Stuart Edwards in Bucharest, Romania, with American political consultant Michael Griffith. At least I think it was Michael Griffith. I'm not sure. He was pretty subdued tonight."

Chapter 61

The cadre of persons who made their way across the tarmac of Bucharest airport looked different than any other group of executives headed to their corporate jet.

"Company plane?" Argo asked Kline as they approached.

"Yup," replied Kline with a sly smile. "Registered to some nondescript American corporation, I suspect. I've got this little Irish mug back at the headquarters who always takes care of me. Kropper outdid himself this time."

"Shit," said Argo. "At the FBI, we're used to traveling coach."

"You ought to change agencies. Come work for us, Leo. I'll put in a good word. We could be partners."

"After this week?" replied Argo. "Not on your life. I've had my share of international intrigue." He paused and somberly reflected on the fate of Benny Vesper. "Not on your fucking life."

As they stood at the steps of the jet, Michael Griffith was the first to break the awkward silence. "Well, Yorgi boy. I guess this is it. I'm not much for tearful good-byes, especially with a Russian intelligence paid interpreter. Take care and pardon me if I say that I hope to hell I never see you again."

"Michael!" exclaimed Sue.

"What?" replied Griffith.

"That's just rude."

"Not to worry, Miss Sue," replied Yorgi. "I'm not here to say good-bye. I'm here on direct orders of the Kremlin to confirm that Mr. Griffith gets on the plane and leaves the country."

"Well," said Sue. "In any event, good-bye."

"And, Miss Sue," said Yorgi with a sly tone to his voice.

"Yeah?"

"Stay away from the ballet."

Sue laughed and pointed her finger at Yorgi in a mocking accusatory gesture. She and Griffith made their way up the steps to the plane. Argo and Kline followed, with a simple nod as a gesture of professional courtesy to Yorgi.

The Fat Man waddled to the plane just a few steps behind Argo and Kline. "Never met a real commie before," he said tipping his New York Yankees hat to Yorgi as he passed. "And after this, I hope I never meet another."

"We feel the same way about American lawyers," said Yorgi with a wicked grin.

"Touché," said The Fat Man as he too, boarded the plane.

Thompson and Ann, with Josh in close tow, were the last to board. "I can't thank you enough for what you did for us," said Thompson on behalf of the trio. "Josh is alive because of you. I'll never be able to thank you enough for what you did."

"Call it our own private little détente," replied Yorgi.

Ann leaned forward and gently kissed Yorgi on the cheek. "Thank you," was all she could muster.

"The boots look good on you, Congressman," smiled Yorgi.

"Please don't encourage him," Ann injected.

"You guys go ahead and get on the plane," said Josh. "I'd really like to talk to Yorgi alone if you don't mind."

"I understand," said Ann. "Come on, Rick. Let's get on the plane."

"Don't give away any government secrets," mocked Thompson. "He's the enemy, you know."

"Yeah," said Josh. "I know." He looked Yorgi squarely in the eye. "They are right, you know. You saved my life. Thank you."

"Not a problem, young man," replied Yorgi.

"I have one favor," said Josh. "That is, if you don't mind me asking you one question?"

"Don't you think that asking a favor at this point is a bit inappropriate? I think I'm ahead in the favor category."

"I understand," said Josh. "But I have to ask you something or I'll spend the rest of my life wondering about the answer."

"Okay," replied Yorgi. "What's your question?

"Why'd you shoot Noua?" asked Josh. "I mean, she was your ally. She was trying to rebuild the Communist Party in Romania. She believed. You could have easily shot me and gotten away with it. Instead you shot her. I'm just wondering why."

"Well, Josh," replied Yorgi. "I know a little bit about your friend Griffith. It's said that he likes the movies called *The Godfather*. Is that right?"

"Yeah, but I don't follow you."

"Let's just say that I do a good job at keeping my friends close and my enemies closer." He winked at Josh. "Those movies are popular over here, too."

"But which one was I?"

Yorgi stuck out his hand and Josh returned the grasp in-kind. "Good day, Meester Yoshuua," he said, accentuating the fake accent he used when he had first met Josh. As he spoke, he clicked his heels together and bowed sharply at the waist. "Have a great life."

As Josh started up the steps of the plane, Yorgi called after him, "Hey, Josh."

Yorgi approached the steps and handed him a news paper. "Give this to the Congressman. He'll want to read it before he lands."

Josh looked back at him quizzically. "Okay," he said.

"And Josh …"

"Yeah?"

"It will serve you well to spend the rest of your life wondering."

All were silent until the plane slowly lifted off the runway. The jet made a quick ascent and a sharp turn towards the west. “We’re clear,” said Kline, breaking the uneasy silence.

“Thank God,” said Griffith. “Hey, Josh, what was all that crap between you and the Commie back there at the airport?”

“I just wanted to say good-bye,” said Josh.

“In other words, you’re not going to tell me,” said Griffith.

“You are damn right,” replied Josh. “Hey, Boss, I almost forgot. Yorgi said to give this to you. He said you’d want to read it before we got home.”

Josh handed a *USA Today International Edition* to Thompson. Thompson read the top headline: **Presidential Chief of Staff Killed in Random Street Shooting.**

Thompson read on: “The White House today announced that Presidential Chief-of-Staff Benny Vesper has been killed about two blocks from the White House in what has been described as a random street mugging gone bad. The White House released a video from a nearby security camera showing Vesper as he was shot after leaving a walk-up automated bank teller machine.

“In a written statement, President Jack Mocker said ‘Benny Vesper was a great American, patriot, and a dear friend. He died as he lived, in service to this nation.’ President Mocker stated that the details of Vesper’s death were still emerging and under investigation by the Federal Bureau of Investigation. According to the FBI’s office of public affairs, Special Agent Leo Argo has been put in charge of the investigation.

“Reaction in Washington was swift, Speaker of the United States House of Representatives Damon Koenig said, ‘Benny Vesper was a dear friend …”

Thompson did not feel like reading the remainder of the article or the side-bar article with a pie-chart graph bearing the headline **Street Crime in America: By the Numbers**. But, before tossing the paper aside, he noticed a headline which appeared below the fold: "United States and Russia Strike Historic Oil Pact."

"What is it, babe?" asked Ann, looking at Thompson's furrowed brow.

Thompson folded up the paper and stuffed it in the seat-back in front of him. "Yorgi must have known that I'm a baseball fan. He gave me the *USA Today* sports section."

Thompson leaned back in his chair, popped his iPod buds into his ears and dialed up a song by Warren Zevon.

...Whenever there's a crisis,
The President sends his Envoy.

Epilogue

As completely spectacular as the White House looks from Constitution Avenue, the West Wing itself can sometimes be almost as completely bland from the inside. Take away the ceremonial suites in the building and, after all, it is an office building housing the executive offices of the President. The halls are narrow and the desks in the offices with their doors open are stacked high with papers and folders. People dart to and fro with a jerky pace that resembles an old silent movie.

Richard Thompson had not been to the White House since being a staffer. This was his first visit to the President's home and office since being elected to the U.S. Congress, and the fact that the halls looked like any other old, small office building in the city was not lost on him.

But then Thompson turned a corner and found himself standing in a small reception area just outside the oval office. After giving the President's secretary his name, he stood silently in awe. Even though the door was closed, he understood the significance of where he stood and why. He peered into the Roosevelt Room, where President Teddy Roosevelt's 1906 Nobel Prize for Peace sits humbly on a fireplace mantle. Peace was Thompson's singular thought to himself. His mind was racing much too quickly about the upcoming meeting for him to attempt to contemplate anything further.

The phone on the desk of the assistant rang. She answered and looked at Thompson. "Very well," she said. "Congressman Thompson, the President will see you now."

"Thank you," Thompson replied as he opened the door. When he entered, President Mocker arose from his seat on one of the two light blue couches facing each other in the center of the room. Jane Kline and another man whom Thompson recognized as her boss, Ellsworth Steele, the head of the CIA, sat on the other couch. Two long wooden boxes, containing both Maces, sat open on the floor beside the couch. Kline and her boss also stood as Thompson entered the room.

"Good morning, Congressman Thompson," offered Mocker. "I don't think we've met yet."

"No, sir," replied Thompson. "We have not met before. It's my pleasure." He lied.

"You already know Agent Kline, I presume," said Mocker. Thompson reached over and shook Kline's hand and smiled. Kline did not break as much as a slight grin. "And this is Ellsworth Steele. Mr. Steele is the head of the Central Intelligence Agency. I believe that he is the one who invited you to this meeting."

"Nice to finally meet you, Mr. Steele," said Thompson. "Agent Kline has told me a lot about you. I appreciate that you agreed to include me in this gathering."

"Likewise," said Steele as he and Thompson shook hands. "According to Agent Kline, I didn't have much of an option. She said you can be very persuasive."

Mocker sat down and patted the couch in an offer for Thompson to sit next to him. "We all certainly appreciate everything you did in Romania," said Mocker.

"Thank you, Mr. President," replied Thompson.

"It is me who should thank you," said Mocker. "What you helped orchestrate is extremely important to our national security interests." Mocker paused to try to gauge Thompson's reaction. "And, of course, I do not have to add that the confidentiality of that mission is of utmost importance."

"You have my silence, Mr. President."

"That's good," said Mocker.

"But it will come with a price," said Thompson.

"Excuse me?" Mocker replied, his voice rising ever so slightly. "A price? Ellsworth, are you a part of this?"

"No, sir," said Steele, impressed with the gumption the freshman Congressman was displaying. Steele had lost a young agent on the President's mission and he was more than a little pleased to watch him squirm. "I assure you that I have never met the Congressman before he walked in here today." He failed to mention Kline had been in constant contact with Thompson since their return from Romania coordinating the strategy for this meeting.

Mocker stared at Steele. He did not trust Steele or his response, but Mocker knew Steele held far too many cards to push back. "So a new Member on Capitol Hill is blackmailing the President."

"No, sir," replied Thompson straight-faced. "I am not blackmailing you. I'm simply expressing a very attractive *quid pro quo*."

"You have a big set of balls, son," said Mocker.

"Sir, with all due respect, Mr. President," Thompson replied, "I've had a lot on my mind since returning from Romania. Our Sergeant at Arms is dead. Your Chief of Staff and his agent met the same fate. And all of this was over some silver poles and oil. That's a lot to think about, Mr. President."

"And I assume you've figured out what this burden on your soul is worth?" Mocker snapped.

"I have," replied Thompson.

The President laughed out loud, "Un-fucking-believable. They said you were new and principled. But you are like all the rest of them. What do you want? An Ambassadorship? A Post Office with your name on it?"

"Three requests, sir," Thompson retained his composure.

"Three? Not just one. I guess I'm your genie. Beautiful!"

"Yes, sir," replied Thompson. "First, you are to call home the *chargé d'affair* in Romania and appoint Josh Barkman to the post."

"The kid who was kidnapped?" asked Mocker. "He wants to be the charge in Romania?" The President leaned back on the couch, put his hands behind his head and then looked at Steele. “Ellsworth?”

“We checked Barkman out during the kidnapping,” Steele said. “The kid is clean. He’s not been trained for the Foreign Service, but we can change that pretty easily. We can send him to some intensive training for a couple of months before we send him over. I can make that happen.”

“All right,” said Mocker. “The kid goes to Romania. What else?”

“Second,” said Thompson. “The CIA frees up some funds.”

“Which you want sent to some foreign account in your wife’s name,” interjected Mocker.

The suggestion pissed Thompson off, but he still maintained his cool. “No, sir. I want those funds under the direct control of Agent Kline for use in Romania. Barkman needs resources for what he wants to do over there. I do not want him to have to fight with the appropriation committees for funds. He will let Kline know what he needs and she will have it in her discretion to respond in kind.”

Mocker shook his head in disgust at his situation. “Ellsworth, get an order prepared. I’ll sign it.” He looked at Thompson. He picked up a vase off the end table and rubbed it. “Poof,” he whispered. “And what is your third wish, Master?”

“I do want a building named,” said Thompson.

“Here it comes,” said Mocker.

“I need there to be a Robert Patterson Building,” said Thompson. He looked at Steele. “Of course, to name a building after Patterson there needs to be a cover story that clears his good name. It’s not fair that his name has been drug through the mud because of …”

“Get the fuck out of here,” said Mocker.

“Mr. President,” said Thompson. “You directed Director Steele to create a story for Vesper.”

“That was national security,” said Mocker.

"And your ass was on the line," interjected Kline. "It was not national security. It was your reelection that was on the line."

"Agent Kline," said Steele in a rehearsed response. If anyone was going to be a bad guy here, it was going to be Kline. "You are out of order."

"You certainly are," said Mocker. "You and the Congressman need to leave now … now."

Kline and Thompson got up and made their way to the door of the Oval Office. They opened the door and exited, leaving Steele and Mocker behind. Thompson started to speak, but Kline silenced him. "Wait until we get outside." Together the pair weaved their way to the North Entrance of the West Wing. When they were outside the gates, Kline spoke. "You did well in there."

"Thanks," Thompson replied. "So what happens now?"

"The Director explains the reality of the situation to him," Kline replied.

"And …"

"And," Kline laughed, "the sonofabitch understands you have him by his short hairs. Steele explains if anything happens to you, we release everything. I suspect that by the end of the day, I'm sending visa papers to Josh, planning how to spend some money in Romania and coming up with a cover story on Bob Patterson."

"I am not sure I really like Josh being your eyes and ears in Romania," said Thompson.

"I don't think you have a say in that one, Congressman," said Kline. "The kid was pretty insistent that he get the assignment."

"Yeah," Thompson replied. "You're probably right. Josh is at that stage in his political career where he has 'true-believerism.' I had it once."

"Would you rather have your guy or Mocker's guy watching over the balance of power in Romania?"

Thompson just smiled. “Thanks,” said Thompson, as he stuck out his hand to Kline. “I’ll never truly understand what you do and how you do it. But I think I’m glad you are out there.”

“See ya’ around,” said Kline, laughing at Thompson’s assessment of her job as she returned the hand shake.

“Nothing personal,” said Thompson, “but I sure as hell hope not.”

Kline looked towards Lafayette Park where Ann Thompson was sitting on a park bench in the early morning sunshine patiently waiting for her husband to exit the White House. She was reading a paperback book. Kline saw Thompson was looking at Ann as well and when Kline looked at Thompson she smiled. “She’s waiting for you,” said Kline.

“Yeah,” said Thompson, smiling. “I waited all of my life for her and now she’s the one who waits for me.”

“Take care.”

“You, too.”

Thompson crossed the street and slowly walked into Lafayette Park. He approached the bench and sat down. “Hey, pretty lady,” he said, as he if were meeting her for the first time. “Come here often?”

“I heard that I could meet a Congressman in this park,” she replied and then paused. “And that is the worst pickup line in the history of hookups.”

“Aw, too bad,” said Thompson. “I was hoping you would come with me to meet my wife.”

“Ooh, a three way,” laughed Ann. “Sorry. You don’t look strong enough to handle two of me.” She took Thompson’s hand, leaned over and kissed him gently on the cheek. “Seriously, how was your first official trip to the White House?”

“Official? That’s rich. I don’t expect there will be any record of my visit here today.” Traffic noise filled the cool morning air as they both stared off into the distance. “It looks like Josh will get the Charge post in Bucharest. Jane Kline is going to help usher the paperwork through the State Department."

"That will make him happy," said Ann. "That whole trip has really changed him. He's not the boy we sent over there."

"He's searching for something now," said Thompson. "He's not sure what. But he'll know it when he finds it."

"And what about you, Richard?" Ann asked. "What are you searching for?

"What do you mean?" he replied.

"We've never kept anything from each other, Richard," said Ann. "Right?"

"Right," he replied. "I know."

"So what happened in Romania?" she asked. "Your head has been a million miles away since we got back. What happened up in those mountains?"

"Someday, babe. Not today. Someday."

"I'll accept that," she said. "Just don't forget me when you are ready to talk."

"Let's go get some breakfast," said Thompson, purposefully changing the subject. "The Old Ebbitt Grill is about two blocks away. I told Griff that we'd meet him and Sue there in a bit. I think she may be the one."

"I'm not going to let this go, Richard."

"I know."

"One thing, though," Ann said as they started to walk, hand in hand across the park.

"What's that?"

"It's the boots," she said as she looked down at a new pair of black snakeskin boots that Thompson had just purchased after coming home from Romania. "It's going to take me a little while to get used to the boots."

"Yeah, me too, babe. Me, too."

The end

Introduction to
Writ of Mandamus

By
Rick Robinson
(due out 2011)

Jane Kline reveled in the fall drive along the George Washington Parkway from her small townhouse in Old Towne Alexandria. The morning was just warm enough to put the top down on her old red Miata convertible and the wind whipped through her dark hair whenever she was able to get the break through the stop-and-go D.C. traffic long enough to get her speed above 20 m.p.h.

It had been several years since Kline left the covert side of the Central Intelligence Agency and joined the rank of desk jockeys at the Company. Kline liked to jokingly include herself within the ranks of "desk jockeys," but her past work in the field had earned her a reputation of being something more. Administrative personnel with covert field experience were hard to come by and, since her arrival at headquarters, she had risen quickly in the ranks. In just over three years she had become the Deputy Director of the Central Intelligence Agency—Number Two behind Ellsworth Steele.

At first, Kline was upset with the move to headquarters, but she had come to enjoy the authority she was able to exert at the Company. She knew the field and that experience allowed her to influence decisions at the highest level of authority. Anyway, although she stayed in shape and could outwork most of the new recruits, she knew there was a natural life-span to her activities in the field. Running around the foreign country side looking for bad guys was a young person's job.

President Jack Mocker was gone. The American people had seen the thin veneer of his political smile and un-elected him a year earlier. His replacement was President Nathan McKinley. An unknown politician four years earlier, Kline considered McKinley as clueless as Mocker had been evil. Unfortunately for her, she could not figure out which attribute was worse for the country.

The move to the administrative side of the CIA also offered some much needed stability to Kline's personal life. She owned her own home for the first time in her adult life and a black lab named Hoover now accompanied her each morning on her five mile run.

Moreover, Kline was now seeing someone on a regular basis. She got to know FBI Agent Leo Argo on their long flight home from Romania. Shortly thereafter, when Argo's latest relationship had failed (mainly due to his being more committed to his job than his girlfriend), he called Kline to commiserate his predicament. They soon became lovers, although they both knew their jobs stood in the way of anything really serious. Occasional sex led to real dates and sleepovers. Over time, Leo Argo and Jane Kline had become something more than friends with benefits and something less than committed lovers.

Once past the bottleneck by Arlington National Cemetery, the road opened up and Kline pushed the accelerator of the Miata a bit lower, weaving in and out of cars as if she was driving a cross-country race for a million dollar prize. She slowed as she came to the traffic light which stood at the entrance to CIA Headquarters. She silently cursed as the light turned red prior to her approach. A left turn lane had the green arrow and she waved at CIA Director Ellsworth Steele as he drove across the GW Parkway onto the access road which led to the headquarters.

When the large flash of light first ignited, Jane Kline's field training kicked in. She quickly ducked her head onto the passenger seat as the explosion of fire and sound ripped past her car, shattering the windshield. She reached into the glove box and pulled out a revolver. Once the initial reverberations had roared past the Miata, Kline threw her car into park and raised herself out of the vehicle. A man who Kline recognized as someone from IT sat stunned in the car behind her, his face covered with blood from the shards of glass that had exploded in his face.

Weapon now drawn, Kline ran towards the Director's car. The fire was just starting and smoke from the explosion rose in a plume above the car. That's when the second explosion hit. The man from IT watched as Jane Kline was thrown twenty feet backwards by the blast. A large piece of metal from the Director's car ripped through her right leg as she flew.

Five days later Jane Kline opened her eyes in a private room at Walter Reed Medical Center. She tried to speak, but something was in her throat. There were lots of people standing around the room; some she recognized from the Agency, some she didn't.

"She's awake," said one of the nurses.

Kline immediately struggled to get up. She pulled at the wires strapped to her body.

"Stay down, honey," said the nurse. "You've been in a bad accident."

Kline's actions became more deliberate. Her eyes moved wildly around the room as people closed in around her. She pulled at the tube in her mouth.

The nurse called for a doctor on her monitor. "Everyone please leave the room. We're going to need to sedate Ms. Kline."

When she continued to struggle, Kline heard a familiar voice. "Jane, calm down. It's me. It's Leo." Argo positioned his body so Kline could see him hovering over her. He put his hand on her shoulder and leaned forward so he could whisper in her ear. "You need to calm down. Okay? Otherwise, they are going to shoot you full of drugs. Trust me. Calm down. Okay?"

Kline nodded her acceptance. Unable to speak, she looked wide-eyed at Argo and breathed hard. He knew what she was trying to express.

"You've been here for a couple of days. They've had you in a drug-induced coma. There's been a bad accident. You were in the middle of it. You had a severe concussion and a serious injury to your leg. Got it?"

Kline again nodded yes.

The doctor walked in, but Argo waved him off. "She's fine now, Doc." The doctor moved away while Argo leaned back down to talk to Kline. "Jane, look at me. Do you remember anything that happened?"

This time Kline nodded a negative response.

"There was an attempt on Steele's life. A real professional hit. Someone blew up his car at the entrance to the Agency. You had the misfortune of being in the wrong place at the wrong time."

Kline shifted her eyes around the room to the other men and women looking at her. "Steele is dead. They are your body guards. As Steele's Deputy, you are now the acting Director of the Central Intelligence Agency."

Appendix

The American institutes (Republican and Democratic alike) were all born of a speech that President Ronald Reagan made to the House of Commons in 1982. Over the years, the six political institutes have sent staff and volunteers around the globe to fight for free elections all over the world. In large part, the work these institutes did for democratic reform became the final chip which led to the fall of the Berlin Wall and the end of the Cold War.

For those who enjoyed the historical aspects of this book, I thought Reagan's speech would be a good read. Enjoy.

"The Evil Empire," President Reagan's Speech to the House of Commons, June 8, 1982.

We're approaching the end of a bloody century plagued by a terrible political invention— totalitarianism. Optimism comes less easily today, not because democracy is less vigorous, but because democracy's enemies have refined their instruments of repression. Yet optimism is in order because day by day democracy is proving itself to be a not at all fragile flower. From Stettin on the Baltic to Varna on the Black Sea, the regimes planted by totalitarianism have had more than thirty years to establish their legitimacy. But none — not one regime — has yet been able to risk free elections. Regimes planted by bayonets do not take root.

The strength of the Solidarity movement in Poland demonstrates the truth told in an underground joke in the Soviet Union. It is that the Soviet Union would remain a one-party nation even if an opposition party were permitted because everyone would join the opposition party....

Historians looking back at our time will note the consistent restraint and peaceful intentions of the West. They will note that it was the democracies who refused to use the threat of their nuclear monopoly in the forties and early fifties for territorial or imperial gain. Had that nuclear monopoly been in the hands of the Communist world, the map of Europe—indeed, the world—would look very different today. And certainly they will note it was not the democracies that invaded Afghanistan or suppressed Polish Solidarity or used chemical and toxin warfare in Afghanistan and Southeast Asia.

If history teaches anything, it teaches self-delusion in the face of unpleasant facts is folly. We see around us today the marks of our terrible dilemma—predictions of doomsday, antinuclear demonstrations, an arms race in which the West must, for its own protection, be an unwilling participant. At the same time we see totalitarian forces in the world who seek subversion and conflict around the globe to further their barbarous assault on the human spirit. What, then, is our course? Must civilization perish in a hail of fiery atoms? Must freedom wither in a quiet, deadening accommodation with totalitarian evil?

Sir Winston Churchill refused to accept the inevitability of war or even that it was imminent. He said, "I do not believe that Soviet Russia desires war. What they desire is the fruits of war and the indefinite expansion of their power and doctrines. But what we have to consider here today while time remains is the permanent prevention of war and the establishment of conditions of freedom and democracy as rapidly as possible in all countries."

Well, this is precisely our mission today: to preserve freedom as well as peace. It may not be easy to see; but I believe we live now at a turning point.

In an ironic sense Karl Marx was right. We are witnessing today a great revolutionary crisis, a crisis where the demands of the economic order are conflicting directly with those of the political order. But the crisis is happening not in the free, non-Marxist West but in the home of Marxism-Leninism, the Soviet Union. It is the Soviet Union that runs against the tide of history by denying human freedom and human dignity to its citizens. It also is in deep economic difficulty. The rate of growth in the national product has been steadily declining since the fifties and is less than half of what it was then.

The dimensions of this failure are astounding: a country which employs one-fifth of its population in agriculture is unable to feed its own people. Were it not for the private sector, the tiny private sector tolerated in Soviet agriculture, the country might be on the brink of famine. These private plots occupy a bare 3 percent of the arable land but account for nearly one-quarter of Soviet farm output and nearly one-third of meat products and vegetables. Over centralized, with little or no incentives, year after year the Soviet system pours its best resources into the making of instruments of destruction.

The constant shrinkage of economic growth combined with the growth of military production is putting a heavy strain on the Soviet people. What we see here is a political structure that no longer corresponds to its economic base, a society where productive forces are hampered by political ones.

The decay of the Soviet experiment should come as no surprise to us. Wherever the comparisons have been made between free and closed societies — West Germany and East Germany, Austria and Czechoslovakia, Malaysia and Vietnam — it is the democratic countries that are prosperous and responsive to the needs of their people. And one of the simple but overwhelming facts of our time is this: of all the millions of refugees we've seen in the modern world, their flight is always away from, not toward the Communist world. Today on the NATO line, our military forces face east to prevent a possible invasion. On the other side of the line, the Soviet forces also face east to prevent their people from leaving.

The hard evidence of totalitarian rule has caused in mankind an uprising of the intellect and will. Whether it is the growth of the new schools of economics in America or England or the appearance of the so-called new philosophers in France, there is one unifying thread running through the intellectual work of these groups — rejection of the arbitrary power of the state, the refusal to subordinate the rights of the individual to the superstate, the realization that collectivism stifles all the best human impulses....

Chairman Brezhnev repeatedly has stressed that the competition of ideas and systems must continue and that this is entirely consistent with relaxation of tensions and peace.

Well, we ask only that these systems begin by living up to their own constitutions, abiding by their own laws, and complying with the international obligations they have undertaken. We ask only for a process, a direction, a basic code of decency, not for an instant transformation.

We cannot ignore the fact that even without our encouragement there has been and will continue to be repeated explosion against repression and dictatorships. The Soviet Union itself is not immune to this reality. Any system is inherently unstable that has no peaceful means to legitimize its leaders. In such cases, the very repressiveness of the state ultimately drives people to resist it, if necessary, by force.

While we must be cautious about forcing the pace of change, we must not hesitate to declare our ultimate objectives and to take concrete actions to move toward them. We must be staunch in our conviction that freedom is not the sole prerogative of a lucky few but the inalienable and universal right of all human beings. So states the United Nations Universal Declaration of Human Rights, which, among other things, guarantees free elections.

The objective I propose is quite simple to state: to foster the infrastructure of democracy, the system of a free press, unions, political parties, universities, which allow a people to choose their own way to develop their own culture, to reconcile their own differences through peaceful means.

This is not cultural imperialism; it is providing the means for genuine self-determination and protection for diversity. Democracy already flourishes in countries with very different cultures and historical experiences. It would be cultural condescension, or worse, to say that any people prefer dictatorship to democracy. Who would voluntarily choose not to have the right to vote, decide to purchase government propaganda handouts instead of independent newspapers, prefer government to worker-controlled unions, opt for land to be owned by the state instead of those who till it, want government repression of religious liberty, a single political party instead of a free choice, a rigid cultural orthodoxy instead of democratic tolerance and diversity.

Since 1917 the Soviet Union has given covert political training and assistance to Marxist-Leninists in many countries. Of course, it also has promoted the use of violence and subversion by these same forces. Over the past several decades, West European and other social democrats, Christian democrats, and leaders have offered open assistance to fraternal, political, and social institutions to bring about peaceful and democratic progress. Appropriately, for a vigorous new democracy, the Federal Republic of Germany's political foundations have become a major force in this effort.

We in America now intend to take additional steps, as many of our allies have already done, toward realizing this same goal. The chairmen and other leaders of the national Republican and Democratic party organizations are initiating a study with the bipartisan American Political Foundation to determine how the United States can best contribute as a nation to the global campaign for democracy now gathering force. They will have the cooperation of congressional leaders of both parties, along with representatives of business, labor, and other major institutions in our society. I look forward to receiving their recommendations and to working with these institutions and the Congress in the common task of strengthening democracy throughout the world.

It is time that we committed ourselves as a nation — in both the public and private sectors — to assisting democratic development....

What I am describing now is a plan and a hope for the

long term — the march of freedom and democracy which will leave Marxism-Leninism on the ash heap of history as it has left other tyrannies which stifle the freedom and muzzle the self-expression of the people. And that's why we must continue our efforts to strengthen NATO even as we move forward with our zero-option initiative in the negotiations on intermediate-range forces and our proposal for a one-third eduction in strategic ballistic missile warheads.

Our military strength is a prerequisite to peace, but let it be clear we maintain this strength in the hope it will never be used, for the ultimate determinant in the struggle that's now going on in the world will not be bombs and rockets but a test of wills and ideas, a trial of spiritual resolve, the values we hold, the beliefs we cherish, the ideals to which we are dedicated.

The British people know that, given strong leadership, time, and a little bit of hope, the forces of good ultimately rally and triumph over evil. Here among you is the cradle of self-government, the Mother of Parliaments. Here is the enduring greatness of the British contribution to mankind, the great civilized ideas: individual liberty, representative government, and the rule of law under God.

I've often wondered about the shyness of some of us in the West about standing for these ideals that have done so much to ease the plight of man and the hardships of our imperfect world. This reluctance to use those vast resources at our command reminds me of the elderly lady whose home was bombed in the blitz. As the rescuers moved about, they found a bottle of brandy she'd stored behind the staircase, which was all that was left standing. And since she was barely conscious, one of the workers pulled the cork to give her a taste of it. She came around immediately and said, "Here now — there now, put it back. That's for emergencies."

Well, the emergency is upon us. Let us be shy no longer. Let us go to our strength. Let us offer hope. Let us tell the world that a new age is not only possible but probable.

During the dark days of the Second World War, when this island was incandescent with courage, Winston Churchill exclaimed about Britain's adversaries, "What kind of people do they think we are?" Well, Britain's adversaries found out what extraordinary people the British are. But all the democracies paid a terrible price for allowing the dictators to underestimate us. We dare not make that mistake again. So, let us ask ourselves, "What kind of people do we think we are?" And let us answer, "Free people, worthy of freedom and determined not only to remain so but to help others gain their freedom as well."

Sir Winston led his people to great victory in war and then lost an election just as the fruits of victory were about to be enjoyed. But he left office honorably and, as it turned out, temporarily, knowing that the liberty of his people was more important than the fate of any single leader. History recalls his greatness in ways no dictator will ever know. And he left us a message of hope for the future, as timely now as when he first uttered it, as opposition leader in the Commons nearly twenty-seven years ago, when he said, "When we look back on all the perils through which we have passed and at the mighty foes that we have laid low and all the dark and deadly designs that we have frustrated, why should we fear for our future? We have," he said, "come safely through the worst."

Well, the task I've set forth will long outlive our own generation. But together, we too have come through the worst. Let us now begin a major effort to secure the best — a crusade for freedom that will engage the faith and fortitude of the next generation. For the sake of peace and justice, let us move toward a world in which all people are at last free to determine their own destiny.

Acknowledgments

I could not have written this book without the assistance of many people. I'll start the list with Shelley and Ed Stewart and their pals from the International Republican Institute, Catherine Barnes and Meg Thompson. They worked on campaigns all over the world and, yes, they were in Romania in 1990. To the best of my knowledge, neither Ed, Catherine nor Meg ever killed anyone while in Bucharest. One of my EKU Phi Delta Theta brothers, Mark Oschenbein, was in special forces for twenty years. Thanks to Osch, I now know how to properly clear a room. Thanks for your service to our country.

Thanks to Phil Tatro who taught me to play Zevon and Prine on acoustic guitar. We're still working on Meat Loaf.

Like my other titles, *Manifest Destiny* made it to print with a lot of help from sample readers: Vicky Pritchard, Jeff Landen (who—as usual—did enough work that he should be credited on the front cover), Debbie Streitelmeier, Mark Morris, Karen Renz, Jim Brewer, and Eric Haas.

Jack Kerley has offered great advice and guidance. Now, if I could just learn to write like him. Thanks to my old Phi Delt pledge brother, Steve Lyons, who lets me ramble on the pages of his e-zine, OneNewEngland.com, every now and then.

I enjoy visiting book clubs. The people who attend are great at giving advice and assisting with future works. Two book clubs stand out, and I want to thank Barrie Theilman and Lori Recktenwald for inviting me to their clubs. A lot of your suggestions are in these pages.

Father Joe Pennington gave me such a great tour of Trinity Episcopal Church that I joined the congregation. Thanks to Jim Lokesak for letting me use his river cabin to write.

Those who follow me on Facebook had the chance for input into this book. Thanks to Pat Flannery and Ira Robbins from Trouser Press for coming up with the name of the CIA Director, Ellsworth Steele. Add me as a Facebook friend and you'll get similar opportunities in the future. I'm also on Twitter and MySpace.

No reader gets my attention more than my wife of 25 years, Linda. She offers great assistance in both prose and life.

Finally, Cathy Teets and all of the fine folks at Publisher Page (an imprint of Headline Books) continue to believe in me and deliver quality books to my readers. Thanks.